SAINT

A NOLAN BASTARDS NOVEL

AMY OLLE

Copyright © 2019 by Amy Olle

Editing: Hot Tree Editing
Cover Design: Michele Catalano Creative
Cover Photography: Wander Aguilar
Cover Model: Andrew Biernat

ISBN: 978-1-944180-11-9

This book would not have been written without the support and friendship of Jennifer, Olivia, Heather, Rachel, and Nicole.

CHAPTER 1

They say time heals all wounds, but what the hell do they know?

Twelve years was a long time. A long time for Brynn Hathaway's heart to heal.

But it hadn't.

The old wound throbbed. The pain was relentless.

Time hadn't healed Brynn's hurts, but had merely allowed space for the pain to expand and rot.

They'd know that if they'd ever fallen in love with somebody incapable of loving them back.

Or if they'd been a source of misery for everyone they cared about in the world.

Or if they'd been so stupid as to sleep with their stepbrother, a known manwhore and womanizer, only to watch the whole scandalous affair blow up in their face.

And they'd be painfully, horrifyingly, aware of that fact if they'd ever sat at the dinner table in their parents' home, smack in the middle of making a sales pitch to the one client they couldn't afford to lose, with their (sort of) boyfriend sitting beside them, when that same stepbrother showed up unannounced for the first time in years.

Midsentence, Brynn's words trailed off, and she stared open-mouthed at the man suddenly filling the doorway. Through the windows behind him, the fiery glow of the setting sun torched the late summer sky.

The fire reached his eyes. Gold and amber embers blazed in his dark irises. Dark eyes that'd once been the center of her world.

Dark eyes now locked on her and brimming with hatred.

The wound in her chest gave an agonizing wrench, and with it, a gasp slipped between her lips.

"Aiden?" Brynn's stepmother, Siobhan, sounded as shocked and dazed as Brynn felt. "What are you doing here?"

Twelve years.

Twelve years since her dad had caught Aiden in Brynn's bed and thrown him out of the house.

Out of the family.

Twelve years since she'd been in the same room with him longer than mere minutes.

Twelve years, and then suddenly, he was here.

Her memory hadn't sufficiently held onto the details of his appearance. Like layers of dross buffed from silver, his features appeared brighter, sharper than she remembered. His dark hair and intense eyes more vibrant.

He was leaner and taller.

Harder and darker.

She gulped.

A lot darker.

Her heart thrashed, and with every wild beat, shock pumped into her.

"This is my oldest son, Aiden," Siobhan explained to Brynn's potential client, Mrs. Everly. "He's been... traveling and hasn't been home for... for a very long time."

Aiden didn't blink or appear even to breathe while he stared daggers at Brynn.

With every aching second that passed, those eyes, that cold expression, jabbed and pecked, puncturing her composure.

A ripple of nervous unease curled through the room.

"Why don't you join us?" Siobhan's voice sounded unusually buoyant. "We have so much to talk about."

"No." Aiden dragged his gaze away from Brynn to glance around the table. "I'll come back."

"We're almost done here." Brynn's dad, Alan, studied Aiden with an intense frown. He'd been so distracted and erratic of late that Brynn might've been relieved to see the return of his sharp focus if it wasn't fixated on Aiden. He pointed to the empty chair. "Sit."

Fury swept across Aiden's striking face. "I have nothing to say to you."

He turned to leave, but just then, a chair leg scraped across the wood floor, and their half-sister, Brie, sprang up from her seat.

Aiden glanced back over his shoulder.

Brie shifted her body as if to hide her slight frame behind the chair's high back, but at twelve years old, she no longer disappeared behind the velvet-upholstered wingback. Uncertainty crowded her small features.

Aiden tipped his head and caught her shy gaze. His dark eyes gleamed like burnished jewels.

A heartbeat of hesitation passed, then Brie's smile erupted, and she bounded across the room. When her little body crashed into his, a morsel of laughter knocked from him.

Pain knifed Brynn.

The twelve-year-old pain.

The same pain *they* said should have healed by now.

In twelve years, this was only the fourth time she'd laid eyes on him. The first time was at Christmas three years after he left. Neither had spoken, but they'd shared a long, heated look that had fried every brain cell Brynn still possessed in his presence before he'd stalked out.

She didn't see him again until Brie's eighth birthday party, when he'd brought his girlfriend of the moment, and Brynn had feigned a sudden illness to flee. Though honestly, the sight of Aiden with another woman had made her physically ill.

After that, he stayed away until last year, when she'd arrived at the hospital to be with Cian for his first treatment, and glimpsed Aiden's retreating back on her way indoors.

And now. Only the fourth time he'd come home.

In. Twelve. Years.

But while he hadn't cared enough to reach out to Brynn in all that time, he'd obviously nurtured a bond with Brie. And given Siobhan's puzzled expression, he'd done so without their mother's knowledge.

Brynn struggled to breathe. He'd taken care with Brie's soft heart, despite believing that he needed to hide the relationship from their mother.

"You can sit by me." Brie tucked her hand inside Aiden's large palm and tugged him toward the table.

"What a surprise," Siobhan said with a stiff smile for Mrs. Everly. "When you run a family business, sometimes business dinner becomes family dinner."

Panic clawed its way up Brynn's throat.

"Have you met Jared?" her dad asked.

Queasiness rippled through Brynn as Jared pushed to his feet and reached across the table. "Nice to finally meet you."

Aiden looked down at Jared's outstretched hand for a long, uncomfortable moment. Then, without accepting it, his dark eyes swung to Brynn.

Her heart leaped with wild recklessness, even as his beautifully formed features twisted into a fierce scowl. His gaze fixed on her face, he slowly lowered his body into the empty chair between Brie and Mrs. Everly.

Brynn could only stare back at the man seated across from her who resembled the Aiden she remembered, but possessed no hint of the boy she'd once loved. He was a stranger to her now.

An enemy.

Suddenly, she doubted her memories. Had there ever been a time when he hadn't despised her? Had it all been a dream? A figment of her imagination? Perhaps Aiden had never looked at her with love in his eyes. Maybe he'd never touched her naked body with gently questing hands.

P she'd never spread her legs for him and thrown away all her silly schoolgirl dreams about true love right along with her virginity.

Words piled in her throat, but an invisible hand squeezed the narrow passageway and prevented their escape.

Awkwardly, Jared withdrew his hand and eased back down beside her. "So, Aiden, what do you do?"

Aiden's lips curled into a vicious sneer. "We're not really going to do this, are we?"

"Yes, please, let's finish dinner—" Brynn swallowed the rest of her shaky plea when Jared trampled over it.

"Why not? You're my girlfriend's brother. Tell me something about yourself."

"I am not her brother." The lick of fire in Aiden's voice singed.

Brynn flinched. A trickle of sweat that had nothing to do with the late September heatwave slid between her breasts.

"So stepbrothers aren't siblings now?" Leaning back, Jared balanced an ankle on his knee and slid his arm across the top of Brynn's chair. "Wait until my stepfamily hears about this."

"Jared, please don't—"

Jared cut her off once more. "Tell me, what do you do for a living?"

"Freelance," Aiden bit out.

"Freelance?" Scorn infected Jared's tone. "What are you? A drug dealer?"

The strangled sound came from Brynn. "Mrs. Everly, did you receive the packet of information we sent?"

The fading sunlight illuminated Mrs. Everly's immaculately styled white hair when she nodded. "Your portfolio is stunning."

"She's the best in the entire city," Brie stated. Her little arms opened wide. "The entire world."

"No, but seriously," Jared interjected. "What is the actual work you do?"

Aiden's eyes narrowed dangerously. "I flip failing businesses."

"How's that?" Brynn's dad hunched forward. "Like flipping houses?"

Aiden's scowl darkened. "No."

The room took a dizzying swoop, and Brynn gripped the edge of the table.

"Brynn designed every room in this house," Siobhan said to Mrs. Everly. "I still can't believe I live in a home so beautiful as this one."

Brynn forced the corners of her mouth upward. While the home's over-the-top décor was not to her taste, she'd designed the spaces for Siobhan—who was dazzled by vivid colors and ornate styling—when she and Brynn's dad had moved into the opulent mansion two years ago.

"It's a lovely home." Mrs. Everly reached for her wineglass. "I adore the plans you've come up with for my house."

The panic continued its steady creep up Brynn's spine. Soon, it would consume her. "We can make any changes you'd like to the color schemes or the layout."

"There is one thing—"

Brynn's dad drowned Mrs. Everly's next words out. "What businesses?"

Irritation simmered in Aiden's dark scowl. "Bars and restaurants, mostly. Some retail."

Her dad plucked up his wineglass. "How do you turn them around?"

"It depends why they aren't successful. Look, I didn't come here for the mindless chitchat." Aiden twisted toward Siobhan. "I need to talk to you. Alone."

Beneath the table, Brynn's fingers twitched, unconsciously grasping for the string of beads.

When the first panic attack had gripped her, she'd fumbled through the shoebox tucked away in the back of her closet and found the old rosary hidden there. Somehow, rolling the smooth beads between her fingers had helped her survive those earliest episodes. Possibly because they reminded her of a time when she'd felt safe and loved.

Now, whenever the panic tore at her, she fumbled for them.

"You can't make any money doing that," Jared said, a nasty smirk making his handsome face ugly to her.

"You'd be surprised what someone will pay to save their livelihood." Every one of Aiden's words dripped with disdain. "I'm sure you know all about hard work and the desperate struggle to provide for yourself and your family."

"His dad bought him a boat," Brie said, swinging her legs under the table. "You should see it. It has a living room and, like, four bedrooms."

"Is that so?" Aiden's spiteful smirk rivaled Jared's.

Besieged by the gathering storm of panic inside her,

Brynn hadn't noticed Jared's movements until his hand touched her shoulder. The contact sent a jolt of terror flying through her and she jerked so hard that she knocked over a glass of water beside her plate.

Frozen in panic, she sat paralyzed while a burst of exclamations flew across the table and ice-cold liquid seeped through her lightweight cotton sundress.

In slow increments, she realized the room had fallen silent, and all eyes around the table were fastened on her.

Because the shawl she'd draped around her bare shoulders had slipped down her arm, and Jared had only moved to tug the delicate fabric back into place.

Heat seared her cheeks when she closed her fist tight around the shawl and hauled it up under her chin.

Jared hated the thick, pink scar that ran from the base of her collarbone to her shoulder, once telling her that she should keep it covered so that no one had to look at it.

While it was true the scar was repulsive, she hadn't completely forgiven him for his careless words. She'd rather he lie to her and say the imperfection didn't bother him.

Instead, he'd blurted out the truth, and then he wondered why she still hadn't slept with him after nearly a year of dating.

Because if the scar on her shoulder disgusted him, what would he think of her other wounds? The ones concealed beneath her clothing?

Jared's mouth pinched into a thin line when he withdrew his hand from her shoulder. Dimly, she understood he was angry at what he perceived to be her enduring aversion to his touch.

But his frosty reaction wasn't what set off the trembling inside her.

Across the table, Aiden's curious golden-brown eyes had observed the entire fiasco as it played out before him.

She bent her head to hide her face. "I'm sorry," she muttered. "If you'll excuse me...."

Her soaked dress clung to her body when she darted from the room.

At the end of the hall, she ducked inside the bathroom and barred the door.

But the barbs of fear and panic followed her into the small space. They stabbed and pierced until she sagged against the wall in defeat.

Her heart slammed against her breastbone, and she pressed her palm over the painful thuds as if to halt the agonizing wallops. Never once had she been able to stop the pain or the fear from taking over.

Helpless to the storm raging inside her, she could only hunker down and wait for the chaos to pass. Eventually, it would.

In time.

She needed only to wait it out.

What was he doing here?

With greedy gulps, she dragged air into her aching lungs and prayed for the minutes to tick by. A sob filled her throat, and she clasped a hand over her mouth to cage it inside her.

Why had he returned now?

Her knees buckled, and she sank to the cold tile flooring.

How had seeing him again after so long reduced her to a trembling, sobbing mess on the floor of their parents' bathroom?

She didn't know how much time had passed before the first tiny break in the storm appeared, arriving as a bright spot of sunshine to chase away the black clouds of her despair.

It didn't matter why he was here. He wouldn't stay long. He never stayed.

She needed only to wait him out.

Relief poured over her. Wiping tears from her cheeks, she climbed inelegantly to her feet and shuffled over to the sink.

By the time her dress had dried, he'd be gone again.

He never stayed.

CHAPTER 2

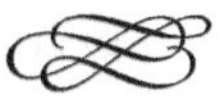

*A*iden Nolan stared hard at the empty doorway where she'd fled, his muscles bunched with the need to go after her. In his bones, the yearning ached.

It was a fool's longing.

He should leave instead.

He never should've come back to Chicago.

From the first moment he saw her all the way until now, he'd only ever caused her misery.

With a vicious wrench, he jerked his head around, returning his gaze to the table.

Surrounded by strangers and enemies in the grotesquely opulent home of the family that'd cast him aside, years of resentment surged.

Then spilled out of him.

"Dinner's over," he announced.

The preppy little prick, Jared, erupted with anger. "Who in the hell do you think you are?"

With the colorful words he uttered next, Brie dissolved into giggles, and Siobhan pleaded for calm while Mrs. Everly clutched the pearl necklace at her throat.

Aiden relished the turmoil. He had little sympathy for the people who looked at him like he didn't belong. Who had thrown him away like he was nothing more than the bastard son of a pathetic man.

Which he was.

Still, he felt no mercy. Even if his fury was unfounded, their rejection had carved out his heart.

"That's enough." Alan's booming voice shattered the chaotic din of noise.

Silence dropped like a stone in the center of the table.

Chair legs grated across the floor when Alan stood. "Brie, honey, why don't we show Mrs. Everly your favorite room in the house?"

Brie straightened in her seat. "Right now?"

"Yes, sweetheart, right now." Alan moved to help Mrs. Everly with her bulky chair. Over the white puff of the woman's hair, he flung Jared a meaningful look and thrust his chin toward the doorway.

Jared's cold, colorless eyes found Aiden's in a challenging glare.

Bored, Aiden sighed.

With deliberate slowness, Jared rose and strutted from the room.

At Aiden's elbow, Brie appeared.

She regarded him with solemn, light green eyes that reminded him of her sister's. "Brynn is taking me to the beach next weekend. You wanna come?"

The pang struck Aiden in the center of his chest. "Sorry, squirt. I cannot stay that long."

"Your brother is very busy," Siobhan said, twisting the knife of his pain.

"Okay." Brie studied the toes of her shoes. "Maybe next time."

Behind Jared and Mrs. Everly, Brie filed through the doorway.

Beneath the arch, Alan paused, and a thoughtful frown cluttered his neat features while he considered Aiden.

A coil of alarm snaked through Aiden. He'd expected his stepfather's anger, possibly even his rage. But the older man's quiet study lifted the hairs on the back of his neck.

With his tongue, Aiden worried the slight, puckered scar on the inside of his lip, put there by his stepfather twelve years ago.

"Don't upset your mother," Alan finally said.

At the hint of threat, Aiden bristled. "You'll not ask me for any more promises, Al. We finished with that a long time ago."

"Promises?" Siobhan asked. "What promises?"

The two men locked gazes.

As Aiden watched, a splinter of fear fractured his stepdad's stern expression.

"Alan? What promises?"

Alan's throat spasmed when he looked at his wife. "It's nothing. Have a nice visit."

With the room emptied, his mom reached over and squeezed his forearm. "I'm so happy you're here. You shouldn't stay away for so long."

He stared at her hand a moment while the shock of it all overwhelmed him once more. "Why didn't you tell me the truth?"

In the beat of silence, unease rippled.

She withdrew her touch. "I'm a middle-aged woman, dear. You'll have to be more specific."

Emotion choked him when he lifted his gaze to hers. "You should've told us about our dad."

Her smile cratered. "What about him?"

When Aiden set out to find the man that'd given him life

but had never been his father, he'd been thinking only of Cian and what might be necessary if his illness continued to progress. He'd hoped to find living relatives, in case they needed family histories, or donors.

In that respect, he'd hit the jackpot.

"Did you know he had another family?"

Her gaze slipped away. "Now, wherever did you hear that?"

"I met his sons." The truth tasted thick on his tongue. "I met my brothers."

Stunned, she gaped at him while the color seeped from her face.

"Did you know?" He spoke in a low voice.

"That he had a wife and kids?" Her hand trembled so badly, the fork she held clattered against the china. "Yes."

"Did you know she was dying?"

By her expression, he could see that she had known.

"Do not look at me like that," she snapped.

He couldn't hold back his dismay. "How could you?"

"Is this the only reason you've come home?" She abandoned the fork and snatched up her wineglass. "To pass judgment on me?"

"You should've told us." Anger raised his voice.

"Why would I?" With a defensive shrug of her shoulders, she waved the wineglass through the air. "Once I realized he would never marry me, what was the point?"

"You kept our family from us. We had a right to know."

She shook her head. "What if they didn't accept you? I was protecting you."

His fury lashed like a whip. "That wasn't your choice to make."

"What do you want me to say? I'm sorry?" The defiant tilt of her chin was unapologetic. "Whatever your father is or isn't, he gave me you boys. I won't regret it."

"Keep your damned apologies." He stood so abruptly, his chair rocked. "They mean nothing."

"Aiden, wait. Don't be mad—"

Halfway to the door, he stopped, then turned slowly. "Mad? You want me not to be mad, Mother?"

"Yes. You're so angry."

"Mad doesn't begin to describe how I'm feeling right now."

With a thud, she plopped the wineglass onto the table. "Why are we even talking about this? It's in the past. Can't we just let it go?"

"It's not in the past. It's who I am. Every day. All day. I'm Daniel Nolan's bastard."

"Don't say that word."

"What word? Bastard?" He savored the vile obscenity, rolling it around on his tongue and in his mind. Never hiding from it. Never denying what he really was. Indeed, he preferred to keep the facts of his birth and his place in this family at the forefront.

Never again would he forget what he really was to them.

"I will not have ye saying that word about us. You are my son." She struck her fist against her breast. "My heart."

A bitter laugh rattled in his chest. "Is that right?"

"Yes, that's right."

"You have no problem throwing me out of the house, but that word is too much for you? Do I have that right?"

She muttered a prayer, asking the Lord for patience.

"Why?" he barked. "Why did you give us his name?"

"Because..." She lurched to her feet. "Because I thought...." With a hand on her head, she paced away from the table.

"What did you think?" Blood whooshed past his ears with the thunderous roar of his heart.

Twisting around, her arm dropped heavily to her side. "I

thought one day he might want us. But he didn't. Are you happy now?"

A toxic mix of anger and shame swirled inside him, poisoning his soul. "No, Ma, I'm not happy."

That made two families that didn't want him.

His feet pounded the wood floor with each of his long strides. He burst into the hallway, only to rear back at the sight of her standing with her back pressed against the wall.

Pain ripped through him.

Brynn.

Light green eyes gripped him by the balls.

Goddamn, she was beautiful. Despite the new maturity in her delicate bone structure, it might as well have been the first moment he'd spotted her in a crowded airport when they were only seventeen years old.

Then, like now, his body had a visceral reaction to her.

His heart lurched.

His cock ached.

Every time he gazed upon her, the world stopped. In that moment of singularity, he drew his first and his last breath all at once.

Every. Fucking. Time.

He couldn't bear to look at her.

He couldn't tear his gaze away.

It'd always been so. From that first moment to now. Today.

Her lips parted, and for the space of several heartbeats, they stood staring at each other, still as statues on opposite sides of the vast hall.

Unwilling to stay, but unable to go.

When she fussed with the ridiculous scarf slung over her shoulders, he saw that her hand shook. That he made her nervous should have elicited a punch of satisfaction, but there was none.

He frowned. "Do you have something to say, because if not—?"

"She should've told you." The trembling in her hands reached her voice. "You should've known you had a-another brother."

Damn her. He wanted to hate her.

He *needed* to hate her.

"Where's Jared?" he drawled.

"He... had to go." Sorrow chased the warmth from her voice. "How did you find out about your brother?"

"Brothers."

The honey-colored streaks in her light brown hair shimmered when she gave her head a small shake. "What?"

"I have five half brothers."

Her eyes went wide. "Five brothers? That's.... Wow. That's... a lot."

Unbelievably, a smile quirked. "Tell me about it."

"Have you met them?"

The softness in her eyes terrified him. "I have."

"Once, I suddenly gained three brothers." One corner of her mouth tilted upward. "It can be overwhelming."

If he was too weak to hate her, then he needed *her* to hate *him*. He'd never been able to resist her soft heart, and without her hatred, he'd be lost.

That, too, had always been so.

Unable to bear her kindness, he lashed out like the wounded animal he was. "Well, I don't plan to fuck any of them, so it shouldn't be too bad."

Anguish slashed across her face.

The pang that struck him was a one-two punch of grief and regret. With the wrench, he bore down on the front door, desperate to escape her, to escape this house, this city.

Outside, the sun's heat lingered, and a cotton candy

sunset painted the sky with purple and orange hues. He charged down the stone steps.

"Seriously?" From the top of the porch stairs, fury heated the word on her tongue. "Twelve years—twelve fucking years—and that's all you have to say to me?"

An avalanche of resentment caved in on him. "What do you want me to say?"

"Where have you been?" She scurried down the stairs after him. "All these years…? Why didn't you come home? Why didn't you ever come for me?" Her voice broke. "Where did you go?"

"To hell," he hissed. "Where you sent me."

"Wh-what does that mean?" she whispered.

He dragged his car keys from his pocket. "Nothing. It doesn't mean anything. Are we done here?"

"No. I want to know what you meant."

"You gave up your right to demand answers from me twelve years ago." He slid his thumb over the key fob, and the lights on his car flashed when the locks gave way.

With a violent tug, he yanked open the door.

"So that's it? You're just going to barge in here, blow up everyone's life, and walk out again? What the hell is wrong with you? No, you know what?" She backed away from his car. "Forget it. I should've known you haven't grown up."

"You know nothing about me."

"Don't I?" She crossed her arms. "How's Kaylee? Or is it Madison? No, wait. Let me guess. It's someone new. Of course it is. It's always someone new. What's this one's name? Skylar? Brandy? Teresa? You're not the enigma you believe yourself to be."

He shook his head, a contemptuous sneer tipping up one corner of his mouth.

"Am I wrong?"

"There's a good little girl. Believe all of daddy's lies without questioning a single one of 'em."

She frowned. "What lies?"

"That you have to ask tells me all I need to know about you." He turned his back on her.

"Fine. Go. Run away, like you always do."

Cold fury ignited. He slammed the car door shut and whirled on her. "Don't you dare do that."

Alarm flared in her eyes, but she stood her ground. "Do what?"

"Pretend it was all my fault." He advanced until they stood toe to toe, their faces inches apart.

"You left and never came home." The hitch of her vulnerability shattered him. "That is your fault."

"I asked you to come with me. You said no." Standing so close, her light scent tortured his senses. "That's on you, not me."

Her expression crumpled, and she ducked her chin, hiding her face from him.

"I'm not your mom, Brynn. I did not abandon you."

When she lifted her head, huge tears clung to her eyelashes. "You lied to me."

"What did I lie about?" At the lethal edge in his voice, she remained silent. "I did not lie to you about Samantha Whitaker."

"You told me you weren't sleeping with anyone else, so how did she wind up pregnant?"

"I told you then, if she was pregnant, it wasn't by me. You chose not to believe me."

"You didn't give me a chance—"

"You didn't give *me* a chance." He erupted with the words. "You blindly accepted everything your dad said."

Doubt disturbed her eyes. "Why would he lie about something like that?"

"I don't know. Have you asked him that?"

Pink stained her cheeks.

He steeled himself against her softness. "Maybe he lied, or maybe he was lied to. I don't really give a fuck which it is. I was there. I knew. You should have trusted me."

Right then, he should've left. He should've climbed into his car and driven away without a glance in the rearview mirror.

Instead, he stayed.

"Everything happened so quickly, and… I… I…." The tip of her tongue peeked out to take a nervous lick of her bottom lip.

In the dying ember of dusk, a cascade of memories rained down on him.

Bare skin against bare skin. The sound of her soft, eager moans. The tight warmth of her body clamping around him.

His gaze fastened on her mouth.

Her breath caught.

Need and want swelled his cock, and he bent his head low.

Her lashes swept down.

Hate and lust collided in his chest, because dammit all if he didn't still want her.

More than ever, the urge to possess her was unrelenting. Inescapable.

For twelve years, she'd haunted him. Stalked him like a phantom. She was the reason for everything he did or didn't do.

Aching with need, is mouth hovered above hers.

When he didn't kiss her, her heavy lashes fluttered open.

Her dark pupils had expanded to swallow the fading sunlight, but in her pale green irises, he glimpsed a profoundly different woman from the girl he'd once loved. The one with her heart in her eyes.

"What happened to you?" he murmured. "You've changed."

Shadows rushed in to darken her face.

He frowned as the darkness stole all her heat and light.

While her fingers fumbled for the edge of her scarf, she eased away from him.

"Brynn...?"

"You're right. I have changed." Her spine rigid, she leveled him with a cold, hard stare that didn't quite hide her heartbreak. "I'm not that naïve girl you remember, and I haven't been for a very long time. Not since I fell in love with the wrong boy."

CHAPTER 3

So he still hated her.

That fact didn't surprise her, but her lack of shock didn't make the truth hurt any less.

On shaky legs, Brynn scrambled to her SUV and dove inside. With a gush of relief that she'd chosen to meet Jared for dinner rather than ride with him, she stabbed the key into the car's ignition and yanked on the gearshift.

The vehicle lurched forward, but at the end of their parents' short, circular driveway, the security gate blocked her escape. While she waited for the ornate iron doors to draw open, panic heaved.

She choked it down. She couldn't let it out. Stuffing it down to sit like a leaden ball in the pit of her stomach was the only way. Her gut churned.

How had he known something had happened to her? That something had changed her forever? Had he seen her scar? Had she said something to make him suspicious?

Before the black gate had finished pulling apart, she squeezed the SUV between them and veered onto the quiet street in the upmarket neighborhood.

In the car's rearview mirror, the four-story stone mansion loomed like a menacing monster. She forced her eyes back to the road ahead of her, but her mind replayed the angry, hurtful words they'd flung at each other.

Her recollections latched onto one sharp memory.

He'd said she'd sent him to hell.

What did that mean?

They were only eighteen years old when her dad had kicked him out of the house. Where had he gone? What had he done for money? For food? Where had he lived?

Why didn't he want to tell her?

Vicious tentacles of shame lashed at her, and her vision blurred. She swiped at the tears with the tips of her fingers and propelled the vehicle through the dark streets of the north side Chicago neighborhood.

To the pangs in her heart, the voice in her head argued. If he'd suffered, well, he'd taken much from her, too. When he left her, he took far more than her innocence with him. He'd stolen her hopes and her dreams. He'd shown her there was a fate far worse than not being loved at all.

Was there a worse pain than being loved and having that love withdrawn? That his affection and passion turned so quickly, so completely, to disgust and indifference was a betrayal she'd never forgive.

In the passenger seat, her purse vibrated.

Stretching, she rummaged through her handbag and plucked her cell phone from an inside pocket.

When her best friend's name flashed on the phone's screen, Brynn winced but slipped the device into the hands-free cradle and accepted the call.

"Hey, Molly."

"Where are you?"

"At my dad's." The lie dropped quickly from Brynn's lips.

"You're still coming out with us later, aren't you?"

"I don't know." Brynn hedged while she grasped at an excuse.

She couldn't tell Molly that she'd talked to Aiden again for the first time in years, and now all she wanted to do was go home and cry into her pillow. Or puke.

She couldn't tell Molly that, because she'd never confessed to her best friend what they'd done all those years ago.

At first, Brynn hadn't been able to bring herself to speak the words out loud—that she'd had sex with her stepbrother and torn their family apart.

Later, too much time had passed, and by then, Brynn's wounds had ached and festered so severely, and for so long, she couldn't bear the thought of revisiting them.

It wasn't the only secret she'd kept from her best friend.

Nor the biggest.

"You can't blow us off again." No irritation heated Molly's words, but a resigned tedium at having the same conversation yet again tainted her tone. "Corinne's going to think you hate her."

"Tell Corinne I don't hate her," Brynn said. "And I'm not blowing you off. I don't know when I'll be done here."

It amazed Brynn that Molly still bothered to include her.

After high school, they'd roomed together at Northwestern, where Molly had thrived and made friends easily while Brynn had retreated into her shy, awkward shell.

By their senior year, Molly had blossomed into a tall, gorgeous blonde with curves that fascinated all the boys and a trendy wardrobe all the other girls envied.

Brynn had focused on her studies and graduated with honors.

"I don't care what time you finish," Molly said. "We're going to the old neighborhood. Promise you'll meet us. One drink. That's all I ask."

"That sounds fun," Brynn lied. "But I have to—"

"Work," they said together.

"I know." Molly sighed. "You have to work."

"I'm sorry." Brynn bit down on her bottom lip.

"Don't be. It's why you're rich and have a great man, and I'm poor and single."

Brynn repressed a groan at the mention of Jared, who'd left her dad's place in a huff of annoyance. He would not find the events of that evening amusing, she knew, but she couldn't decide if she cared or not.

"Plan on next weekend?" Molly asked.

Brynn's stomach lurched. "I promise I'll try."

It was a lie, of course.

One more lie in the long list of lies Brynn told herself all the time, every day for as long as she could remember.

She lied a lot. To herself, mostly, but also to anyone else who bothered to ask. Some big, some small, all lies.

How are you?

Great.

Lie.

How was your weekend?

Good.

Lie.

Are you okay? You look tired?

I'm fine.

Lie.

If she kept repeating the lies, eventually she'd start to believe them, and if she believed them, then they'd become true.

Wouldn't they?

Brynn disconnected the call. When she approached the highway interchange, she eased to a stop at the traffic light and switched on her turn signal for the northbound ramp that'd take her to her condo north of the city.

In the quiet inside the car, the panic threatened from the shadows.

The light changed, and she silenced the car's indicator at the same time she stomped on the accelerator. Shooting through the traffic light, she flipped on her turn signal and cut in behind another car to ease onto the southbound freeway.

She couldn't go home to be alone with her painful thoughts, but neither could she meet Molly at the bar to drink and laugh as though she were a normal woman.

Her fingers moved over the hands-free console.

When she heard the gruff voice crackle over the car's speaker, guilt pinched her. "Hi, Curtis. How are you?"

"Ah, Ms. Brynn. I'm doing all right. How 'bout yourself?"

"I'm good." Her stomach roiled with the lie. "I need to swing by the office for a bit. Can you meet me in the garage?"

"Sure thing. I'll head down now and watch for ya."

"Thank you, Curtis."

Fifteen minutes later, she exited the highway and rolled into downtown. At the Hathaway Group offices, she pulled into the underground parking garage, then slipped into her reserved spot by the bank of elevators.

Dressed in his black uniform, Curtis heaved his massive body up off the concrete safety bollard and moved to open her car door.

Apologies gushed out of her. "I'm so sorry to bother you."

"It's no bother at all." His gigantic hand shoved her car door closed behind her. "Always brightens my day to see you."

The concrete parking structure held the summer heat. Sounds from the city streets above reached them as Curtis walked with her to the elevator. She speared the button with her finger and the doors slid open.

Inside the metal box, the elevator whisked them up. Brynn's stomach roiled with the motion.

Curtis kept his gaze affixed to the gleaming sliver doors. "You sure you're all right? You look a little seasick tonight."

Brynn nodded when her stomach heaved. "I'm all right."

Or, she would be, once she'd submerged herself in her work.

Work was her life raft. Her security blanket. When the panic attacks had begun, work was the escape hatch she'd used to avoid the worst parts of herself. Before that, after Aiden had left and taken her dreams with him, work was the only place she had to put the shattered pieces of her broken heart.

In truth, she'd started to unravel years before, after her mom had abandoned her just as the full weight of teenage insecurity was descending.

Now, whenever she thought to dream, or the panic threatened to overtake her, she wrapped the mantle of confident businesswoman over her shoulders, pushed it all aside, and got to work.

The business she'd built with her dad was all she had to hold on to. If she lost it now, she'd lose the last thread of herself.

Then there'd be nothing to stop her final unraveling.

Miraculously, they reached the main lobby before Brynn lost her stomach. Though a small accomplishment, she knew she should be proud of herself. Because that was how far she'd fallen, that not losing her stomach in the office elevator was a victory.

When the doors eased apart, Brynn shot from the tin canister.

"Don't work too late," Curtis called after her, knowing full well she might stay all night, as she'd done many times before.

She might as well work. After seeing Aiden, she wouldn't be able to sleep that night anyway.

~

AIDEN CLAIMED an empty stool at the bar and lifted a hand to signal for the bartender.

When the shaggy-haired blond glanced up, a wide grin split his face. "Excuse me, sir, this is a respectable establishment. I'm going to have to ask you to leave."

A spot of laughter knocked around inside Aiden's chest.

"How you doing, man?" Ben pressed his palms against the bar's scarred surface. "It's been a long time."

"I hear you've been busy," Aiden said, sidestepping Ben's question.

"Oh, man, you're not kidding." Ben plucked a clean pint glass from the rack. "Six months of married bliss and now Carrie's pregnant. It's so wild."

"Congratulations, man."

"How about you?" At the beer dispenser, Ben tugged the tap, and Guinness flowed into the glass. "You found a girl yet? Or a job?"

Aiden pulled a face. "Now, why would I want to go and do a thing like that?"

Ben set the Guinness on the bar in front of Aiden. "I've come back from the other side to tell you it's not that bad."

"Not that bad?" A sardonic smile tilted up the corners of Aiden's mouth. "I think I'll wait."

Ben laughed as though Aiden joked, but he meant every word. He made no commitments. Ever. Not to any employer and certainly not to any woman. He wasn't about to lock himself in a toxic relationship. Not professionally, and sure as shit, not personally.

Especially not personally.

"How's your brother?" Aiden asked.

"You're not going to believe this." Ben pushed his horn-rimmed glasses up his nose. "They promoted him. Made him lieutenant or Jedi Commander or some such shit."

Ben's brother, Xavier, had served in the Chicago police force for the past several years.

"Good for him," Aiden said.

At the opposite end of the bar, a new customer pulled Ben away.

Aiden scanned the barroom. With no sign of his brothers, he sipped from his pint and watched the football game on the TV behind the bar.

When his cell phone vibrated in his hip pocket, he retrieved the device and glanced at the screen.

Then, as he'd done with all the other calls, he let it go to voicemail.

Beneath the bar, his knee bounced, and he searched the faces in the crowd of pub dwellers for Cian or Rory. With his search unsuccessful, he returned his attention to the football game.

But the action on the TV couldn't keep his thoughts from straying back to her. Like his tongue worrying the scar on the inside of his lip, he always came back to her.

Their angry words wove through his memories as he tried to reconcile the fiery woman with the sweet, vulnerable girl.

An image of Brynn beneath him, quivering with desire and begging for his cock, had him grasping for his drink.

While he gulped down a desperate swallow, a cloud of sweet-smelling perfume materialized beside him. He set his glass on the bar, then his gaze slid to the woman who'd claimed the barstool next to him.

Leggy, blonde, and stacked, she offered him a smile.

He smiled back.

Interest flared in her bright blue eyes. "Hi."

"Hi." He sipped his drink.

"It's Molly." She placed her elbows on the bar, which had the effect of lifting her incredible breasts.

His blood stirred.

The heat from his gaze deepened the blush of pleasure on her cheeks.

If he and Molly shared a drink, mutual attraction might arouse their desire. Perhaps she'd invite him back to her place, and he'd drown out the torturous memories of Brynn's honeyed heat in some other sweet pussy.

Maybe that's what it'd take to make him forget Brynn for a few hours, at least.

With open appreciation, he studied her beautiful face.

CHAPTER 4

"Mind if I sit with you while I finish my drink?" Molly's bright eyes danced with an inner light that appeared dull when compared to the gutting directness of Brynn's pale green gaze. "I think my friends stood me up."

While he talked with the gorgeous woman, who was smart and seemed genuine, he couldn't stop himself from noticing all the ways her striking features differed from Brynn's softer beauty. Molly's straight nose lacked the small upturn Brynn's took near the tip, and her mouth, while nicely shaped, seemed too wide and thin compared to Brynn's puffy, pouty lips.

Soon, exhaustion dragged at him. Molly was attractive and intelligent, and nice...

And all he could think about was his stepsister.

Brynn.

She dominated his thoughts. Memories of her soft smile, and the way the sunlight caught the streaks of caramel and honey in her hair, tormented him.

He couldn't stop pondering the shadow lurking in her eyes.

That was new.

The weary sigh might've pulled from him now or twelve years ago. His hunt for the woman who could make him forget her was endless.

Useless.

Truthfully, he'd forgotten more women than he remembered, because he only remembered one woman. Nothing short of a bullet to the head could stop him from wanting Brynn.

When Molly finished her drink, Aiden thanked her for keeping him company while he waited for his brothers to arrive.

With a sad smile, she slipped off the barstool and melted into the crowd.

For a time, he stared into his empty glass and wondered what the hell was wrong with him.

When he looked up again, Cian was balancing his large, lean frame on the barstool Molly had vacated.

His hazel green gaze flitted from the napkin where Molly had scribbled her phone number to Aiden's face. "So, you saw Brynn, did ya?"

A sound like a growl vibrated in the back of Aiden's throat.

One side of Cian's mouth pushed up. "Met Jared too?"

"Aye, I met him." Aiden signaled Ben for another Guinness.

"If it makes ya feel any better, she doesn't want to marry him."

Aiden's head swung to Cian. "Marry him? Who said anything about marriage?"

Cian scratched the scruff on his jawline. "You've been away for a long time. There's a lot you don't know."

A possessive fury snaked through Aiden's gut. "Why don't you fill me in?"

Cian narrowed his eyes. "I thought you wanted us not to tell you about her."

The grind of his molars crunched inside his skull, and he made an impatient gesture with his hand.

"Alan's pushing her to do it," Cian said.

A curse shot from him. "Why the hell for?"

Cian rolled his broad, bony shoulders. "Who knows? Jared's in the same line of work, and my guess is he wants a business merger. With Al, it's always about business."

When he reached for his pint, Aiden's hand shook.

After a beat, Cian spoke in a low voice. "She doesn't want to marry him."

Aiden searched his expression. "Did she tell you that?"

"No." He shifted on the stool. "But it's obvious."

Dark, poisonous memories marched through Aiden's mind. "She wants to make her dad happy."

Which meant it was a done deal.

"I guess we'll find out soon enough." As Cian said the words, a shadow darkened his face.

Aiden turned as Rory slid onto the barstool beside him.

Tension crackled when Rory's gaze met Cian's briefly, then slid away.

With a brother on either side of him, Aiden's head swiveled between them. Despite their differing features, their matching scowls produced the sensation of gazing at two sides of the same mirror.

"Everything all right?" he asked.

"Everything's fine," Rory muttered at the same time Cian snapped, "It's all good."

"Uh, oh. What's with the frowny faces?" Ben lined up three pints of Guinness on the bar in front of them. "Let's flip those frowns upside down."

Two dark scowls blasted him.

"What?" Ben looked from Rory to Cian. "You act like he stole your girlfriend or something. Oh, wait—"

The tension sparked like a live wire.

Aiden's head swung to Rory. "Tell me you didn't."

"Are we not laughing about this yet?" Ben winced. "Is it too soon?"

Cian lifted his hand, then closed his thumb and forefinger until a whisper of space existed between them. "A bit."

When Ben retreated to tend to more customers, Rory snatched a pint off the bar and tossed back a healthy swallow.

"I hope she was worth it," Aiden said.

Rory shot him a dark look. "Was Brynn?"

The verbal sucker punch knocked the air from Aiden's lungs. Defenseless, he tumbled down the sweet, devastating tunnel of his memories, recalling with powerful, aching clarity.

At first, she'd been shy and uncertain around him. Then, lusty and needy. Witnessing the transformation had been one of the most special experiences of his life, and despite years of trying, he'd never forgotten a single, searing moment of being with her.

Of being inside her.

Nor had he been able to replicate anything remotely similar with any other woman.

Was she worth it?

Hell, yeah, she was worth it. Every heart-pounding, heart-breaking second of it.

Even the years of misery and isolation that had followed.

His agony must've shown on his face, because Rory quickly backed down. "Look, I can't stay. You wanna tell us your news?"

Aiden grimaced. "Not particularly."

"It won't get any easier." Cian lifted his glass to his lips. "Might as well get it over with."

"It's about our dad," he began.

Then, with a pang of regret for the mindfuck he was about to deliver to them both, he started talking. Though he kept the details to the bare minimum, wild swings of emotions played across their faces as he spoke.

When he'd finished, he fell silent.

"So let me get this straight." With his elbows propped on the bar, Rory folded his arms. "He was fucking our mother while his wife was at home, with his five sons, dying of cancer? And Ma knew all this and didn't tell us?"

Aiden's head bobbed. "Pretty much."

"Five brothers?" Cian's hand opened and closed. "That's… a whole fistful."

Aiden pushed on, eager to finish. "He died young. In his fifties, I think. Of a heart attack. He was a heavy drinker and a smoker."

Rory scrubbed his hands over his face. "He sounds like a real charmer."

"I think I remember him." Cian spoke quietly. "I saw him at the house once."

Surprise knocked into Aiden. "When?"

"I must've been five or six. Ma kept me home from school with a stomach bug." A scowl marred Cian's features as his mind chased the memories. "They were yelling at each other, and he hit her."

Dark rage spiraled through Aiden.

"I tried to fight him." Cian brushed his fingers over his mouth. "The bastard gave me a fat lip."

"I remember that. You bit his leg." A faint smile touched Rory's lips. "You think that was our dad?"

"Fits the description," Aiden said.

Two questioning gazes snapped to his face.

"He…" Aiden took a desperate gulp from his pint, but the beer curdled in his gut. "He beat his kids. Our half brothers."

"How do you know that?" Rory asked.

"I met them." Aiden's cell phone was heavy in his pocket. "I think they want to meet—"

Just then, a commotion erupted across the room.

As one, they turned. A man had pinned another on top of a table and pressed a pool stick across his throat. Behind them, a woman with huge, terror-filled eyes cowered as two men backed her against the wall.

Cian lurched to his feet.

"Settle down, Rocky." Lifting the bar flap, Ben darted out from behind the bar and moved toward the ruckus.

Cian nipped at his heels. "Oh, c'mon. I haven't had a good fight since I quit the circuit."

Drinks in hand, Aiden and Rory slid off their barstools and followed them.

"Sorry, guys, we can't have this kind of thing going on in here." Ben placed his hand on the pool stick-wielding man's shoulder. "Take it elsewhere."

Slowly, the man straightened. Over his shoulder, the two other men abandoned the woman and crowded close.

"Mind your own business, wimp." He shoved Ben's thin shoulders, and Ben stumbled back.

"Hey," Rory bellowed as Cian steadied their friend. "He may be a wimp, but he's our wimp."

Setting Ben aside, Cian stepped forward until he stood nose to nose with the man.

Though Cian was taller, the man must've outweighed him by fifty pounds, a fact that Cian seemed oblivious to when he stood facing the trio of burly men as though the muscles he'd painstakingly built over the years still hung on his now skinny frame.

With Rory on Cian's right, Aiden added his presence to the left side.

Casually, Rory sipped his pint.

With a snarl, the man slapped the drink out of Rory's hand.

Before the glass shattered on the concrete floor, Cian lunged.

"Aw, c'mon." Rory swiped a pool stick off the table. "That's a waste of perfectly good beer."

Cian had taken the beefy man to the ground and rained blows on his meaty head when one of his buddies zeroed in on Aiden.

Aiden tracked the man's lumbering approach, and when he drove too soon, Aiden feinted left but dodged right.

The man staggered, and Aiden stuck his foot out in time to send him tumbling to the ground. Before he'd hit the floor, Aiden landed on his broad back. Straddling him, he rolled the man over and unleashed two well-placed hooks to knock him out cold.

Two large hands grabbed Aiden's shoulders and spun him. A fist crashed into his face, then a driving shoulder hurtled into his torso. When he hit the concrete, the wind left his lungs in a painful whoosh.

Above him, the man drew back his arm, but before he released the brutal blow, Rory's pool stick caught him under the chin, and he fell limp on top of Aiden.

With a groan, Aiden rolled the man's unconscious body off his. His lower lip burned with pain and he touched the aching spot with his fingers. He winced.

Cian appeared over him and offered his hand. When Aiden reached up, Cian hauled him to his feet.

Chest heaving with his heavy breathing, a wicked smile curved Cian's mouth. "Feels good, doesn't it?"

Adrenaline pumped through Aiden's body, taut and exhilarating. He gave a curt nod.

"Almost better than sex."

Aiden lifted his arms and laced his fingers behind his head. As oxygen filled his chest cavity, he sliced Cian with a look. "Not that good."

Within hours of his return to town, he'd been embroiled in two brawls. Though the three large men were nothing next to the beat down Brynn had delivered earlier that night.

But as Aiden dragged air into his lungs, he had to wonder what other fresh hell awaited him before he could hightail it out of this godforsaken city?

HE WOKE to the annoying buzz of his cell phone. Rolling to his side, Aiden reached for the device on Rory's coffee table —then the sharp bite of pain struck his ribs.

He gasped and fell back onto the couch pillows.

The annoying buzz persisted.

Slowly, he pushed upright and swung his feet over the side of the sofa. He gritted his teeth and snagged the phone off the table. With a few swipes of his thumb, he accepted the call from the number he didn't recognize in case it was a potential new client.

"Aiden Nolan." He winced at the movement of his sore lip.

"Aiden, it's Alan."

"How did you get this number?"

"I need to talk to you. It's important."

Dread drummed through him, and he dragged his stiff body off the couch. "That wasn't my question."

"Your mother had it," his stepdad admitted.

"Does she know you called me?" While he waited for

Alan's response, he touched his lip, his fingers brushing the split in his skin at the corner of his mouth.

Going forward, he'd stick to sex.

"I want to keep this between us."

Dread morphed into alarm. The last time his stepdad had contacted him with no one's knowledge, Aiden had regretted everything that'd followed.

"Whatever you have to say, don't," Aiden said. "I'm not interested."

"Wait—"

Aiden hung up.

In his hand, the phone immediately started buzzing.

"Don't test me, Al."

"I get it. You don't want to talk to me, but I think you'll be interested in what I have to say." An edge of desperation cut into Alan's voice. "Why don't you come by the house? What I have to say needs to be said in person."

"Say it now or I'm hanging up," Aiden said.

"Don't be unreasonable—"

Aiden hung up.

He dropped his phone on the coffee table, where it buzzed as he trudged down the hall and locked himself in the bathroom. In the shower, the hot spray of water soothed his aching muscles, and he lingered beneath the invigorating stream.

When he returned to the living room, the phone was quiet, though a quick check told him he had five missed calls.

As he cradled the device in his palm, it began to vibrate.

He swiped with his thumb. "I can do this all day, Al."

"It's about Brynn." The plea in Alan's voice struck Aiden in the chest.

A direct hit.

"What about her? What have you done?" Aiden tangled a

hand through his wet hair. "So help me, Al, if you've hurt her I will—"

"She's okay," his stepdad interrupted. "But it's important that we talk. Privately."

The muscle in Aiden's sore jaw ticked. "When?"

"Now. Will you come by the house?"

His gut twisting into knots, Aiden bit back the words he really wanted to say. "I'm on my way," he muttered instead.

In record time, he dressed and flew across town to the north side Chicago mansion, reaching the black wrought-iron gate within the hour.

The gate, which had been propped open the previous night when he'd arrived, was now closed, and while he waited to be let onto the property, he struggled to control his emotions. His knuckles turned white on the steering wheel.

Instinct told him to run. Get out, now, before his stepdad blackened another part of his wretched soul.

The gates drew open, and Aiden punched the car's accelerator.

He bounded from the vehicle and his long strides ate the ground as he plowed through invisible barriers. His heart thrashed when he took the stone steps three at a time and burst through the front door without knocking.

His stepdad waited for him in the front hall. At his side, Brynn stood clutching a file folder overstuffed with papers.

Seeing her, Aiden drew his first full breath in an hour.

"You're still here," she said, her tone dryer than the desert. "That's a record."

He drew his lips back in a sneer. "Miss me, did ya?"

A frown formed between her brows. "What happened to your lip?"

"Nothing."

She drew close. "It's not nothing."

Alarm shot through him, and he jerked his head back, away from her touch. "It was just a bar fight."

Hectic color rushed into her cheeks, and she pulled her hand away. "What did you do? Hit on someone's girlfriend?"

"You guessed it."

He expected her animosity and thoroughly enjoyed her obvious jealousy, which reminded him of the possessiveness she used to show for him. But the anguish that tore across her face left dumbfounded.

While his mind still grappled with the cause of it, she blanked her expression. "What are you doing here?"

"I asked him to come," Alan said.

Startled green eyes darted to her dad. "Why?"

Alan tucked his hands into the pockets of his dress slacks. "To talk."

"To talk about what?"

"He's my stepson." Alan lifted his shoulders. "It's been years since we talked."

Bitterness lashed at Aiden. "It's been years since we've talked because you threatened to have me arrested for rape."

Brynn sucked in a sharp breath.

The asshole laughed. "Let's not get into all that now. It's behind us."

"And yet it feels like only yesterday," Aiden said through clenched teeth.

"Brynn, honey, will you give us a minute?"

She gaped at her dad a moment, then said, "I think I'll stay."

Aiden's eyebrows crept skyward. Was that the closest she'd ever come to defying her father?

He didn't mean to judge her for it. Her dad had stood by her when her mother abandoned her, and even though it was literally the least any halfway decent parent would do, she felt indebted to him.

He got that. He really did. She was loyal. Faithful.

To her dad, at least.

But it pissed him off.

"Not this time, sweetheart." Alan patted her on the arm. "Aiden and I need to talk. It's man's business."

"Man's business?" She repeated the ridiculous phrase while Aiden's stupefied chuckle echoed around the foyer.

"Geez, Al. That's not insulting or anything."

"I'm sorry." Fatigue dragged at Alan's grizzled features. "Just give us a minute alone, would you? Aren't you shopping today? It's Sunday."

"Most people go to church on Sunday." Aiden shook his head. "But not you. You go shopping."

Pale green eyes flayed him. "When you've been around more than a couple of hours, you can have an opinion about how I spend my time. Until then, keep your opinions to yourself."

When she pushed past him, her light, clean scent wafted up to assault his senses.

While she stormed off in one direction, his stepdad moved in the opposite.

"This way," Alan called out.

Aiden's head pounded from the ache caused by grinding his teeth.

He moved down the hall, but pulled up when a painting on the wall snagged his gaze. Fascinated, he stared at the intricate brush strokes.

He leaned closer, and his jaw went slack. "You own The Wanderer?"

A distracted frown touched Alan's features. "The what?"

Aiden stabbed a finger at the wall. "This painting. It's called The Wanderer. It sold at auction last month."

For many millions of dollars. Ten times the amount of its assessed value.

"Oh." His stepdad's distraction only intensified. "Yeah."

Then he disappeared through a door.

With difficulty, Aiden dragged his eyes from the painting and followed Alan into the wood-paneled room.

Behind them, Alan slid the heavy pocket doors closed. "I wouldn't have asked you here if it weren't important."

"I have no doubt you must be desperate if you've come to me."

The plush oriental rug covering the wood floors swallowed Alan's footfalls. "Have a seat."

Aiden dropped into a leather armchair in front of the massive mahogany desk. "What's the matter? Bought one too many paintings?"

His stepdad eased into the high-back executive chair behind the desk. "I want to make you an offer."

The only thing Aiden had ever wanted from the man was his daughter, and they both knew Brynn was not available to the likes of him.

"There's nothing you could offer me that I want," Aiden said.

One of Alan's eyebrows lifted in challenge. "What about Hathaway Group?"

"Your company?" Aiden shifted uneasily in the chair. "What about it?"

"I want to give it to you."

CHAPTER 5

Shock slammed into him. "This is a fucking joke, right?"

"Not at all," Alan said.

"But…" Aiden's mind reeled, spinning scenarios and running probabilities, but no logical motive kicked out. "Why?"

"I'm going to try something new." Alan drew open the top drawer of the desk and withdrew a brown leather cigar box. "I've built one successful business, and I want to try my hand at another. I'm opening an art gallery."

"That's it." Aiden surged to his feet. "I'm out of here."

The drawer fell shut with a bang of sound. "Sit down."

Fury lashed Aiden at the command.

"Please," Alan added.

His muscles twitching to flee, Aiden lowered his body into the chair once more. "You have two minutes."

"As president of Hathaway Group, you'll be compensated handsomely."

"How much?"

Alan raised the lid on the box, and the faint scent of tobacco floated up. "Far more than you're accustomed to."

"You have no clue what I'm accustomed to."

"Fair enough. I'm sure we can come to terms that satisfy us both. But keep in mind, I'm not asking for a full-time commitment. Everything is on autopilot." Alan tipped the box toward Aiden. "You don't even have to show up if you don't want to."

With one hand, Aiden waved off the offer for a cigar. "How will I get paid my fat corporate salary if I don't show up to work?"

"My accountant, Philip, takes care of everything." Alan selected a cigar for himself. "He'll mail your checks to you anywhere you are in the world."

"So I'd be a figurehead?"

"It's vital that the company maintains the appearance of strong leadership." Alan rolled the cigar between his fingers.

"Tell me again why that person won't be you?" Aiden wanted to know.

"I'm starting a new company, and I want to keep it separate from Hathaway Group."

"You're divesting?" Aiden reclined back into the chair. "What happened to me not having to do any actual work?"

"I must divest, legally." With the flick of a lighter, Alan took several puffs of the cigar.

"Legally if not truthfully?" Aiden's sneer tasted as bitter as the words. "Wouldn't want to risk ruining Chicago's reputation for corruption, now would we?"

"If things go well, in a year or two, I'll fold both businesses under the Hathaway Group umbrella." Smoke and the sharp scent of tobacco permeated the cloistered room. "The art market is hot, but volatile. In case things don't go well, I want the two businesses kept separate for now. All you have to do is keep Hathaway Group afloat until I'm able to return."

He should do it. He should call the bastard's bluff.

With the thought, a slow smile worked its way across Aiden's face.

All he had to do was say yes, and he won. Either he'd gain the satisfaction of proving Alan a liar, a prize not to be underestimated, or his stepdad meant the offer and a whole new world of possibilities opened up to him, every one of which added up to Aiden exacting a little revenge on the man who'd taken everything from him.

What would it be? Would he gleefully run the company into the ground? Co-opt it and turn it into some entirely new venture that'd drive his stepdad crazy, like a homeless shelter or a home for runaway, or disowned, youth?

Better yet, Aiden could use his newfound power as head of the company to torture the woman who'd so easily tossed him aside twelve years ago. His smile widened.

Alan met Aiden's gaze with a direct, level look. "I wouldn't ask this of you if it wasn't absolutely necessary."

"What about Brynn?"

Unease settled on Alan's shoulders. "She's the vice president and will remain so."

"I mean, shouldn't you be giving the company to her?" Aiden said. "President, vice president. That's kind of the point, isn't it?"

"I can't do that."

"Why not?"

Alan's cheeks puffed as he took several heavy pulls of his cigar.

"Whatever." Aiden stood. "Work out your issues with your daughter, but leave me out of it."

Smoke billowed from Alan when he exhaled. "It's complicated, okay."

"Then you better start explaining it to me."

"She's... she's not ready to run a company this large." Alan sputtered with his lies.

"But I am?"

"She's too soft to be on her own."

"She's a grown-ass woman, Al." At the ugly pallor of Alan's skin, alarm crept up Aiden's spine. "It can't be that bad, can it? You sell houses."

Alan's chair groaned when he leaned forward and snuffed out his cigar in the ashtray. "This business, it's cutthroat. Vultures are always circling. With Brynn at the head of this company, they'd smell blood. They'd swoop in and pick her apart in a matter of months." With his cigar extinguished, Alan rocked back. "She'd know it was all her fault, and she'd be devastated. I need someone who can keep the sharks at bay, and you're as unfriendly a guy as I could come up with."

At that, Aiden almost cracked a smile. "Flattery won't help you."

"I don't want to upset her."

"If you think appointing me head of Hathaway Group won't upset her, you don't know your daughter very well."

"She'll understand." Alan waved off the worry with a large sweep of his hand. "Eventually."

Dropping back down into the chair, Aiden set one heel, then the other, on top of Alan's desk with boorish thuds. "I should say yes just to see her reaction."

"I know we haven't always seen eye to eye, but when it comes to my daughter, I think we're on the same team."

Aiden's smile fell. "You'd be wrong about that."

Alan's shrewd gaze made an open assessment of him. "Would I?"

Aiden didn't like the perceptive gleam in his stepdad's eyes. "So let's recap," he said. "You want to give me the company you've spent the last decade building so that you can—what was it?"

"Pursue new opportunities."

"I'll be president—"

"And CEO."

"—and CEO, but I don't have to do any actual work or even show up if I don't want to, and for my unemployment, you'll pay me a massive salary?"

Oblivious to the irony, Alan held out his hands. "What do you say?"

Aiden set both of his feet on the floor. "Find someone else."

"There isn't anyone else."

"Cian or Rory would help Brynn."

A wrench of genuine distress pinched Alan's features. "Cian has enough on his plate right now."

"Rory, then."

Alan shook his head. "Rory and Brynn are too alike in this. Rory's a diplomat. I need a fighter."

"And that's what you think I am? A fighter?"

Serious eyes, light like his daughter's, landed on Aiden's face. "I don't know what you are. We never got to know each other all that well."

Aiden refused to blink. "And why is that?"

"I was protecting my daughter then. Just as I am now."

"So we've come full circle, have we?" In his chest, Aiden's heart pounded with his contempt. "You ruined my life to keep me away from her, and now you'd ruin it to make me protect her?"

Alan's eyes narrowed to tiny, calculating slits. "One thing I do know about you, you're a bastard, and I'm not talking about the circumstances of your birth."

Aiden's hands curled into fists.

Abruptly, Alan stood. "You know what? You're right. Forget I said anything." He strode toward the office door. "I'll speak with Jared about all this. I'm sure we'll be able to come to an agreement."

The mention of Jared drove Aiden to his feet. "Excuse me?"

"I'm sorry I wasted your time." At the door, Alan faced him. "Jared and Brynn will be married within the year, and there's no reason he can't take over the business. Actually, it makes perfect sense. I should've thought of it before now."

The words coiled through Aiden, twisting and winding his innards tight.

It was a setup. An ambush.

Of course it was.

Alan knew Aiden couldn't be blackmailed. Not this time. He may have gotten away with it once years ago, but this time, things were different, and Alan must've known if he wanted to pull the strings to make Aiden dance, he had to come up with a damned good motivator.

He had to dangle the only thing Aiden had ever wanted from him.

His daughter.

Goddammit.

BRYNN NEVER REALIZED how well the door to her dad's study had been soundproofed. The work crammed inside the file folder she clutched in arms was long forgotten as she paced the hallway outside the door.

When finally the heavy wooden door whisked open, Aiden shot from the room like a missile at the launch.

She started after him, but at the snap of her dad's voice, she jolted.

"Aiden, wait."

Aiden skidded to a stop, but he didn't turn.

In the heavy silence, her dad clenched and unclenched his fists. "I need you," he said. "*We* need you."

Panic ricocheted through her veins. "Dad? What is going on?"

In slow increments, Aiden turned. The two men shared a long look that sent her heart plummeting to her toes. Then one of Aiden's straight, dark brows quirked.

A challenge.

Her dad made a sharp half-turn toward her. "I've asked Aiden to step into my role at Hathaway Group."

The blood drained from her head in a rush. With the dizzying swoop, the file folder overflowing with notes and receipts slipped through her fingers, and papers scattered across the marble floor at her feet.

"I'm stepping aside." Her dad wouldn't quite meet her eyes. "Effective immediately."

"Because of your heart?" Her brain tripped to catch up. "Did the doctor say something to you?"

"It's not my heart," her dad said.

"Then… why?" she asked.

"Remember that new venture we discussed?"

"The art gallery?" She blinked stupidly at him. "You were serious about that?"

Her dad's mouth pulled into a tight line. "Yes, I was serious. And now is the time to move forward with it."

At her feet, papers crinkled when she stepped forward. "I told you, I don't mind taking over your responsibilities until you're ready to come back."

But her dad was shaking his head. "You have your own work to do. The company needs you doing it."

"But…" She risked a glance at Aiden. "Why are you bringing him into this?"

"The company needs a forceful leader at the top," her dad said.

Treachery stole her breath. "It has one. More than one. You, Uncle Mike. Me." Her voice faltered. "What about me?"

They'd built the business together. It'd taken years of hard work, and through it all, she'd assumed that when the time came, she would be the one to lead the company. Now her dad would cut her out?

In favor of Aiden?

Aiden!

"Trust me, it's better this way. You can keep doing what you love to do. Design. Decorate. Make things pretty. Leave the business stuff to us. You don't want to be bothered with all that man stuff."

Brynn recoiled. "Man stuff?"

The daggers of betrayal were coming too fast and too painfully.

Darts of self-doubt stabbed and punctured. Wasn't she good enough? Hadn't she proven herself?

Sure, she had much to learn, but not that much. Not as much as Aiden.

Aiden!

The person who hadn't been around in years. Who knew nothing about the company. Who hadn't spent more than a few weeks one summer helping her uncle demo a couple of houses.

What. The. Hell?

"Man stuff?" Aiden cringed. "Really, Al?"

"The job requires someone tough. Someone willing to do what's necessary." Her dad's voice rose with his conviction. "It needs someone with balls."

The strangled sound that erupted from her might have been a laugh or a sob.

Her racing heart outpaced her rapid-fire thoughts. What was happening?

Why was it happening?

Had her dad always been such a misogynistic jerk?

And how had Aiden come to be here at this exact moment? To witness every awful second of her heartbreak and humiliation?

Her cheeks on fire, she whirled on him.

Indeed, he watched her closely. A small crease puckered the space between his eyebrows as he absorbed every detail of her embarrassment.

He must be enjoying this.

He'd hated her for so long, she couldn't rule out the possibility he'd orchestrated the whole thing. Had he planned it out over weeks? Months? Years?

From the moment her dad threw him out of the house?

The thought struck her like a hammer driving a nail head through solid wood.

"Why did you come back?" she asked him.

A dangerous light flickered in his golden-brown eyes.

She ignored it. "This is why, isn't it? You did this to get back at me for what happened?"

The muscle along his jawline ticked. "This was not my idea."

Her suspicion ran too deep. "Do you want me to apologize? Admit I was wrong?"

He rolled his shoulders as if shaking off some minor irritation.

"Fine." Suddenly adrift on a sea of churning emotions, her stomach heaved. "You were right about everything, and I was wrong, okay? You win. Are you happy? Will you please go away now?"

The dangerous light in his dark eyes turned downright lethal. "Once again, you're blaming the wrong guy. I didn't ask for this. I don't want your company."

"Then why is my dad trying to give it to you?"

"Good question." Aiden's voice dripped with sarcasm. "You should ask him."

Frustration closed the back of her throat when she faced her dad. She had asked him, and she'd gotten some ridiculous answer about testicles.

"Nothing has changed," her dad said, an edge of impatience sneaking into his voice. Soon, he'd be done with this conversation and that would be that. "You're still the vice president of Hathaway Group. The only difference is, you work for Aiden now."

"I have not agreed to anything." Aiden's words coiled with tension, like a trap ready to be sprung.

After a beat of surprised anger, her dad snapped. "Well? Yes or no? Which is it?"

"I have one condition."

"You have—?" With a patronizing bark of laughter, her dad shook his head. "All right, let's hear it."

"You will divest," Aiden said. "For real."

All traces of humor leached from her dad's expression.

"If I'm in charge, I want to be in charge, and I don't want you meddling from the sidelines." Aiden's brutal gaze pinned her dad inside the trap. "If you interfere with my work, I'm gone. If you sabotage me in any way, I'm gone. If you undermine me or so much as steal my lunch from the break room, I'm gone."

Her dad sputtered as color crept into his cheeks. She'd never seen him so flustered.

A slow smile curved Aiden's mouth. "If you want my help, that's the only way you're going to get it."

Suddenly, the stammering ceased. "It's a deal." Her dad turned on his heel and retreated down the hall. "But don't muck it up. I'm counting on you."

With a thump of finality, the door to his study slid closed.

Brynn's heart spasmed.

That was that. It was over.

Somehow, someway, she'd just lost her life raft. Her life's work, the company she'd founded and nurtured, no longer belonged to her.

It belonged to Aiden.

From the shadows, panic pounced. The edges of her vision trembled.

Years of emotion crashed down on her and she dropped to her knees. With wide, wild sweeps of her arms, she gathered the papers littering the floor and tried to ride out the onslaught.

For twelve years, she'd pined for him, and all the while, he'd been plotting her demise. Twelve years of tears and regret, shame and self-doubt, and finally, total devastation.

Climbing awkwardly to her feet, she hugged the fluttering documents to her chest like a shield.

Beneath his intense gaze, she began to shake.

"I hate you." Her watery voice dowsed the heat from the words.

Still, he winced as though she'd wounded him. "I'm sorry."

"I will never forgive you," she said. "Once again, you've taken everything from me."

It was the wrong thing to say.

On his face, a black cloud materialized. "*I* have taken everything from *you*?"

"Yes."

"They threw me out of my home. I had nowhere to go. No job. No food." His tongue whipped and lashed, taking bites of her flesh. "I had nothing and no one to turn to."

Her heart gave an agonizing wrench.

"I know it's real convenient for you, but you can't keep pretending that you're the victim in this, Brynn."

Her throat ached with the effort to hold back tears. "You

don't get to judge me, Aiden Nolan. You have no idea what it was like for me."

"Don't I? You had everything you ever wanted. You had a family." His palm smacked his chest. "*My* family."

"Because you left," she cried. "You left while I stayed. I had to face them. All of them. Every day. I had to watch our parents' marriage fall apart, knowing we were the reason for it. I had to watch Rory and Cian lose you. I did that. All by myself. Because you weren't here."

"That was your choice to stay." His cool tone sent a chill through her.

"It was an impossible choice."

"But you still made it. I wanted you to come with me until things settled down. I never would've kept you from your dad." He thrust a finger at the closed door of her dad's study. "He made you pick. Not me."

Tears blurred her vision. "So, this is my punishment?"

"I told you, I didn't ask for this."

The old, unhealed wounds throbbed in her chest. "But you sure jumped at the chance to hurt me."

He gave a slow, disbelieving shake of his head. "Why don't you marry Jared?"

She rocked back on her heels. "Wh-what?"

"Your dad wants a pair of balls, so go and get yourself a pair of balls." Mockery poisoned his tone. "Marry Jared, and the company is yours."

Fresh wounds formed on top of the old ones. "If I marry him, it won't be to take control of the company I already own. The company *I* built."

His shoulders moved with his callous shrug. "I'm just sayin'. It'd solve a lot of your problems."

"I don't have a lot of problems." She fixed him with a dark look. "I have one problem. Only one."

His eyes narrowed dangerously. "You think I cannot do it."

"I know nothing about you. Do you have any experience running a company this large?"

One dark eyebrow inched upward. "Do you?"

"I built this company."

"You've mentioned that."

His scorn poked holes in her self-confidence. "In this entire city, a handful of people could make the argument that they are more qualified than me to run Hathaway Group. You are not one of them."

White teeth flashed in his humorless face. "I get it. You want me to leave."

She didn't deny it. "I see now that you were right to stay away. It was easier for everyone without you here."

Anguish touched his expression a moment before the anger crowded it out. "Is that right?"

She experienced a twinge of regret.

"Who is it easier for if I leave?" His wintery tone sent a chill through her. "Your dad? You? My brothers? Brie?"

"That's not what I meant—"

"It's what you said. It's what you believe. Why don't you just admit it?"

"You're p-putting words in my mouth."

His icy glare froze her heart.

"I suppose it doesn't matter what you believe," he said.

At the odd catch in his voice, fear squeezed the air from her lungs. "Wh-what do you mean?"

"I'm done being polite." Disdain burned in his fiery brown eyes. "I'm done giving everyone else what they want. I will not stay away anymore just to make it easier for all of you."

"Easy?" Her bitter laugh sounded shrill in her own ears. "You think it was easy on any of us? On me? You don't know what you're talking about."

"I can see what it cost you." His harsh gaze raked up and down her body. "Must've been excruciating for you, living in a big fancy house and working a cushy job at daddy's multi-million-dollar corporation."

A tear spilled over to slide down her cheek, and she swiped at it. "All you see is the money. You don't know what's in my heart."

"You have one?"

"Screw you," she choked.

"Been there, done that."

"You are such a jerk."

"Don't get me wrong, it's a tantalizing offer." His mouth twisted with a cruel sneer when he threw her words back at her. "But I'm afraid it wouldn't be appropriate, what with me being your boss and all."

CHAPTER 6

*A*iden should welcome her hatred, but with Brynn, "should" never mattered for long.

The pain in her eyes destroyed him. Like poison-tipped daggers, each look of betrayal and every word of hatred pierced the protective armor he'd spent twelve years fashioning.

So while he should welcome the poisonous regret seeping into his bones, he didn't.

He loathed it.

And he loathed his stepfather for bringing them to this moment.

Alan had told him that Brynn was too soft, too sensitive to run the company in a business full of cutthroat competition, but by now, Aiden knew his stepdad well enough not to take him at his word.

Did Brynn lack toughness? Or was there some other reason Alan wished to prevent her from assuming control of the family business? Because, while she was wrong about a lot of the things she'd said, Brynn was right that she was infinitely more qualified than Aiden to run the company she'd helped build.

So what was Alan's game? And how did Aiden fit into it?

That's what he intended to find out.

Unable to sleep more than a few hours on Rory's lumpy couch, he showered and made his way downtown early the next morning. Driving in from the neighborhoods, the city reared up from the ground, forbidding and proud.

The Hathaway Group offices were in a converted factory on the banks of the Chicago River, surrounded by looming skyscrapers that encroached as if to devour the smaller building from another age.

Since he'd arrived well before the start of normal business hours, the security guard, Curtis, buzzed Aiden in. Though an older man, Curtis had a large barrel chest and massive biceps.

"Mr. Hathaway told me to expect you." Curtis led Aiden across an open lobby with an understated water feature and a conspicuous number of green ferns.

"How long have you worked for him?" Aiden asked conversationally.

"Oh, I've been with the family since the beginning." Warmth affected his deep baritone.

"Do you like your job?"

"I like it all right. It's quiet, and it pays well."

In his mind, Aiden began ticking through his list. After an initial, first-impression assessment of any business, he could often glean much about the company's health from the state of the facilities and the employees he encountered.

After a quick ride in the elevator, Curtis led Aiden through a tidy cubicle farm to an office door in the far back corner. Bending over the doorknob, Curtis fiddled with the lock, then the door swung open on an oversized office with an impressive view of the river.

Sleek black furniture and luxurious carpeting contrasted the décor in the rest of the building, which was in keeping with the brick and wooden bones of the old warehouse.

"Welcome to Hathaway Group, sir."

"Thank you, Curtis." Aiden stepped into the office. "Can you tell me where to find Philip?"

"Mr. Griffin's office is upstairs. Room 441."

While Aiden waited to be given access to the Hathaway Group servers and financial records, he figured he'd go directly to Alan's trusty accountant, Philip, to grab the files he needed to get started.

Upstairs, Philip visibly bristled when Aiden requested the company's financial statements. "I am responsible for the entire finance division here at Hathaway Group."

"Right." Aiden glanced around the opulent office. "That's why I came to you. I want to see the ledgers."

"Is there something specific you're looking for?" Philip's chair groaned when he leaned forward and filched a pencil off his desk.

After college, Aiden had worked at a hedge fund for a few years until he could no longer stand the cubicle and suits, so not only did he need to understand the company's financial health in order to do his job, but a professional curiosity tempted him.

This was his vehicle now, and he wanted to peek under the hood. "I want to see at all of it."

"Of course." Philip scribbled a note on a yellow Post-it. "I'll write you up a summary when I get a chance."

"That's not necessary." A sliver of annoyance wedged beneath Aiden's skin. "I have a business background and I know how to read a spreadsheet. Just email me the files."

Philip's tight smile revealed over-bright white teeth. "My financial documents are very complex."

Aiden's eyes narrowed as suspicion replaced annoyance.

"I'll ask if I have questions."

"Why don't we schedule a time to sit down and I can give you an overview?"

"Let's do that." Aiden turned. "In the meantime, send me the files so I can be ready with my questions."

"Anything you say, boss."

Aiden didn't miss the edge of mockery that Philip hooked onto that last word.

By the time Aiden found his way back downstairs, a niggle of dread had taken root. If Alan's sudden interest in artwork hadn't set off his bullshit detector, Philip's borderline hostility sure had.

It was possible Alan hadn't informed Philip of his decision to hand over his company to his disfavored stepson, and shock was the cause for Philip's distrust.

But again, Aiden had learned long ago to use caution where his stepfather was concerned. If Alan was up to no good, Aiden needed to figure it out as soon as possible.

And if it involved his daughter, there'd be hell to pay.

AFTER A SLEEPLESS NIGHT spent tossing and turning, Brynn dozed off on the sofa near dawn and slept through her alarm clock as it blared in her bedroom down the hall.

Which meant, for the first time in years, she wasn't at her desk before anyone else had arrived at the office.

Brynn detected the soft tap of Donna's fingers as they flew over the keyboard when she shuffled by. "Good morning."

"Good morning," Donna called out in return. "How was your weekend?"

"Great," Brynn lied, craning her neck. "If anyone's looking for me, I'll be in my off—"

She plowed into a solid, masculine torso.

Her gaze traveled up, past the side of his neck where a trio of black cross tattoos peeked out at the neckline of his crisp white dress shirt, to his kissable mouth.

Aiden's soft, full lips moved when he said, "Glad you could join us this morning."

"Oh, sorry. Did I miss your introduction?" She winced. "Gee, I feel really terrible about that."

The gold flecks in his eyes glinted with a mischievous light. "You're just in time."

"If I could have everyone's attention." Her dad's voice boomed through the large room. "I have an announcement."

Her stomach dropped.

When Aiden stepped around her, she turned slowly.

The well-cut charcoal gray suit he wore melded to his lean, muscular frame when he sauntered through the small crowd of employees as though he owned the place.

Which, technically, he did.

In the wake of his splendor, a soft buzz started to churn.

"This is my stepson, Aiden Nolan." Her dad smacked Aiden on the back. "He'll be stepping into my role as president and CEO of Hathaway Group."

The buzz swelled to a drone.

"I'll be stepping away from the real estate business for a while to pursue some new opportunities, but I think you'll find yourselves in very capable hands."

Curious glances from her coworkers prickled Brynn as she stared straight ahead.

What were they thinking? Were they wondering why her dad hadn't chosen her to step into his place as head of the company? Did he think she wasn't smart enough? Or didn't work hard enough?

A few glances were pitying.

While her dad praised her stepbrother's talent and business acumen, her thoughts spiraled downward. What if it wasn't her work performance that had convinced her dad to pass her over? What if it was the panic attacks? What if her dad believed she was too weak, too messed up, to take over the business?

Feeling agitated and insecure, she kept her eyes fixed on the front of the room.

As though the past twelve years had never happened, her dad beamed proudly at his stepson. "Aiden, would you like to say a few words?"

"Thank you, Alan." Calm and confident, Aiden immediately captured the room's rapt attention.

He spoke a little about his experience and his plans for the company, and while he talked, the staff she'd hired to work for her and her dad slipped under his spell.

At one point, he made a lame joke, and his sudden, crooked smile flashed, startling in the severity of his striking face, and a murmur of appreciation mingled with the crowd's obliging laughter.

When he finished, a throng of bodies pushed forward, excited to meet their new boss.

Angling sideways, Brynn squirted out the back of the crowd and stole away to her office. When she pushed the door shut behind her and sagged against it, she expelled a deep, shuddering breath.

Which was cut off when a light rap sounded. Before she could hustle out of the way, the door swung open, and she grunted when it hit her in the backside.

Aiden loomed in the doorway. "Hiding from the boss?"

Tall and broad-shouldered, his dark hair begged her to push her fingers through the thick, wavy locks, and his potent gaze made her heart trip inside her chest.

She scowled. "What do you want?"

"I need you to show me around." He leaned with a

shoulder against the jamb. "Apparently, you're the best person for the task. Everyone says so."

"My dad can do it."

"He's already gone."

"What?" Disappoint gripped her.

She'd wanted to try talking to him. If she could get him alone, she might convince him to reconsider this crazy, rash plan of his. Maybe it wasn't too late to change his mind and save her company from Aiden's evil clutches.

"He got out of here so fast, you'd think he was retiring and not starting a new company." He folded his arms across his chest. "Now, about that tour…?"

"Why bother? You won't be around long enough to do the job."

"I told you, I'm not leaving."

The steel in his tone lodged a sliver of unease in her chest. "You never stay."

"Doesn't mean I can't."

The sliver twisted.

"You said it yourself. I have a lot to learn." His wide shoulders hitched. "I suggest we get started."

While she sputtered her outrage, his arms fell to his sides, and he moved toward her.

"If you expect me to train you to do the job that should be mine, you are delusional."

"You work for me now." His words sounded like a threat. "You have to do what I say."

She craned her neck back to look up at him. "Or what?"

He smelled delicious, like sunshine and soap.

"I could fire you."

An anvil of fear slammed into her.

Warm brown eyes watched her face closely. "You could lose everything. Your business, your fancy home. Your entire lifestyle could go up in smoke."

He garnished every word with a dash of disdain.

"You think I only care about the money?" In her surprise, she failed to banish the hurt from her voice.

"Don't you?"

The gut-punch knocked a puff of air from her lungs.

It hurt more than it should have. But, she supposed, that's what happened when fantasies were crushed.

Because until that moment, she'd held out some small hope that what they'd had together twelve years ago had been real. It might've been brief and ill-fated, but there had been genuine affection between them, and passion.

Suddenly, and entirely too late, she realized it was all a lie. He'd never loved her, and indeed, his hatred for her ran far deeper than she'd wanted to believe.

His face swam before her eyes. "You know me. You know where I grew up. I don't care about that. You know I don't."

His features held their hard edges. "You've changed."

With the slash of pain, a gasp slipped from her.

Just then, her design assistant, Felicity, breezed into the office. "Good morning. Sorry I'm late—" At the sight of Aiden, Felicity drew up short. "Ooooh. Hello, there."

His mask of effortless charm dropped into place.

Without taking her eyes off him, Felicity spoke to Brynn through the side of her mouth. "Who is this?"

"This is Aiden." Her emotions roiling, Brynn's voice sounded weak. "My stepbrother."

Felicity gasped. "Wait, is this the oldest one? The saint, right?"

Brynn snorted.

They thought he was perfect. A saint. No one ever bothered to look past his dark beauty and seductive charm.

But Brynn had. She knew the truth about him.

He was a liar. A manwhore.

He was pure and utter sin.

"Nice to meet you, Aiden," Felicity purred.

The crooked smile played on his puffy lips. "It's a pleasure, Miss…?"

"Felicity. I'm Felicity."

"Felicity." He let her name linger on his tongue. "What a lovely name."

Pink stained Felicity's cheeks.

"Aiden is the new President of Hathaway Group." Brynn slanted forward, drawing close to Felicity's ear. "He's your boss."

"Oh." Felicity's mouth dropped opened. She blinked rapidly. "Wow, I was only a few minutes late. It seems like I missed a lot."

Brynn gestured to the conference table at the far end of her office. "We should get started."

Aiden remained root to his spot. "How about that tour first?"

Felicity rushed forward. "Sure thing—"

"Felicity is busy," Brynn snapped.

"I'd like you to show me around." One corner of Aiden's mouth tilted. "As my assistant—"

"I am not your assistant," Brynn ground out. "I am the vice president."

He flicked his wrist. "Same thing."

"No, it is not."

Felicity crossed to the table. "Go ahead. I need a few minutes to set up, anyway."

At Aiden's smug smile, Brynn's scowl deepened. "Donna can show you around."

He frowned. "Donna?"

"She's our executive assistant."

"Ours?" he asked. "We share her?"

"Yes. She keeps our calendars, schedules any meetings we need setup, that sort of thing." Brynn wiggled her fingers toward the door, as if to shoo him away. "She knows where everything is and can get you whatever you need."

"But I don't want Donna." His voice dropped a couple of octaves when he said, "I want you."

Her skin flushed hot. "Well, I'm not available."

"Well, make yourself available." A menacing edge crept into his tone.

She gasped her exasperation. "You are unbelievable."

"Thank you."

"That was not a compliment."

"You two are adorable," Felicity said. "You fight like brother and sister."

"He is not my brother," Brynn said at the same time Aiden declared, "She is not me sister."

A hiss of annoyance leaked between Brynn's teeth. "Fine. Let's just go."

But the moment they stepped into the hall, she whirled on him. "I have worked very hard and have made this company a lot of money. They pay me well to do what I do, and I am not ashamed of that."

Something like remorse flickered in his eyes. "Nor should you be."

"Then, please, stop looking at me like I'm the scum on the bottom of your shoe." The hitch in her voice whipped color into her cheeks, and she twisted away from him.

Everything that had happened in her office with Felicity recurred again and again on their brief tour of the building.

The ladies in the front office nearly swooned when Aiden stopped to chat with them.

As did the design team.

In accounting and acquisitions, he drew the men to him just as easily and without sacrificing an ounce of his charming appeal.

It was like high school all over again.

Brynn had hated high school.

By the time Justine in the contracts department invited him for a drink after hours, jealousy burned through Brynn.

Even though she had no right to feel possessive of him.

Even though they were no longer eighteen, and he was no longer the boy she'd been obsessed with. Far from it.

Even though he'd stolen all her dreams.

She was jealous that he was so willing to give to others what he withheld from her.

The rest of the tour was more of the same. More flirting. More dazzling smiles. More flashbacks of high school as people she'd known and worked with for years suddenly displayed personalities she'd never glimpsed before. Funny and kind, bright and witty, he drew the best out of every one of them.

Finally, somewhere between the payroll and compliance departments, the reality she'd crafted over the last twelve years suffered a fatal fracture and crumbled completely.

She'd tried telling herself the chemistry she and Aiden shared was the reason she'd never fallen for another man or even met one who captured her interest beyond a few dates.

Bitter-washed memories assailed her, and through that lens, it hit her. Their chemistry wasn't unique. It wasn't special to *them*, to him and her together.

It was special to *him*, and only to him, and he shared it with anyone and everyone he interacted with.

When they'd completed the tour and arrived at the door to his office, her head ached with the emotional toll the past thirty-six hours had levied on her.

"Now where to?"

Her hands trembled, and she tucked them into the pockets of her black dress pants. "I have meetings with my staff the rest of the morning. Maybe you can find something to do for a few hours?" She turned toward her office. "Or just go play on the internet for a while and try not to break anything."

But rather than turn toward his office, he followed her.

She glanced over her shoulder, then tripped to a stop. "What are you doing?"

"I'm coming with you."

She twisted around. "Oh, please don't."

"On-the-job training is the best way to learn." He brushed by and barged into her office ahead of her.

Her design assistants, Felicity and Alison, had pulled up the software program they used to play with color schemes and layouts for every room in every house they renovated. The kitchen of their latest project displayed on the enormous TV screen hanging on the far wall.

"We got a problem," Felicity announced, as Brynn moved toward the conference table.

A delay had occurred at the warehouse shipping the custom cabinets they'd ordered for the Wicker Park project, and suddenly the entire renovation risked not getting done in time for the open house in two weeks.

Worse yet, a delay on one project meant they needed to shift the work crews around, and they couldn't change the crews' schedules without reworking the complex project schedules of five other ongoing renovations.

Throughout the meeting, Aiden remained quiet, which should've pleased her but instead frayed her already thin nerves instead. She could imagine what he was thinking, watching her scramble to find a solution to the crisis. How many mistakes had he picked her apart for making? Which of her weaknesses had he zeroed in on to ridicule her about later?

Lord knew she had enough of them to justify the troubled frown marring his perfect features.

When they'd finally nailed down a new schedule, Felicity and Alison emptied out of her office.

She held the door for Aiden, but he hesitated.

"So you oversee project management for the entire company?" he asked. "For every project?"

She nodded. "I also make all new residential acquisitions. My dad handles—handled—commercial development. It's unfamiliar territory for us, and he's overseen that expansion."

His thoughtful frown swept suddenly away. "So? What's next?"

"Lunch." She scooted him out the door.

"Excellent. I'm starved." The crooked smile played on his soft lips. "Where're we going?"

In that moment, when he looked at her without disdain or loathing, her heart skipped with wild, reckless abandon.

"I'm going to grab a sandwich downstairs." In the hallway, she pulled her office door closed behind them. "You can go wherever you want. Like you always do."

Inwardly, she cringed. She was just being peevish now, but she couldn't stop the words from popping out of her mouth.

Before more petulant attacks dropped from her tongue, she fled.

On the sun-warmed sidewalk outside, she inhaled her first full breath of the morning. She'd never been able to breathe deeply when Aiden was around.

A light breeze lifted the ends of her hair and kissed her skin as she crossed the bridge over the river to her favorite food truck. Waiting in line, she checked her phone messages and while the sun heated her back, tried to pretend her world hadn't been flipped upside down.

When a presence appeared at her elbow, she knew it was him before he spoke.

"Do you want to know why I never came back?"

CHAPTER 7

*B*rynn sucked in a sharp breath and stared up into his beautiful face, which was taut with emotion. Certain whatever he said next would shatter her, she could only nod.

"I was eighteen. Homeless. Broke. Hungry." A hitch of vulnerability roughened his voice. "There was no way I could afford college tuition on a bartender's salary."

The line moved forward, and so did they.

"When your dad found me, I hadn't eaten for days."

Her heart lodged in her throat. "My dad found you? When? Where?"

"Here. I was crashing at friends' houses when I could." The breeze blew a hank of dark hair across his forehead. "I had no money and no way to leave the city. I couldn't afford a meal, let alone a plane ticket."

The line shifted again. With a weak smile for the vendor, she stepped forward and mechanically ordered her usual number four. Hands shaking, she fumbled clumsily for a bill in her wallet.

"I had nowhere to go," he said. "I was sleeping under the pier so the cops wouldn't find me and send me to a shelter."

With the wrench of her pain, her fist clenched, crumpling the billfold in her palm. "Did he know you had no place to go? What did he say to you?"

Aiden's sharp jaw clenched tight. "He made me an offer I couldn't refuse."

Frozen in fear, she stared at his beautiful, pain-riddled face. "What does that mean? What offer?"

"He would pay for my airfare and tuition as long as I left the country and never came back."

The air whooshed from her lungs. "He paid you?"

"He blackmailed me." Anger sliced through his tone. "He knew I was desperate, and he extorted promises from me."

"Ma'am," the vendor barked, and she jolted.

She handed the man her money and plucked her sandwich off the metal counter.

When she'd scrambled out of the way, Aiden stepped up to the window and placed his order. While he made his exchange with the vendor, Brynn stood on the crowded side-walk with her sandwich in one hand and her wallet in the other, her world collapsing around her.

Was it true? Had her dad really done it? He'd known she was heartbroken when Aiden left. They all knew it, because Brynn couldn't hide her utter devastation. He'd known Siobhan was heartbroken, too. He *knew*, and yet he kept Aiden away from them, anyway?

Grief overwhelmed her. Grief for the boy abandoned and left on his own. Grief for the girl who was too scared and didn't know what to do. Who didn't have the courage to follow her heart. Who worshipped a father undeserving of her trust.

When Aiden had paid for his sandwich, he slipped from the line.

Her heart in her throat, she looked up at him. "I didn't know...."

"I know you didn't." His fingers picked at the sandwich's cellophane wrapping. "That was part of the deal."

"But you took his money? You went to school in Ireland?"

"Aye, I took his money." Anger radiated off him, but so too did shame and regret. "I took it because I wasn't coming back, anyway."

As his emotions became hers, a trembling started in her chest and moved outwards. "You weren't?"

The soft curve of his mouth hardened. "I didn't want to be where I wasn't wanted."

With that, he eased back a step, then turned and ambled away. She watched his dark head until it blended in with the horde of pedestrians packing the busy sidewalks.

On her walk back, her eyes swam with tears and she struggled not to bump into anyone or trip on the uneven pavement.

That afternoon, she'd planned to check on the progress at a few houses, so rather than return to her office, she headed to the parking garage.

But as she approached her SUV, Aiden leaned against the trunk of the black Charger parked next to her in the spot reserved for the Hathaway Group president, eating his sandwich.

Her feet stumbled.

When he saw her, he stopped chewing.

She ducked her head and tossed her lunch in the trash bin, then she took a straight path to her car door. Her fingers fumbled with her car keys, then the locks clicked open, and she yanked on the handle.

But before she slipped inside her car, she whipped around.

"I'm sorry." The words erupted from her. "I'm sorry you thought no one wanted you here."

Over the roof of his car, he watched her, his features set in stone but his eyes bright with question.

"For twelve years, you were very—" Her throat squeezed. "—*very* missed."

Slowly, he stood.

Choking down a sob, she rushed on. "I'm glad you took his money. I'm glad you went to college, and I'm glad that you ate." Her voice broke, and she swallowed several painful gulps. "I'm just very glad about all of that."

With a gutting wrench of pain, she whirled and dove inside her vehicle before he could laugh at her or say something cruel.

In the quiet interior, she teetered on the verge of losing her battle against the tears when the passenger side door swung open and he slid into the seat beside her.

The door slammed shut, and many long moments passed while he stared hard at the car's dashboard.

When finally he turned his head to look at her, the fiery flecks in his golden-brown eyes blazed. "Thank you for saying that."

The spasms squeezing her heart eased somewhat, and she pushed a shuddering breath between her lips.

For a time, they sat in silence.

Unhurriedly, he lifted his sandwich to his mouth and tore off a bite. He chewed slowly, then swallowed.

Her gaze bounced between him and the sandwich. "I'm going to be out of the office this afternoon while I check on the project sites."

"Okay." He ripped off another hunk of bread with his teeth.

"I'm leaving now, so…."

He reached back and dragged the seatbelt across his body, then clicked it into place.

With a small headshake, she gaped at him. "What are you doing?"

~

What the hell was he doing?

"I'm coming with you." He heard the words as though someone else had spoken them.

Someone confident, and sure, and not at all devastated by one small, simple, softly spoken apology.

The last traces of upset faded with her confusion. "You don't even know where I'm going."

In the confines of the vehicle, her airy scent invaded his senses, and while he shouldn't have climbed into her car, he couldn't bring himself to regret it.

"You're working, though, aren't you?" He suspected she never stopped.

By her expression, he'd guessed right.

With a punch of satisfaction, he settled deeper into the passenger seat. "I want to see what you do all day."

Her light eyes narrowed to tiny, suspicious slits. "You're not a micromanager, are you?"

"I prefer to call it job shadowing." He took another bite of his sandwich.

With an aggrieved sigh, she flipped the key in the ignition, and the engine fired.

It was a warm day, one of the few remaining of the summer, and as she maneuvered the treelined city streets, people packed the sidewalks and patio cafes.

Despite his better judgment, Aiden had agreed to his stepdad's ridiculous offer to take over the family business mostly so that he could make sure Brynn wasn't in over her head. To do that, he needed to get close to her.

At least, that's what he told himself about his reasons for riding along with her while she worked. It had nothing to do with wanting to catch more glimpses of her incredible ass, like he was that same horny teenager who could never resist her.

Damn, she smelled good. Like honey and fresh sea air.

His body reacted with a wrench of lusty yearning. With the tip of his index finger, he speared the black button on his door and eased open the window.

Minutes later, she turned the vehicle onto a quiet side street and eased to a stop in front of an old, drab house.

"This is the Bucktown project," she said, and climbed out of the car.

On the sidewalk, he looked up at a brick two-flat house.

"It's a popular neighborhood that we target often for quick flips." She moved to stand next to him and her gaze followed his. "They built this house in 1918. It has three bedrooms and one bath, so we're adding a full bath upstairs and a three-quarter bath in the basement. That'll add another eight hundred square feet of livable space and take the total square footage to twenty-four hundred feet."

She started toward the house, and he trailed behind her.

With every swing of her round bottom in those snug black pants, he grew more distracted.

"At that size, in this neighborhood," she was saying, "we'll list it at one point four, but if we can get it on the market before the winter slump, we might get as much as one point five or even six for it."

Inside the house, a wall of noise struck them. The heavy fall of a hammer echoed through the large open space, and a radio blared with the tinny chords of an old rock song. Over the clamor, loud voices called out to one another.

They picked their way across the war zone, stepping around an array of discarded power tools and debris. As they moved through the house, the dozen or more men packed inside took notice of their presence. One called out a greeting, and Brynn waved.

Her alert gaze inspected the work being done, and as she progressed deeper into the home, she sprinkled a bevy of compliments for the crew that left even the burly, gray-haired man with arms full of ink blushing with pride.

To one man, she introduced Aiden. "Hey, Joey, do you remember Aiden?"

Brynn's cousin, Joey, who Aiden had worked with for a brief time years ago, extended his hand. "Of course. Hey, man, how you been?"

"Not bad." Aiden slapped his hand into Joey's palm. "Yourself?"

"Can't complain."

"Aiden's going to be filling in for my dad for a while," Brynn said.

Joey's blue eyes grew enormous, and he used one hand to comb his thick beard. "Is that right?"

"My dad is stepping down." Brynn tipped her head to one said. "Did Uncle Mike say anything to you about it?"

"Not a word." His gaze shifted to Aiden. "They never tell us anything. Welcome aboard."

Aiden inclined his head. "Thank you."

Brynn exchanged a look with her cousin, which she quickly concealed when she caught Aiden watching.

She gave Aiden her back. "Do you have a minute to talk about the kitchen?"

"Yeah." Joey abandoned his hammer and followed Brynn to the wide-open space at the back of the house. The kitchen, presumably.

With a tape measure and a sharpie, they carried on an

animated discussion about the layout, including the placement of the cabinets and appliances. Interruptions from the crew came in a steady stream, as most seemed eager to catch Brynn either to ask her questions while she was available to them or to show her something they'd finished.

One guy brought her a bucket and plopped it down at her feet.

When she peered inside, her face lit up like a billboard in Times Square. "Where did you find these?"

"I pried them off all the old windows before we hauled them out." The guy pulled his baseball hat off his head, then tugged it back on. "I thought you'd want us to keep them."

She bent over and lifted a hunk of tarnished metal out of the bucket. The clump in her palm, she brushed her fingers over the antiquated piece of hardware. "You found all this here?"

"Sure did."

"These are amazing." More pieces of rusty hardware made their way into her small hands. "Is there anything we could use them on?"

After a brief discussion that involved input from everyone within earshot, they decided they'd use the old pieces on the built-ins they'd custom designed for the basement, to give the illusion that the brand-new shelving was original to the house.

When she'd finished at the house in Bucktown, they piled into her vehicle and headed to the next house.

At a red light, she switched on her left turn signal.

He studied her profile. "Does your cousin know about us?"

The car blinker ticked several times before she answered. "There is no us."

Though technically true, he wanted to argue with her. "How about Jared? Did you tell him we were lovers?"

Hectic color stained her cheeks. The light turned green, and she executed the turn.

"So he doesn't know." The knowledge moved through Aiden like a quiet storm. "Are we hiding it from him?"

"What I discuss with Jared is none of your business."

He tsked. "Hiding things from the man you're marrying."

Her surprised laugh held no humor. "I am not marrying Jared. I can't even—"

She pursed her lips as if to hold back whatever words she'd been about to say.

"You can't what?"

"Never mind." She turned her face away to glance at her side mirror. "I would like to keep our past quiet from everyone else, though."

That poked a sore spot. "Is that so?"

At his tone, she shot a curious glance at him.

Bitter resentment twisted in his chest. "Are you ashamed you got it on with your stepbrother?"

Startled green eyes flew to his face, then darted back to the road. "I'm not ashamed."

He turned his head and watched the scenery whiz by.

"We did nothing wrong." Her voice gentled. "It's just… I've spent the past ten years trying to prove I'm more than daddy's little girl. If they learn I slept with the new boss, I'll never earn their respect."

They stopped by two more houses, and while the homes' styles and crews varied, Brynn's efficiency and easy rapport with the workers did not.

Most businesses he'd helped to rehab had suffered the same fatal flaw—poor management. So far, that didn't seem to be an issue at Hathaway Group, as everything he trained his clients to do, Brynn seemed to be already doing.

That morning, she'd deftly resolved what appeared to be a potentially catastrophic scheduling conflict and settled a dispute between her design assistants by incorporating the best of what they'd each brought to the table, and she did it all on the fly. With him in the room.

It was…impressive.

Whether she'd learned it in college or through her years on the job, it appeared natural. Effortless. He suspected it was.

She was just being herself.

And if he were being honest, he would've told her she'd already earned her coworkers' respect.

It was an hour past closing when they arrived back at the office and she reclaimed her parking spot in the garage.

"You going up?" he asked.

She nodded. "For a bit."

As they approached the elevator, a man suddenly appeared off the street and planted himself in their path. Before they'd realized what was happening, he'd pushed a camera in Aiden's face and clicked the shutter button.

Aiden lifted a hand against the bright flash. "What the…?"

With a ping, the elevator door slid open, and Brynn moved to step around the man just as he shifted to block Aiden.

Their bodies collided, and his larger frame knocked Brynn back against the wall.

Like a bomb going off in his mind, Aiden's arm shot out and squeezed the man by the neck.

"Do not touch her." Time slowed as ribbons of rage sloped through his bloodstream. The ribbons tightened, and he squeezed until he felt the man swallow.

"It's okay." Her soft voice filled with fear when she laid her hand on his arm. "He's not worth it."

Eyes bulging, the man raised his camera between their faces and clicked.

Against the bright flare of the camera's flash, Aiden winced, and the man scrambled away.

She held the elevator door for him.

"What the hell was that?" he asked, joining her inside the car.

"He works for the *Daily Sun*." She pressed the button, and the doors eased shut.

"The what?"

"It's a tabloid."

He gaped at her for a moment. "Why is a tabloid taking our picture? We're not celebrities."

"I think he was taking your picture." She kept her eyes on the elevator doors. "And, well, you did date that supermodel for a while last year."

Her obvious jealousy might've pleased him if not for the touch of hurt in her voice.

"To whom I haven't spoken since." He straightened his shirt collar.

With a sigh, her narrow shoulders lifted. "I guess they see a young, single, great-looking guy newly in possession of a small fortune and they can't resist you. You're like crack to them."

A smile pushed up one corner of his mouth. "You think I'm great-looking."

She shot him a side-eyed glance. "You know you are."

"Yes, but I didn't know you think I am."

She regarded him solemnly for a moment. "It's an objective fact."

"Still, it's nice to hear." When the elevator doors slid open, the smile lingered on his face.

Dammit.

He played a dangerous game, staying close to her. But he'd hoped to last longer than one fucking day before her sweetness drew him in again.

Was it the first time she had looked at him without wary suspicion or contempt?

He liked it. A lot.

Which meant he needed to remind her, and himself, that he wasn't her friend.

CHAPTER 8

ithin minutes of sending the all-office email, Brynn appeared at his office door.

One hand perched on her hip. "What the hell do you think you're doing?"

"Running a company."

By the end of that first week, he'd completed phase one of his unofficial audit. He'd spoken with every employee in the building to assess their workloads and inquire about any areas of concern they may have and had collected a trove of useful information.

"Work from home?" She snapped her fingers. "Just like that."

"Just like that," he said. "Being boss is fun. You should try it. Oh, wait…."

"Are you trying to ruin the company?"

"Not at all."

He'd made a career out of helping others build successful businesses, and given the opportunity, it was almost too much to expect him not to run with his own long thought-out ideas. After freelancing so long, finally sinking his teeth into something tasted good.

Slowly, he pushed to his feet. "There's no reason they need to be sitting in this building all day. We have forty full-time employees and they're averaging more than an hour commute every day. That's time away from work and their personal lives. That's wasted time."

Uncertainty softened her features.

He rounded the desk and eased his body down onto the corner surface. "Half of them perform eighty percent or more of their duties online or sitting in front of a computer screen. A computer screen that can be physically located anywhere in the city. They spend the rest of their time in meetings or on conference calls. Truly, only a handful need to be physically present in the office more than a few days a week."

Her hand slid off her hip. "What if you need them?"

"Then I'll call them. Or I'll talk to them the next time they're in the office."

"What if they don't answer, and they don't call you back right away?" she challenged.

"They aren't my servants." He folded his arms over his abdomen. "As far as I can tell, you've hired hard workers and trained them well. We all have work to do and are busy doing it. What do I care where they are when they're getting shit done, as long as they're getting it done?"

"But what if it's an emergency and you can't reach them?"

"Then we'll have a problem."

Her internal struggle played out on her pretty face. She wanted to fight, but she was running out of ammunition. It was kind of adorable, actually.

"We're just going to try it out," he said. "Everyone gets one day a week to work from home. If it goes well, we'll discuss more days."

"One day a week?" Her rigid shoulders relaxed. "Did you say that in your email?"

"I did." He clicked his tongue because he knew it'd annoy her. "You didn't read all the way to the bottom, did you?"

The flash of fire in her eyes heated his cock. Always pretty, she was a downright stunner when she was mad. All fierce and fiery. She rarely became angry, except with him.

"They're adults, and I'm choosing to treat them as such." He stood once more. "If they prove me wrong, they'll lose their flexibility. They know that. Let's see how they handle it before we assume they can't."

"Fine." She shot him one last death glare, then swept out of the room.

A soft chuckle rumbled in his chest.

The next day, he knew he needed to be armed with facts and data before he hit the Send button on his email.

She appeared at his door on a cloud of honey and indignation. "Really?"

"You're against healthy lunches now, too?"

Streaks of caramel and gold shimmered in her light brown hair when she shook her head. "You're just bribing them so they'll like you."

"Think it will work?"

He could tell by her frown that she did.

"I don't mind changing up the food available in the building, but an onsite gym?" She stepped through his door. "Are you kidding?"

The desk chair creaked when he leaned back. "Why not? Someone was brilliant enough to buy this massive building. We have plenty of space for it."

"It's not free. You know that, right? There's equipment, showers, new flooring, a sound system." She ticked off each item with her fingers.

"Philip assures me we can afford it. They're practically printing money upstairs."

Her hand still hanging midair, she pulled a face. "Did he say that?"

"I'm paraphrasing." He leaned forward and propped his elbows on the desk. "I'm not talking about state-of-the-art machines. Just something so everyone who wants to can squeeze in some exercise. Chicago winters are too long and cold to expect them to get outside every day. Besides, renovations are our business. Joey said we can have it all done in a month, and the cost is negligible when compared to the benefit of a happier, healthier staff. The potential health care savings alone make it a no-brainer."

She threw her hands up. "Why not put in a pool? How about a sauna? Oh, I know. We could offer massages."

"Good idea."

The exasperated sound she made originated from the back of her throat.

"Not the pool. That's ridiculous," he said. "But bringing in a masseuse once a week is doable. I see why your dad valued your input so much."

Her frown faltered, as though she couldn't determine whether he teased her. Unable to decide, she flung him a parting scowl and shuffled from his office.

Damn, this was fun.

He knew she challenged him because she resented his presence here, but when it came right down to it, she couldn't resist his ideas for improvement, and she couldn't resist them because she cared. She cared about her employees and she wanted them to be happy.

He respected that, even if she was a pain in his ass.

Unfortunately, Brynn wasn't the only pain in the ass at Hathaway Group.

Well into Aiden's second week on the job, Philip

continued to stonewall him on the ledgers. The tech guys had given him access to the company's servers, but the financial records available on it were scant.

So Aiden went to Philip's assistant director of accounting, a lovely woman named Jacklyn, and made the same request he'd made to Philip.

Within the hour, Jacklyn had emailed him the files.

He opened the first spreadsheet, which was indeed large and complex, and began his review of the Hathaway Group financials.

Right away, he spotted an error, but after a little digging, he discovered it was simply a transposing error and made the correction.

Outside his office door, he heard Brynn at Donna's desk, talking with their executive assistant. The sound of her voice, soft and husky, sent a rush of heat to his groin.

He refocused on the numbers, and found more errors, some of which he could easily fix or account for, but others that didn't have an obvious solution. He needed to drill deeper, so he called Jacklyn, who brought him a file folder stuffed with invoices and receipts.

He spent the rest of the day, and the next morning as well, sorting through it all.

When he'd narrowed down the stack to only a few suspicious culprits, he headed for Brynn's office.

Except she wasn't in her office.

"Donna, do you know where Brynn is?"

"Shopping."

He stopped at her desk. "Excuse me?"

Donna pulled the wire-rimmed glasses down the bridge of her nose. "She is shopping, sir."

"Right now? In the middle of the day?"

"Yep."

Was she trying to prove a point about his flex time policy?

"Do you want me to call her?" Donna asked.

"Yes, please." He stood at her desk and waited while Donna placed a call to Brynn.

When she hung up the phone, she handed him a slip of paper with an address on it.

"Can you please give me her number, too?" He slid his car keys from his pocket. "In case I can't find her."

Donna handed him another slip of paper and he tucked it inside his phone case, then headed for the parking garage.

Minutes later, he pulled into the lot of Olde Chicago Antiques, and a low key rumble of laughter tumbled from him. He should've known she wouldn't be shoe shopping on The Magnificent Mile.

When he entered the old brick warehouse, dust and the faint smells of wood and mildew filled his nostrils. The floorboards creaked beneath his feet as he searched for her among the acres of antiques. Hand-carved wood furniture cluttered every walkway, and a horde of old stained-glass lamps dangled from the exposed rafters.

He found her in one of the narrow, cluttered aisles, crouched down and picking through a basket full of grungy doorknobs. Sunlight streaming in through the windows warmed the honey-colored streaks in her hair, and when she looked up at him, no shadows hovered in her eyes.

In that moment, while his gaze devoured her, he wanted to take it all back. All the years away. The layers upon layers of hurt shared between them. All the times he'd wanted to return, but stayed away anyway.

That, most of all.

Then the dark mistrust encroached, and she pushed to her feet. "What do you want?"

He forgot why he'd come, so he leaned over a display counter and peered down at the collection of old war medals. "Did you see my email?"

"I saw it." She dragged her fingers over the top of a wood dresser, then turned and headed up the crowded aisle.

He walked behind her, keeping pace. "I didn't see your reply."

"Because I didn't send one." With a sigh, she faced him. "It's a good idea. One I argued in favor of for years. I'm glad you're implementing it."

Surprise knocked into him, which he concealed with a lopsided grin. "I figured paid parking was the quickest way to their hearts."

Turning, she resumed her hunt through the piles, but not before he caught the soft smile that touched her full mouth. "They'll love it. Just as they've liked all the changes you're making."

"But…?"

"No buts." Her small shoulders lifted, then dropped. "They like you."

The irregular ticking of many aged clocks thrummed while he absorbed her words. "Score one for good old-fashioned bribery, then."

"They like you because you listen to them." She plucked a white pitcher off the table, flipped it over, then set it back down. "And because you trust them."

Years ago, it was her trust that he'd wanted. More than anything.

"You still think I'm plotting to ruin the company?"

A ripple of uncertainty chased across her face. "Honestly, I don't know what you're up to."

"Ah, there it is." The doubt and mistrust he counted on from her. "Come, now. You must have some suspicions. What are they?"

At his tone, anger flashed in her eyes. "I think you're—" With a shake of the head, she cut off her words.

"Go on. Say it. You think I'm what?"

She pretended great interest in some knickknacks for a time, then swiveled toward him and fixed him with her steely gaze. "I think you're angry at me and agreed to my dad's plan only to get back at me. I think you blame me for things that weren't my fault, but also some that were. Mostly, I think you want to show my dad that you're better than him."

"I am better than him," he said through clenched teeth.

"I think you have a hidden agenda." The pulse at the base of her throat fluttered wildly. "One you won't admit, even to yourself."

Standing among the heaps of junk with her heart in her eyes, she was so beautiful it made his chest ache to look at her.

"I'm sorry you feel that way."

"Am I wrong?" Her voice held a teardrop of hope.

Hope he couldn't give her. "You're not wrong."

IT WASN'T until the next morning when he sat down to wrangle with Philip's ledgers once more that he realized he'd forgotten to ask her what he'd tracked her down to ask.

Before considering what he was doing and whether he should do it, he'd flipped to her number in his contacts and tapped on it.

When her husky voice reached through the phone, he experienced a pang beneath his ribs. "Where are you?"

Her wary hesitation screamed through their connection. "I don't have time to fight."

"I don't want to fight. I only need a few minutes. There's something I need to talk to you about."

"I'm looking at a house. I'll be in a little later today."

"What's the address?" he asked. "I'll come to you."

Overnight, the rains had moved in, and as he crisscrossed the city, dark clouds crouched so low that the peaks of the steel high-rises dotting the skyline disappeared into their menacing mists.

Thirty minutes later, he pulled up to the curb in front of a house that'd inhabited one of his childhood nightmares. With a fair bit of trepidation, he climbed the front porch stairs and poked his head inside the front door, which had been left propped open.

She stood in the center of a small, dank living room, absorbing every detail in the vacant room, dingy with age and neglect, by slow half-turns.

Silhouetted against a bank of windows, the outline of her shapely figure set every vein in his body ablaze with desire. She'd removed her jacket and wore a flimsy, sleeveless blouse tucked into a black, form-fitting skirt. Neither tall nor short, every inch of her was a fascinating composite of voluptuous curves and mysterious shadow.

Amidst the grimy surroundings, her face was a beam of sunlight. "Isn't it amazing?"

He dragged his hungry gaze away from the nourishing sight of her to sweep across the room.

It looked like a trash heap on top of a landfill buried beneath a layer of orange shag carpeting and vegetable-themed wallpaper. Smelled like it, too.

"Don't look at the garbage," she said. "Or the carpeting. Or the heap in that corner. I think something died over there." She lifted her hands in front of her face. "Imagine all of that gone, and in its place, dark hardwood flooring and a fresh coat of paint."

She strode across the room and pressed her palm flat against the wallpapered fiasco. "We could knock down this wall and open up the entire first floor. There're four ginormous bedrooms upstairs, plus a basement where we could add more livable space. It's a great school district, close to public transportation. Omigosh, wait until you see the oak tree in the backyard. It'd be perfect for a treehouse. Can't you just imagine the family that'd want to live here?"

Her smile punched a hole in his chest.

"I can see it," he said softly.

For the past two weeks, he'd been studying her, cataloguing the differences between the girl he'd loved and the woman he desired, and trying to puzzle out what had changed. Like the homes she flipped, the foundation remained the same, and many of the features that'd made her unique to begin with had been preserved, but everything else was changed, and the difference was startling.

Finally, in this moment of her fresh joy and openness, he solved the riddle.

It was in the way she held herself, never standing too close to or being too open with anyone. Gone was the affectionate, touch-starved girl eager to be close to others. Back then, she didn't avoid the intimacy, but sought it. Didn't fear it, but craved it.

Now, she was different. Distant.

His chest squeezed with grief at the loss of that girl.

"Sorry," she said, her smile turning rueful. "What's up?"

Yet again, he'd forgotten his purpose in coming.

He slipped a hand inside his suit coat and pulled out the folded note. "I was wondering, what can you tell me about this?"

She took the paper, and as she read it, a frown knitted her brows. "It's a receipt for…? It doesn't say what it's for."

"You don't recognize the company?"

"I've never heard of them." Her troubled look mirrored his own. "I can't believe we spent this much at one time."

Spent that much and at a company she'd never heard of?

His dark, ill-defined dread grew. Several more examples

existed like the one he'd brought Brynn just now. Was this what Al had hoped to shield her from? Had he been trying to stop her from discovering his shady accounting practices?

If his precious daughter had become CEO, she would've learned the truth about dear old dad, and Al would rather give the business to Aiden than allow that to happen. Is that what all this was about?

"Let me do a little digging." She refolded the receipt. "Maybe I'm just forgetting...."

"Sounds good." He doubted she'd forgotten a thing. "Let me know what you find."

Though he should've left right then, he lingered instead. His gaze touched her face, then slipped lower, to the place where the fabric of her blouse gaped.

Several buttons near the top were popped open and, seeking warm flesh and hot memories, his eyes probed the decadent swells of her breasts—

He blinked.

He stared for a long time—too long—but the puzzle gripped him. Was it a trick of the light that gave the appearance of something he knew for a fact was not there?

His mind reeled. Had he forgotten?

He'd been in her bed. His hands, his mouth, his gaze had explored every inch of her naked body. He'd licked the very spot where he now stared.

The skin, once smooth and undisturbed, now... wasn't.

He lifted his eyes to hers and found the shadow gone. In its place was stark fear.

"Let me go," she whispered, terror wrapped around each letter.

Unaware he'd grasped her arm, he released her as though she'd suddenly caught fire. "What happened?"

Her hand shot up to clutch her blouse where it parted. "I—I—I... there was... an accident."

"A car accident? When?" His breath came in short, sharp bursts. "How badly were you hurt?"

"Last year." She wedged her tight fist under her chin and scrambled toward the door. "It was nothing."

"It was not nothing." With a lunge, he blocked her escape. "Why didn't anyone tell me?"

Anguish tore across her face. "Because you weren't here."

The words gutted him.

"I—I'm sorry. That's not…." Huge, round eyes pleaded with him. "I have to go."

He didn't want her to go. He wanted her to stay and talk to him. He wanted her to tell him about the scar on her collarbone and a thousand other things.

While he stood frozen and reeling, she banged out of the house.

His muscles twitched, desperate to go after her, but he clamped down on the need with vicious force. Still, his legs carried him to the door.

He stepped out onto the small front porch. "Will I see you later?"

She'd reached the bottom stair and tripped on the uneven concrete. Shaking her head, she grasped the rusty handrail. "I'll be at the venue all day getting ready for tomorrow."

"Tomorrow…?" he repeated dazedly.

"The charity ball." Still clasping her blouse, she glanced up at him. "Are you coming?"

He'd forgotten about the ball, too. "What's the cause?"

"Cancer research."

A pang struck him. "I'll be there."

With a last lingering look, she fled.

The heavy mantle of despair fell over his shoulders, and he sank down on the front stoop as she scurried to her SUV and slid behind the wheel. A few moments later, her vehicle rocketed away from the curb.

Air rattled through his lungs with the pain that constricted his chest.

He'd known it would come to this. He'd known it all along. He couldn't be near her and not want her. He couldn't be so close to her and not want to love her.

He couldn't want those things and not hurt her.

For so long, he'd wanted to return to her, when he'd thought he couldn't because of her dad, and when he knew her dad couldn't stop him, even if he'd tried.

For twelve years, he'd longed to come home.

He'd always stayed away, anyway.

Because he knew if he didn't, he would find himself in this moment.

He knew he'd want to stay but have to leave.

CHAPTER 9

*B*rynn surveyed the grand ballroom while her lungs struggled to draw air. Beneath vaulted ceilings with scalloped edging and plaster medallions, nearly five hundred guests of Chicago's wealthiest and most powerful citizens mingled in tuxedos and glittering gowns. Purple velvet drapes hung from the curved observation balconies ringing the ballroom, and massive tiered chandeliers dropped into a glittering cascade of soft lighting.

Around her neck hung an expensive necklace, and her fingers toyed with the heavy jewels, fighting the urge to snatch it away from her throat so that she could breathe.

Enormous crowds had a way of stirring her demons.

Photographers from the city's largest media outlets moved through the ballroom, snapping pictures of the businesspeople, politicians, and celebrities in attendance. Attentive white-gloved servers circulated with trays of golden, bubbly champagne, and she tracked the one closest to her, desperate to snag a flute now that she'd completed her interviews with the press.

Interviews she'd lined up to discuss the cause and steer

interest toward making donations, but that had instead focused mostly on Aiden.

"How long has your brother worked for the company? Was his promotion expected?"

"What plans does your brother have for the company?"

"Will he be keeping you on as his vice president?"

"Is he married?"

"Is he seeing anyone?"

Into the array of camera flashes and clicks, she'd squinted. "He's not my brother. He's my stepbrother. My *other* stepbrother is the reason we're here tonight."

At her side, Jared's hand moved to her lower back. Instinctively, she stiffened, and his thin lips pulled into a hard thin.

"Sorry," she murmured. "You just surprised me."

Panic thrashed in her chest, gnashing to be let loose, and she clenched her teeth to hold it back. Her throat ached with the effort, but she couldn't give in to the chaos.

If she let it free, it'd devour her.

Cold and numb were better. Safer.

She offered Jared a placid smile.

He offered his arm. "Shall we dance?"

Brynn didn't want to dance, but she was the hostess at a ball, so she slipped her hand under his elbow.

On the dance floor, he pulled her into his arms. Moisture beaded on her skin as the oppressive weight sitting on her chest grew leaden. Fake smiles and shrill laughter swirled around her with a dizzying frenzy.

When Jared's hand moved to her hip, her stomach clenched.

Beneath the fog of her panic, frustration pricked.

Just once, she wanted to forget.

Just once, she wanted to be free of the revolting terror.

Just once, she wanted to be more than a frightened, fractured woman struggling to get through every minute of every day.

Just once, she wanted to let go long enough to enjoy the highest setting on her vibrator.

Around them, the murmur of voices swelled suddenly to a low buzz. She turned her head, and her gaze followed the trail of craned necks to the front of the ballroom.

There, standing beneath the arched entryway, stunningly striking in a tux, was the new president and CEO of Hathaway Group.

And on his arm, looking every bit as stunning, was Brynn's best friend since childhood, Molly.

Pain knifed Brynn beneath the sternum.

To appreciative gazes, Aiden and Molly descended the wide staircase.

Brynn turned away.

"You should try to hide it better than that," Jared murmured near her ear.

She tipped her head back to see his face. "What are you talking about?"

"Your lust for your stepbrother." His cruel scowl made his handsome face ugly. "It's disgusting. And it's bad for business."

He abandoned her there, in the middle of the dance floor.

She stood frozen for a moment while shock and humiliation poured over her. When a swirling couple bumped into her, she scurried out of the way.

At the edge of the dance floor, a waiter with champagne meandered through the crowd, and she plucked a flute off his tray. She tossed back several greedy gulps, but inevitably, her gaze returned to the most beautiful couple in the room.

Molly's pretty face lit up when she spotted Brynn. She waved her arm wildly and then plunged ahead, dragging Aiden along behind her as she made a beeline for Brynn.

Brynn ducked behind a massive support column. Emotions assailed her, emotions she had no right to feel. She pressed her back against the sturdy pillar and swallowed the rest of the champagne.

Another waiter passed by, and she reached for a second glass as Molly swooped down on her.

"Omigod, Brynn, this place looks amazing." Behind her, Aiden's frown deepened. "I can't believe you did all this. You missed your calling as a party planner."

Aiden appeared uneasy. "You two know each other?"

"Of course we do," Molly said. "Brynn's my best friend."

His warm skin tone paled.

Molly tilted her head and slid him a teasing smile. "I knew you didn't recognize me."

"I'm sorry. It's been a long time," he said.

Envy burned Brynn's cheeks, and she frowned down at the empty champagne flute in her hand. "You've changed a lot since high school," she muttered.

While Molly's appearance had changed a lot over the last decade, Brynn assumed Aiden's amnesia might have a little something to do with her friend's breasts, which had increased three cup sizes since they'd enrolled at Northwestern.

At Brynn's elbow, Jared reappeared with a champagne flute in each hand. "Wow. Molly, you look incredible."

The compliment struck Brynn like another hammer of betrayal. Jared had given her, his supposed girlfriend, no such compliments that night. Or any other night. In fact, other than her scar, he'd never commented on her appearance. Which may tell her all she needed to know about his opinion of her.

Molly smiled. "Thank you, Jared. You don't look so bad yourself."

Even by Molly's standards, she looked exceptionally

pretty that night. She'd twisted her flaxen hair into a sleek bun, and her red gown had tiny crystals sewn into the clingy fabric. Her beauty was worthy of the strikingly handsome man who was her date, and next to her, Brynn felt small and unremarkable.

She'd chosen a sleek, midnight blue silk gown that she'd then had altered to add bunches of sheer fabric around her neck and shoulders to hide her scar. At the moment, she was regretting the choice, as the form-fitting bodice constricted around her rib cage.

She filched a champagne flute from Jared and downed it.

When he glanced at Aiden, Jared's features pinched, as though he smelled something offensive.

Then his intimate gaze swept over Molly's incredible figure once more. "I hope your date is not too insecure to allow me to steal you away for a dance."

Aiden's humorless smile held a lethal edge. "If I had any reason to feel insecure, I would object."

Standing side by side, it was impossible not to compare the two men. Though, like Aiden, Jared was dark and attractive, his hair and eyes were a touch less dark. When next to Aiden, Jared appeared less in nearly every way. Less dark. Less tall. Less handsome. Less compelling.

Less… everything.

"If you're inclined to accept, enjoy your dance," Aiden said to Molly.

Not unused to being the central focus of attention, Molly offered both men a sweetly flirtatious smile. Then she leaned into Aiden. "As long as you promise to dance with me next."

He dipped his head. "Of course."

As Jared led Molly to the dance floor, Brynn scoured the area for an attendant with a tray of champagne.

"Brynn, I—"

At the tug of fear about what he might say, she abandoned

her search. "I'm impressed. It's obvious you don't like Jared, but you played nice. Mostly."

The sharp edge to his features relaxed, but his eyes remained hooded. "He's too dense to pick up on the insult."

She moved a hand over her mouth to hide her smile. "Still, I appreciate your restraint this time. I know what you're capable of when you don't approve of my dates."

With the memory, the gold flecks in his eyes flared, and she stared, fascinated.

"My opinions on who you choose to date are irrelevant."

"But they weren't when we were seventeen?"

Some emotion she couldn't name shimmered in his dark eyes. "They were, but I was seventeen, too. And I was jealous. Give me a break."

Though she smiled, her heart cracked open.

He was jealous.

Was.

Then, not now.

With the painful wrench, her lungs wheezed w the air had been knocked from her body.

Quicksand. That's what he was to her. That's what he'd always been. The harder she fought against his pull, the deeper she sank, and in the end, she suffocated, drowned by a lungful of dirt and sand.

Between her fingers, she pinched the delicate stem of the champagne flute so hard she feared it might snap.

Sound swirled around them. The drone of voices, the soft clink of glass, the subtle melody of string instruments being played by the band tucked into one corner of the room.

He held out his hand. "Dance with me."

Her heart leapt.

She should tell him no, not because she didn't want to dance with him, but because she very much did. But even knowing it was a bad idea, she placed her hand in his.

When his fingers closed around hers, a jolt of adrenaline ricocheted through her veins.

He took her empty glass and deposited it on a tray designed for such purpose and led her through the crowd. On the dance floor, he pulled her into his arms.

His touch was gentle but solid, and her stomach dipped with the pleasant sensation but none of the nausea she'd experienced earlier.

At the firm pressure of his hand on her back, more sensations began to flare inside her, like fireworks shooting off on the Fourth of July.

When the length of his body pressed more fully against hers, a heartbreaking surge of longing rushed through her with the memories of the last time he'd touched her. Then, like now, he was strong yet gentle. Then, unlike now, possessive and protective.

Emotion rose in the back of her throat. She hadn't known a touch quite like his since he'd gone away, and suddenly she realized, if she married Jared, as her dad had been hinting at her to do, she'd likely never know it again.

She risked a glance at his face.

Dark eyes churned with the intensity of Lake Michigan on a stormy day. "I didn't know Molly was your friend or I never would've—"

"It's none of my business who you sleep with." She rushed in with the words, afraid he would proclaim his affection for her friend next.

A dangerous light stoked the golden embers near his pupils. "I take it she doesn't know about us either?"

Unable to speak, Brynn shook her head.

At the hitch of pain in his eyes, she dropped her gaze to his throat. "I couldn't tell her about you." She stared at the spot where his tattoo peeked out of the collar of his shirt. "It hurt too much."

His Adam's apple bobbed.

When she mustered the courage to take another glimpse at his face, she expected to see anger or defiance, but all she found was a soft sadness that wrung a pang from her.

The music reached a crescendo and they moved gently, carried along by the rolling waves of the song.

"I have a proposition for you," he said near her ear.

She suppressed a groan. "Am I going to hate it?"

"I rather think you're going to like it, since it includes me leaving Chicago."

Her eyes flew to his face.

"I should have left two weeks ago, but...." His arm tightened around her waist. "I didn't."

In her chest, her heart throbbed with painful thuds while she gaped at him. "What? You're leaving?"

"Your dad made it sound like you weren't ready to run the company." His face was inches from hers now. "I should've known not to believe him."

"But... but... you're leaving?"

His expression filled with the sorrow in her heart.

"When?" she whispered.

"Monday."

Her lips parted with a small gasp of pain. "So soon?"

"There's no reason to wait."

"But... who's going to take your place?" she asked, not sure whether her words referred to the company or something else.

He turned her, blocking her from the path of a rambunctiously spinning couple with his body. "You are."

CHAPTER 10

*H*er feet tangled, and she tripped.

With ease, he steadied her, but she struggled to keep up with his smooth steps for most of the refrain.

"That doesn't make you happy?"

"Of course." But the ache in her heart spread to the rest of her body. "But my dad was pretty clear he didn't want me in charge."

"Your dad is wrong." The certainty in his voice left no room for doubt or debate. "You're the leader this company needs. Not me."

His words reached inside her like a relieving balm. "But I don't see how we can get around him."

"At the board meeting on Monday, he's going to make it official by signing over his shares in the company to me." One corner of his mouth tipped up into a wicked smile. "Once he does, I'll immediately resign and give them to you."

His smile told her he'd enjoy every minute of it, too.

"That'll make you the majority shareholder in the company. With fifty-one percent, no one will hold more power than you."

Her mind grappled with the idea. Would it work?

"I've read the bylaws." He spoke in a low, lethal-edged voice. "There is nothing in them prohibiting it."

How long had he been thinking about this? Only last week, he was determined to make her life a living hell. Now he would give her everything and walk away?

Why? What had changed?

She searched his face for signs of deception or duplicity. Though she found none, she didn't know him all that well anymore. It was possible her ability to read his expression hadn't survived their separation.

But she wanted to believe him. She wanted to believe that despite everything, he could hold her in his arms and offer her the world the way he once had.

The music and soft lighting wove a spell around them, and under the enchantment, she could pretend none of the terrible parts of their past had happened. She could dream that they'd been together for the past twelve years, and their love had grown and deepened. She could imagine that all her broken pieces were now whole, or were never shattered in the first place because she'd been allowed to love him openly and freely and as hard as she'd longed to from the moment they met.

"Thank you." Her voice was thick with emotion.

"You're welcome." In the shifting light, shadows played across his features. "But I have a favor to ask of you."

Unease skittered up her spine. "Okay," she said carefully.

"There's something wrong with that receipt I showed you yesterday and a few others like it."

"What's wrong with them?"

"I don't know," he admitted. "But I need you to look into it."

"Did you ask Philip about them? What did he say?"

Her question hung in the air.

"I didn't ask Philip," he said finally. "I think you should have an independent audit done."

"An independent…?" Whether the effects of the champagne or the dizzying upshot of being wrapped in Aiden's arms, her thoughts came sluggish and jumbled. "Why? Do you suspect him of something?"

"I don't want to speculate about him." The heightened color on his cheekbones made his eyes shine like burnished jewels. "About Al, I feel slightly less restrained. Your dad dropped the ball."

"Are we still talking about the receipt? I'm sure it's only a mistake."

"Mistakes with that many zeros often mean someone's going to jail."

Her stomach dropped to her toes. Beneath her hands, his body had coiled with tension, and in answer, she experienced a tug of rigidity.

But when she gazed up into his face, the enchantment persisted, and suddenly, she saw his anger for what it really was.

Hurt.

On his shoulder, her hand trembled with the desire to soothe away his hurts. "I know you don't like my dad."

"That's true."

"I understand why. I do." She swallowed the ache in her throat. "What he did to you, with my help, is inexcusable. But that doesn't make him a criminal."

"I didn't say he is."

"Then what are you saying?" She searched his hard-set features.

"I'm saying it was his job to make sure everything being done at the company was on the up and up. As president, it'll be yours." All at once, his anger seemed to dissolve. "Look, if it's only sloppy accounting, you'll still need to clean it up. But make sure it's only sloppiness. Promise me you'll look into it."

Her head bobbed. "I promise."

As the song came to a soft ending, she pulled away.

But he didn't let her go, and the band slipped into a new song.

Brynn and Aiden moved together, swaying softly to the mellow music. The sweet, sad melody plucked at her composure. Or maybe it was the overwhelming sensation of being so close to him again after so long.

His heat, his strength, his potency bombarded her until her senses hurt. Everything ached—her head, her skin, her heart. She ached.

For him.

Beneath her lashes, she snuck a peek at him. While she struggled to hold on to her poise after a few minutes in his arms, he appeared unaffected by the moment.

The pang that struck her snatched her breath. She wished she could be free of him the way he was so obviously free of her.

He caught her looking at him.

She ducked her chin. "Where will you go?"

"I don't know," he said after a beat.

"Where did you go all the other times?"

His wide shoulders moved. "Here and there."

Flushed and tipsy, and emboldened because he'd be gone again in mere hours, she lifted her head. "How did you do it?"

He looked at some point behind her. "What's that?"

"How did you forget so easily? How did you move on like nothing ever happened?" Her lungs spasmed. "When did you stop loving me?"

His mask of indifference suffered a crack.

"Please," she whispered. "Tell me how to forget you."

He opened his mouth.

"No, wait." Her hand shot out, and she touched her fingers to his lips. "I don't want to know any of those things."

They stood motionless, like two marble statues amidst the throng of dancing couples.

"I only have one question." Pulling her hand away, she curled her fingers into a ball. "Did you ever love me, or was it all just a game to you? Was I just a game to you?"

The strong column of his throat worked with his heavy swallow.

Molly burst into their sphere of intimacy. "Omigosh, you guys have been dancing forever." With a seductive smile, she sidled up close to Aiden. "Are you going to share your step-brother with me or not?"

Mortification swamped Brynn, and she stumbled back. "I—I—"

"Jared's looking for you," Molly said over her shoulder as Aiden drew her into his arms.

"You two have fun." Brynn twisted around.

She staggered blindly toward the edge of the dance floor. Once there, she didn't stop.

Her heels clacked against the marble flooring as she dashed for the door, desperate to find an empty stall in the restroom to hide out.

At the bottom of the grand staircase, guests clustered and mingled, and she drove through them.

Suddenly, a large body loomed in front of her.

Unable to stop in time, she crashed into the man. She pitched backward, and her heel caught on the hem of her gown. She started to fall, but his hand clamped around her arm and yanked her upright.

She'd only just steadied herself when she glanced down at the hand on her arm. Time seemed to stop, and she stared while the world fell apart around her.

He wore no tuxedo jacket, and he'd rolled the sleeves of

his white dress shirt up to his elbow, exposing the tattoo of a snake that coiled around his wrist and up his forearm.

The memory flashed through her mind, inflicting fresh pain. *The weight of his body dropped heavily on top of her and propelled the air from her lungs.*

She couldn't breathe.

He crushed her ribs. Gravel impaled her palms and the skin on her cheek as he held her face down and clawed at her clothing.

His palm pressed flat against the ground beside her head while he freed himself.

While she stared at the snake tattoo coiling his forearm....

She stared at the same tattoo now.

It was him.

Her heart thrashed wildly against her rib cage while memories of another time and place assailed her. Terror. Pain. Blood. Screams of anguish, her own.

The invisible hand constricted around her throat, crushing the narrow airways.

Look up, look up, look up.

She needed to look up. She had to know who he was.

No matter how hard she willed it, she could not lift her head. Her stomach pitched with the churn of her terror and dread.

In her nightmares, he was always faceless, even a year later. In reality, it'd been too dark to see, and whenever she'd tried to recall the details of his appearance, the panic would overwhelm her. From her fractured memories, his face had never emerged.

The shaking in her body threatened to shatter her completely.

Just then, a steady presence materialized at her side and the man with the snake tattoo quickly melted into the crowd.

"Who is he?" Aiden's voice near her ear sounded echoey, as though he spoke through a long metal tube.

Panic clawed its way up her throat while the truth screamed inside her skull.

Him! It was him!

It. Was. Him.

"Breathe." His hand rubbed a slow, tight circle on her back. "That's good, *a stór.*"

"Oh, no. Not again." Molly's disappointment stabbed Brynn like a brutal barb. "Brynn, you have to relax."

"She can't breathe," Aiden said. "I'm taking her to the hospital."

Brynn clamped her hand over his.

It is him. He is here.

"You're having trouble breathing." Aiden brushed a tendril of hair off her forehead. "Let's get you some help so you can breathe."

She gave her head a furious shake.

"It's a panic attack," Molly said. "Brynn, relax."

Aiden turned to stand directly in front of her, blocking her view of all else but him. He bent close and peered into her eyes. "Just breathe," he murmured.

His hand moved to her nape. Pressing his forehead against hers, he closed his eyes and drew a deep, deliberate breath. Then another, and another.

Soon, her breaths stretched out, trying to match his. The pain in her chest eased, just a touch, as together, they breathed.

"That's so good, Brynn. You're doing great, *a rún.*"

A shudder rattled through her.

"Maybe some fresh air would help?" Molly tucked her arm under Brynn's and steered them along the path Aiden cleared by slicing through the crowd.

On the stairs, her legs were weak, and she clutched the bannister, which was hard and smooth beneath her death grip. When they'd reached the top, white-gloved attendants hauled open the large ornate doors, and she stumbled through them.

Only a few guests lingered in the expansive lobby, and their footsteps bounced off the cold marble floors and walls as they scurried toward the building's main entrance. Her rough breaths echoed in her ears. Then the cool night air smacked into her.

She gulped for air, but it was no use. Wrenching free from Molly's grip, she lost her stomach in the bushes.

Over her shoulder, Aiden and Molly spoke in hushed voices.

They thought she was weak. Fragile.

In truth, it was worse than that. She wasn't fragile, but already broken.

Shattered a year ago when the stranger in the ballroom took everything from her.

Through her devastation, Molly's apology reached Brynn. "I'm sorry, but I think I need to take her home."

"I'll drive" came Aiden's clipped reply.

Brynn wanted to argue. She couldn't leave. She needed to socialize and try to get more donations. The cause was important to her, and so many others, and she was letting them all down. But she couldn't draw air into her lungs.

She couldn't go back into that ballroom knowing *he* was in there.

She wasn't strong enough.

Which was why her dad didn't want her in charge of the company. Her dad was right, and Aiden was wrong about her.

Brynn didn't remember Molly and Aiden loading her into Aiden's car or giving her keys to Molly to lead the way in Brynn's SUV, but by the time steel high-rises and glass behemoths gave way to row houses and Greystones, she'd started the slow return back to herself.

The rustle of her skirt's fabric followed her up the walk-way, in the elevator, and to the entrance of her condo. She fumbled for her key, but her hands shook so badly that Aiden had to take over the impossible task of unlocking the door.

When the door gave way, Brynn rushed inside.

Molly eased past Aiden and moved toward Brynn. "I'm staying with you tonight."

"No. Please." A fresh wave of nausea rose up. "I just need some rest. I'm so… tired."

"Are you sure?" Molly said at the same time Aiden growled, "I'm not leaving."

Brynn nodded. "I'm sure."

A severe scowl darkened Aiden's face while Molly studied her for a moment.

"This episode wasn't so bad," she said, rubbing Brynn's arm. "See? I told you they wouldn't last forever. You're making great progress, sweetie."

Molly stepped out into the hallway and tucked her arm under Aiden's elbow. "I'll call you in the morning?"

"Okay." As Brynn eased the door shut, Molly tugged on Aiden's arm, pulling him toward the elevator.

Alone, Brynn sagged against the door. Her legs gave out, and she sank to the floor in the dark.

Through the door, she heard Molly's voice in the hall. "She'll be okay. She just needs some time. When you see her next, she'll be back to her old self. You'll see."

CHAPTER 11

*H*er old self.

The words still haunted her Monday morning when she woke with a headache and arrived at the office late.

Who was that? She had little memory of the young girl she'd been before her mom went away, and after, it was all crippling doubt and lost loneliness.

Until Aiden.

With him, she'd been a different person. Happy. Light-hearted. Even a little funny. She missed that girl.

As she passed through the reception area, she saw Aiden propped on the corner of Erin's desk. With a friendly smile on her face, Erin toyed absentmindedly with the top button on her blouse while they talked.

The stab of jealousy lacked the scalding heat of previous pangs. This time, the pain was blunt and sobering. Like grief. Grief for her delusions, which were well and truly dead.

Grief that he was leaving.

In her office, she plopped her purse down on her desk, and almost immediately, a soft rap sounded.

She turned to find Aiden standing in the doorway, his dark eyes alight with a probing fire.

Her stomach clenched. She'd been dreading this moment, when he would look at her with questions in his eyes, knowing she had no answers. Heat rushed over her skin.

With cautious steps, he moved into the room. He probably feared she was going to freak out on him again.

Dark shadows lurked under his deep-set eyes. He appeared as tired as she felt.

She didn't want to contemplate what he'd been doing all night if not sleeping.

"You doing okay?" he asked.

Words jammed in her throat. "I'm... okay." She never could lie to him easily, so she ducked her chin to hide her struggle and scooped up some random file on her desk. "Going to be a busy day today."

When he and his watchful gaze didn't leave, tendrils of alarm whipped through her. "I need to get to work. Isn't there a woman somewhere you can flirt with?"

A quiet twinge of disappointment tweaked his features, as though he'd expected more from her and she'd let him down somehow.

She preferred his disdain. "Erin is engaged to be married, just so you know."

"I was not flirting with Erin."

She sliced him with a speaking glance.

The flash of his quick smile struck her like a bolt of wicked lightning. "You're jealous."

Painfully so.

"Jealous?" She scoffed. "You spent the weekend with my best friend and today you're flirting with one of your employees. I'm not jealous, I'm disgusted."

Golden-brown laser beams pinned her. "Nothing happened between Molly and me."

A snort escaped her.

"I did not know Molly was your best friend," he said with quiet emphasis. "I'm not seeing her again."

"Does she know that?" Brynn folded her arms. "When I talked to her yesterday, she seemed to think otherwise."

"I am not seeing Molly again."

She prodded the leg of her desk with her toe. "Whatever."

He dipped his head to catch her squirming gaze. "I am not seeing Molly again."

"You're repeating yourself."

"I'm repeating myself because you're refusing to hear my words." Soft light smoldered in his gold-flecked eyes. "I am not dating your friend and I will not be dating her. If I'd known she was your friend, I never would've invited her to the fundraiser. I am truly sorry about that."

Shame warmed her cheeks. Why was she being such a jerk about this? Molly was her friend, and she wanted her friend to be happy. She really did.

She just didn't want her to be happy with Aiden.

Because when it came right down to it, after twelve years and countless heartbreaks, Brynn still had a thing for her stepbrother. When she was supposed to be dating Jared.

Jared!

Until that moment, Brynn had forgotten about Jared. For all she knew, he was still wandering around that ballroom, wondering what had happened to her.

At the mess her life had become, her head throbbed, and she rubbed the ache over her brows.

"Did you get any sleep last night?"

At the tender hitch in his voice, lies refused to fall from her tongue. "A little."

"Are you ready for today?" he asked. "If not, we can—"

"I'm ready," she burst out. "If you're... still willing to go through with it?"

"Nothing has changed." He spoke gently. "I have no doubt you'll be an outstanding leader for this company."

He contemplated her quietly, and like a sinner in the confessional, the words started pouring out. "That whole thing Saturday… it was nothing, really. Just a panic attack."

More quiet contemplation led to more admissions.

"Last year… was a rough year." Her throat ached, and she swallowed. "I'm getting some help."

"I'm proud of you," he said without a hint of mockery or scorn. "That cannot have been easy."

Her heart fluttered. Damn, but she didn't want to want his approval so badly. "I really should get some work done before the meeting."

He edged toward the door, but before stepping through, he pulled up. "Anything I should know about Mr. Moretti? How is it that anyone not named Hathaway became a member of the board?"

For a moment, her mind struggled to shift topics. "He was an early investor in the riverfront development project. Without him, that project might've ruined us."

Aiden turned fully to face her. "You were in financial trouble?"

She shook her head. "No, but it was one of those projects where everything that could go wrong did go wrong. We just needed a little extra cash so we could deal with the issues and finish the work before things got out of hand."

With a touch of distress, she recalled her dad's uncharacteristic flares of temper and the ugly fights between him and Uncle Mike as the setbacks had piled up.

"When Mr. Moretti approached us with an interest in the project, we were eager to make a deal, so my dad offered him some shares in the company to sweeten the pot."

A dark cloud settled over Aiden's features. "He has a two percent share?"

"It's an irrelevant amount, I know, and I *still* argued against it." She smiled ruefully. "But he's been a sound addition to the board. With him, we've expanded into the corporate development market, which has opened up a whole new vein of income for us."

"How long ago did all this happen?" he asked.

"I guess it's been... three or four years now."

His fierce scowl made him appear far away.

"Is everything all right?" she asked.

With a heavy sweep of his eyelashes, he returned to himself. He shed his troubled frown and backed through the doorway. "Don't be late to the meeting, or I'll be forced to write you up."

Her smile flirted with forming. He couldn't resist one last power trip.

When he'd gone, she settled in behind her desk and flipped on her computer. While she waited for the device to power on, she fumbled through her purse for her cell phone.

But, clutching the device in her hands, she couldn't bring herself to call Jared. She had no idea what to say to him.

Or maybe she did, and that's why rather than have that conversation now, she typed a quick text explaining she'd become ill Saturday night and had to leave suddenly.

Of course, he wouldn't believe her, but he'd let the lie stand, because maybe her reason for not wanting to call him was the same reason he had for not calling to check on her even once in the past thirty-six hours.

The thought gave her some comfort as she dove into her work. After meeting with her designers, she returned to her desk to follow up on a few critical issues, and the rest of the morning flew by in a whirl of activity.

When she was about to wrap up and move to the conference room down the hall for the board meeting, Jared appeared at her door.

"Oh, hey." As she rounded her desk, a hard pit formed in her stomach. The same pit she experienced of late anytime she was with him. "I was just about to head into a meeting."

"Glad to see you're feeling better." He wore his usual unemotional expression. "I thought we'd get some lunch."

He'd never asked her to lunch before, and a pang of guilt struck her beneath the breastbone. "Sorry, I can't."

"Dinner, then."

For about one fraction of one second, she considered what it might be like to marry Jared. She didn't love him. Sometimes, she didn't even like him all that much. But was it possible that one day she might grow to care for him?

Did it matter if she could?

One man had stolen her heart years ago, and he'd never given it back.

While she and Aiden had no future together, the fact was, she wasn't over him. And while it was entirely possible, likely even, that she'd never meet another man who got to her quite the way Aiden had, she couldn't settle for someone she didn't love because Aiden wasn't available to her, or because her dad wanted her to, or because she hated dating.

There was already enough about herself that she didn't like. She couldn't give away her integrity, too. Not so cheaply, anyway.

It wasn't fair to Jared or to her.

If she were being truly honest with herself, she never should have let their relationship drag on this long.

In the moment of her hesitation, Jared heaved a world-weary sigh. "Brynn, this is getting tiresome. How can we be dating if we never go on any dates?"

Tremors of shame quaked inside her, but she clenched her jaw tight against them.

"I'm sorry you're tired," she bit out. "Believe me, so am I."

"Then let's go out. Have some fun. For God's sake, let's do something."

He'd never once shown concern about her panic attacks. He'd never once tried to help her. The way Aiden had. Instead, his frustration with her had added to the gripping panic and the unbearable weight pressing down on her.

Shame had kept her from wishing for more from him. Fear had stopped her from demanding it.

In a puff of air, she expelled a bracing breath. "Jared, I can't see you anymore."

His eyes narrowed. "Excuse me?"

"You've been incredibly patient with me, and I'm grateful for that, but we both know this isn't working."

Tipping his head to one side, he stepped deeper into her office. "Does your dad know about this?"

"No, of course not," she said.

"He's going to be upset."

Her heart softened that he'd worry about her dad. "He's not the one who has to live with this decision. We do."

"We talked about this. I thought we had an understanding." He inched closer.

She took a small step back.

"If you've grown impatient for a ring, you should have told me sooner than this." Color crept into his cheeks. "I'll get you a damned ring."

Though he'd never proposed, he had dropped the topic of marriage into a conversation once, some months ago.

"Did you get milk?" he'd asked.

"I didn't have time to stop at the store," she'd murmured without looking up from the mortgage contract she'd been reviewing.

"When we're married, there'll always be milk in the fridge." Ire edged his tone, and she had looked up then.

"If you want to keep the fridge stocked with milk, I don't mind."

She hadn't realized at the time he'd accepted her cool response as acceptance of a marriage proposal.

"I don't want a ring," she said now. "I don't want to hurt you or disappoint you, or anyone else, but I think it's time we move on."

Anger flooded his face, and his normally passive features contorted with rage. "We had an agreement."

"We didn't—"

"Your dad and I did."

Shock jolted her. "You made a deal with my dad? Behind my back?"

"Of course we did." His sneer curled his lips. "Did you think this was the playground?"

He'd sidled yet closer, and his flash of anger ignited a spark of fear in her chest. He wasn't a large man, but neither was she a tall woman, and the marked difference in their sizes made her acutely aware of her vulnerability.

She eased back another step. "Jared, I want you to be happy, and I know I'm not the woman that can do that for you."

"It's marriage." His disparaging gaze raked over her. "There are plenty of other women to attend to my happiness."

The gasp slipped between her lips.

"Oh, c'mon on. Let's dispense with the pearl-clutching. This was a business arrangement from the get-go. One I expect you to uphold."

"I'm sorry you misunderstood." Fury burned away the last traces of her shock. "But that's not going to happen."

"What's not going to happen is you humiliating me in front of the entire world." Red-faced and wild-eyed, he stalked closer.

"The entire world?" She was late for the board meeting, so she scrambled over to her desk and retrieved her tablet and phone. "The entire world couldn't care less about our relationship."

"People will talk."

"So let them talk." Her voice rose with her exasperation.

"Do you have any idea what you've cost me?" The words shot from him with the force of a pellet gun.

Terror reached up to tighten her throat. "Do not yell at me."

"You're right." He dragged a hand through his dark hair. "We'll talk about this later. When you've calmed down."

"Jared, I will not marry you."

"Shut up," he snarled.

Her jaw went slack. She searched his face for signs of misplaced humor or bravado. What she found did nothing to ease her escalating fear.

"I want you to leave," she said.

"I want you to stop fucking talking."

He stood between her and the office door.

"I want you to leave." Her fear shook her voice. "After today, I will not speak to you again, and you will not speak to me."

She watched the truth materialize in his eyes. Then his normally emotionless expression morphed into murderous rage. His arm drew back, and her world caught fire.

Her head snapped to the side, and her cheek blazed a moment before the burning prickled with numbness. Stinging tears sprang to her eyes, and she looked at Jared, her mind slow to comprehend that he'd hit her.

He bit out a curse. "Look what you made me do."

She explored the pulsing injury on her face with her fingertips. The moment stretched out while her shock and pain expanded, and she stared at him as though he were a stranger to her.

"I hope I'm interrupting." Aiden's lilting brogue filled her with relief.

Without taking her eyes off Jared, she dropped her hand. "Get out." She injected as much strength into her voice as she could muster, but the words still emerged in a watery whisper. "Do not ever come near me again."

Aiden moved to her side.

Jared's expression reverted to the unsettling blankness she loathed, but he didn't leave.

"You heard her." A dark calmness infused Aiden's voice.

When finally, he shuffled through the door, the clamp around her lungs loosened, and air flooded her lungs.

Aiden's head swung to her.

She turned her face away and riffled through a stack of files on her desk, pretending to search for something.

"You two have a fight?"

"We broke up."

Quiet footsteps fell on the carpet, then his large hand appeared in her line of sight and pressed the pile of folders flat onto the desktop.

Unable to find the courage to look at his face, she stared at his hand.

"He hurt you."

She careened toward the door. "We're late."

"Brynn."

Her name on his lips gripped her insides, and she tripped to a stop.

When she couldn't bring herself to face him, he came around to stand before her. His probing gaze was relentless.

"I can't talk about it right now," she whispered.

Slowly, his hand came up and the backs of his fingers lightly brushed the spot where her cheek blazed.

"D-does it look bad?"

With a thick swallow, he gave his head a soft shake.

Together, they moved down the long hall to the last door.

Outside the conference room, he swiveled toward her. "No matter what happens in there, you are the leader of this company. It has your intelligence and your class. It has your heart."

"Please don't be nice to me." She stared at his hand on the door handle. "I can't take it."

"I'm still going to write you up for being late," he said, then the door swung open.

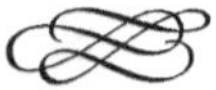

CHAPTER 12

The bastard hit her?

He fucking hit her?

Rage clouded Aiden's vision as he stepped into the conference room.

He fucking hurt her.

By the time he sank into a plush black leather chair at the massive oak table, the spark of his rage had flared into a roaring inferno. The fire consumed him.

Through the furious haze, he glanced around the table. Donna sat at one end with a notepad opened in front of her. Beside him, Alan wiped the sheen of moisture from his forehead.

Across the table, Joey sat between his father, Big Mike, and the only person in the room Aiden hadn't met, Mr. Moretti.

An older man, Manny Moretti may have been handsome in his youth, but his once dark hair had lightened and thinned, and his olive skin appeared pallid. The extra weight he carried sharply contrasted with the lean hunger lurking in his eyes.

Alan slid Aiden a look. "Are we ready to get started?"

Aiden's pulse throbbed painfully when his gaze shifted beyond Alan to Brynn. In a deep red blouse and blazer that hugged her slight frame, she stood apart from the men in black suits, like a rose in a rock garden.

She'd developed one hell of a poker face over the years, and the ever-present shadow in her green eyes provided the only hint of her distress.

"Ready," he said, the word leaking out as a croak.

Alan's mouth dipped into a frown. "As you're all aware, I'm stepping down to pursue other interests and leaving Hathaway Group in the capable hands of my stepson, Aiden Nolan."

With his elbow propped on the armrest, Mr. Moretti cradled his chin in his hand and studied Aiden with open interest.

"Mr. Nolan will gain my twenty-six percent share in the company with his appointment." While he spoke, Alan stared down at the blank screen of his electronic tablet. "If no one objects, I'll call the vote."

"Thank you, Alan." Aiden knitted his fingers and tried to contain the fury clouding his mind. "These past two weeks, I've worked with your staff and observed the work they are doing. You've assembled a talented, dedicated team, and I give you my sincere compliments."

Suspicion narrowed Alan's eyes. "Thank you. I motion to appoint Aiden Nolan President and CEO of Hathaway Group."

Big Mike seconded, and a quick vote went around the table.

"The motion has passed." With an airy sigh, as though he'd thrown off an oppressive weight, Alan pushed to his feet.

Aiden leaned back in his chair and swiveled toward his

stepdad. "That you would attempt to give me such a gift is truly unfathomable. I seriously expected you to dump a steaming pile of crap in my lap."

The room grew quiet, except for the soft scratch of Donna's pen moving across the paper.

"I'm especially impressed by your Vice President, Brynn Hathaway," Aiden continued. "Which is why I'm stepping down and appointing her President and CEO of Hathaway Group."

"What?" The color left Alan's face. "No. You can't do that."

"Nowhere in the by-laws does it state that I cannot." He met his stepdad's gaze directly. "She deserves this. You know that as well as I do."

"But—but—" Alan shook his head in disbelief. "That wasn't the plan."

"Your plan sucked, Al." Aiden took a moment to enjoy his stepdad's misery. "But don't worry. The company will be in excellent hands, with Brynn at the helm."

Flushed now with his fury, Alan glared at Aiden with wild eyes. "I won't allow it."

Over Alan's shoulder, Brynn looked on with a pained expression, her eyes huge in her pale face.

Aiden never could bear her pain. "You're no longer in a position to make that call. I am, and she's proven herself a thousand different ways. She's smart and hardworking, and she knows more about running Hathaway Group than anyone else sitting at this table. A hell of a lot more than I do."

"You son of a bitch," Alan seethed.

"Careful how you speak about my mother."

"If I may say a word." When Mr. Moretti broke in, an uneasy quiet settled over the table. "Your stepson is right. Ms. Hathaway is more than qualified to oversee the day-to-day operations for us."

A warning voice whispered inside Aiden's head.

The corners of Moretti's mouth tipped in a bleak, tight-lipped smile. "Mr. Nolan, thank you for serving Hathaway Group during this time of transition. You can resign knowing that you left us in capable hands." The grimness in his grin moved to his eyes. "But before we vote on Ms. Hathaway's appointment, I'd like to put forward another motion…"

Alarm shattered through Aiden.

"…for a change in the by-laws…"

Brynn's sharp hiss reverberated through him.

"…that when a member of the board of directors resigns, his or her shares in the company will be split evenly among the remaining board members."

"Absolutely not," Alan burst out.

"You're no longer a voting member," Moretti reminded him.

Alan paced away from the table.

"A simple majority vote is all that's required." Moretti captured Aiden's gaze. "Call it."

Blood whooshed past Aiden's ears with the frantic beating of his heart. After a heavy pause, he called the vote.

With Moretti's swift "second", Brynn's full-throated denial came fast, and Aiden mimicked it with one of his own.

Moretti's slimy gaze slithered down the table. "Michael?"

Brynn's uncle appeared queasy when he shifted in his chair. He coughed uncomfortably. "Seems reasonable. I'm a yes."

The air sucked out of the room.

All eyes shifted to Joey, who's gaze fixated on a bead of sweat trickling down the side of his water glass.

"Joey?" Brynn's voice held a gut-wrenching plea. "You're not actually considering it, are you?"

"You have a beautiful family, Joseph." Moretti spoke with

a deceptive casualness. "Did I tell you I met your lovely wife the other day? How'd a guy like you get so lucky to snag a woman like that?"

Joey squeezed his eyes shut and his shoulders slumped. "Yes."

A strangled sound escaped Brynn, and Alan bit out a curse.

"I'm a yes as well." The challenge on Moretti's face taunted Aiden. "Mr. Nolan, we thank you for your service."

White-hot fury screamed inside Aiden's skull.

Whatever the hell was going on with Hathaway Group wasn't Aiden's problem. He could walk away and let his stepdad deal with the snake he'd allowed in the door. He could let Brynn face the consequences of her lifelong loyalty to such a man.

Two weeks ago, if given a chance to ruin his stepdad and prove to Brynn beyond any shadow of a doubt that her loyalties were misplaced, he'd have grabbed it and walked away vindicated.

But now…?

Dammit, but he couldn't do it.

He couldn't break her heart a second time in as many minutes.

Aiden's jaw clenched tight with the effort to hold back his rage. "I'm not going anywhere."

Moretti's eyebrow quirked. "Change of heart?"

Aiden bared his teeth. "Something like that."

The meeting ended with the tension thick and suffocating. Joey darted from the conference room, and Donna snuck out right behind him. Alan and Mike avoided each other's gazes as Mike filed through the door. When Moretti had gone, Aiden kicked the door closed behind him.

"What the hell was that?" Alan bellowed. "We had a deal."

Aiden shot his stepdad a dangerous look. "I promised you nothing."

"For Christ's sake," Alan spat. "I've given you a multi-million-dollar company and you act like I owe something."

"You don't owe me shit." Aiden's lip curled with his disgust. "But you owe your daughter an explanation. She's given you more than you deserve, and this is how you treat her? By trying to rip the company she helped build away from her? Why?"

Alan clasped his hands behind his head and turned away, giving both Aiden and Brynn his back.

"Dad?" The soft hitch in Brynn's voice drew a wrench of pain from Aiden's chest.

Alan whirled. His face splotchy and red, he fumed at Aiden. "You did this, not me. You almost ruined everything, that's what happened."

Brynn lurched to her feet. "Stop it. He didn't do this. He didn't ask for any of this. Why did you make him do it?"

Alan paced away. "I already told you."

"Then please explain it to me again." Brynn's eyes were enormous in her pale face. "Because I don't understand."

"I don't have to explain myself to you," Alan snapped.

Brynn's expression crumpled. "We could lose control of the company. You absolutely owe me an explanation."

Alan thrust a finger at Aiden. "None of this would've happened if he'd done what I told him to do."

Emotions ravaged her face, but she dragged a deep breath into her lungs. When she spoke, her voice was calm. "I've put everything I am into this company, and you're giving it away with no input from me. I want to know why."

"This is ridiculous. I don't need to explain myself to you." With his outburst, her dad banged out of the room, slamming the door behind him so hard that the thin walls shook.

Silence dropped like a hammer.

Her devastation showed clearly when she sank into a chair.

"I'm sorry." His mouth had gone dry, and his words sounded hoarse. "That was my fault."

"Your fault?"

"I was so eager to stick it to your dad that I missed it. I wasn't focused. Not the way I needed to be." Regret shook his voice. "I should've realized the others might make counter-moves. I won't misjudge them again."

She gave her head a firm shake. "This is not your fault."

Her cheek was red where the bastard had hit her.

He swallowed thickly. "It is."

"No, it isn't." Hurt shimmered in her eyes when she looked up at him. "I've worked with these people for years and what just happened... I never would've thought they'd do something like that. *I'm* sorry. I should've realized.... I should've warned you." She rubbed her forehead.

Weariness dragged at his shoulders. "I'm sorry I couldn't turn over the company to you. You still deserve it, and I can't give it to you. Not now."

"You're staying in Chicago?" she asked, a soft catch in her voice.

"I can't leave." He watched her face for her reaction. "Not now."

Understanding dawned as a small gasp. "You're stuck here."

A smile struggled to form on his lips. "It would seem so."

She scrubbed her hands down the side of her face. "I'm so sorry."

"Do not apologize for them."

"I'm not apologizing for them." Solemn eyes gripped his insides. "I've been such a bitch to you, and what you just did for me...."

His heart kicked in his chest. "I think we've apologized to each other enough for now."

"I promise I won't fight you anymore. Whatever you want to do with the company, it's fine with me." She bit down on her bottom lip. "I won't challenge you again."

Her heartfelt vow lifted one corner of his mouth. "If I believed that, I'd be more than a little disappointed."

Her soft smile was fleeting. "What are we going to do?"

The panic in her voice echoed in his chest. "We need to learn everything we can about Manny Moretti. I want to know where he was born, raised, what he eats for dinner. Anything at all we can find out about him. And we need to get our hands on Philip's financial records."

"Philip? What does he have to do with this?"

"He's hiding something, and I want to know what it is."

A frown touched between her brows. "What do you suspect?"

"I don't know." His heart drummed with his dread. "But tonight, after everyone has gone home, we're breaking into his office."

CHAPTER 13

When he spotted her creeping across the dimly lit lobby, he nearly busted out laughing.

Dressed in black from head to toe, she tugged on a pair of black gloves as she scurried toward him. The black pants and turtleneck hugged every one of her shapely curves, and she'd smoothed her light brown hair into a ponytail.

Sweet mother, she was hot. Beautiful and adorable at once.

That much about her hadn't changed.

He chewed the smile from his face. "Where's your ski mask?"

On a gasp, she whirled. "I left it in my car."

He caught her arm. "Forget it."

Reluctantly, he withdrew his touch and punched the elevator button.

While they waited, her wide eyes made another sweep of the darkened lobby. "What about Curtis?" she whispered. "I didn't see him downstairs."

"I gave Curtis the night off so he can take his wife out for her birthday."

She made a soft noise. "I didn't know it was Ruby's birthday."

"Did you know she's turning sixty-four? Or that they went to Navy Pier on their first date?"

She folded her hands over her heart. "Navy Pier? I've always wanted to go there."

He twisted halfway. "You've never been to Navy Pier?"

Her head moved. "Never. Have you?"

"Of course."

With a soft ping, the elevator doors slid open, and they stepped inside the car.

From the corner of his eye, he watched her as they rode up to the fourth floor. The faint shadow of a bruise touched her cheek, but otherwise, she appeared unaffected by the incident with Jared that morning.

Like Molly had told him, she'd bounce back to her usual self in no time. As though nothing had happened.

But he knew something had happened two nights ago. He was there. He'd witnessed Brynn's reaction with his own eyes.

The elevator doors opened on a dark fourth-floor accounting department, and they crept silently through the cubical maze toward Philip's office.

Suddenly, a buzzing sound punctured the quiet.

Aiden jerked with surprise at the same moment a startled gasp tore from Brynn's throat. He slammed his hand against his chest, where the cell phone vibrated in his suit coat's breast pocket. Whipping out the phone, he silenced the incoming call.

"What do you want?" he snapped.

"A fucking foot massage," growled a raspy voice. "What do you think I want?"

Against his will, one corner of Aiden's mouth tipped up in a smile. "I'm busy. I'll call ya later."

"That's what you said last time," Shea reminded him.

"I'm busy."

"When's a good time?"

"I don't know," Aiden hedged. "I'm working."

"Where do you work?"

"None of your business."

"Why don't you want to tell me where you work?" Shea asked.

"What the fuck is this? The Dating Game? I gotta go." Aiden ended the call with his half brother's soft chuckle still rumbling over the connection.

"Who was that?" Brynn asked.

"My…." Aiden swallowed the word. "That was Shea."

Her eyes widened. "Is he one of your half brothers?"

"He is."

"Does he live in Ireland?"

"No." He'd meant to end it there, but big green eyes brimming with questions knocked a sigh from him. "He lives about five hours from here. In Michigan."

"Really?" Surprise lightened her voice. "What are your other brothers' names?"

"Can we talk about this later? Say, when we're not committing a felony?"

"Is this a felony?" Her frantic whisper coaxed another laugh from him.

"Probably not." He shrugged. "I don't know."

She pulled her puffy bottom lip between her teeth. "It feels wrong, doesn't it? I mean, we're breaking into someone's office."

Bent over the keypad, Aiden punched in the five-digit code Brandy from the cleaning crew had given him to gain entry to any office in the building.

"Philip won't mind," he said. "As long as we don't touch his porn stash."

"Ew. Now I have gross thoughts in my head." She smacked his arm. "Thanks a lot."

The keypad flashed green and, laughing, he cranked open the door.

"Let's move quick so we can get out of here." He closed the door behind them.

"What are we looking for?"

"Anything that might hold financial records. Why don't you grab any thumb drives or storage devices you can find?" He slid into Philip's desk chair and switched on the PC. "I'm going to grab a copy of his hard drive."

They lucked out, and Philip's login information populated the access screen fields. Aiden plugged in the external drive he'd brought and set to work copying over all the files on Philip's computer. While he waited for the copying process to complete, he helped Brynn search the desk drawers.

"How long has Philip worked here?" he asked.

"He started about the time we took on the riverfront project."

Aiden glanced up at her. "The same time Moretti joined the board?"

They shared a look.

"Probably just a coincidence," he said.

"Probably." She deposited a handful of flash drives at his elbow.

One by one, he copied them onto his external storage device and handed them back to her to return wherever she found them.

He handed her the last thumb drive. "Is that everything?"

"I think so." She dropped the device into a drawer.

He slid the external drive into the pocket of his suit coat. "Let's get out of here."

When he stood, his body brushed against hers. Heat

seared him as a small gasp slipped from her. Her lips parted to allow the soft catch and release of her ragged breaths, and the blood from his head rushed to his groin.

Then she startled and twisted away.

But in her haste, her hip knocked the corner of Philip's desk, and an abandoned coffee cup teetered, then tipped, splattering a trickle of stale coffee over white papers.

"Oh, no." She righted the cup and lunged to snatch tissues from the Kleenex box. "He's going to know someone was here."

"Don't worry about it." He dropped a pile of soiled tissues into the trash bin. "I'm going to fire him tomorrow anyway."

Confusion froze her. "Then why are we sneaking around like criminals?"

"Because I wanted to grab as much as we could in case he tries to destroy any evidence on his way out the door."

Her expression darkened with her worry. "You think whatever he's hiding is that bad?"

He patted his breast pocket with the small black storage device. "Only one way to find out."

The old Greystone where Brynn lived was only three stories, but an elevator carried them to her top floor unit and delivered them to the small foyer he'd seen the night of the ball.

Brynn unlocked the only door in the hall, and he followed her into a sprawling space with soaring ceilings and warm wood touches. Along the far wall, glass patio doors framed a pitch-black night sky with the soft glow of the Chicago skyline in the distance.

Having seen several homes she'd designed, he'd expected the custom cabinets and sleek stone countertops in the kitchen, but the casual, cozy vibe everywhere else surprised him. Overstuffed furniture beckoned to him, and warm neutral colors relaxed the tension in his shoulders.

The place somehow was impressive and unpretentious at once, and best of all, it smelled like Brynn. Sweet honey and freshly cleaned bedsheets.

Charm and character oozed from every corner, and standing in her home, he could *feel* Brynn. Her warmth and light surrounded him and filled him with the desire to sink into the sofa cushions and never leave again.

"Nice place," he said.

"Thanks."

A cat leaped onto the dining table.

Aiden stared for a moment. "Is that…?"

"Romeo," Brynn said.

"I remember" He scratched the cat's charcoal gray head. "Hey, buddy. How you been, Romeo?"

The cat rolled onto his side, landing with an inelegant thud, and Aiden dutifully rubbed his soft belly. "How old is he now?"

"Almost fourteen." Her mouth twisted. "Old enough to know he's not supposed to be on the table."

"You're in trouble now," Aiden said to Romeo, who purred away, unworried.

While he stroked Romeo's soft fur, Aiden recalled the time Brynn told him her dad had brought the kitten home shortly after her mom left. As though a pet was a suitable replacement for a mother.

She'd tried to smile with the words, but back then, her heart had lived in her eyes. He'd suffered the slash of her pain as she'd relived it in the retelling.

While she cleared a stack of magazines from the dining table, he couldn't stop himself from comparing the woman before him to the sad seventeen-year-old he remembered. For so long, whenever he thought of her, he experienced the ache of loss and regret right along with his festering resentment. Now, only a hammer of sadness struck his heart.

She retrieved the laptop from the living room and deposited it on the dining table, then plugged it into a wall socket and switched it on.

When she settled in front of the computer, he handed her the external drive. She slid the connector into a port, then popped up out of the chair and bolted for the kitchen.

"Do you want some coffee?" she called over her shoulder.

"Uh, sure."

While she set about the task, he claimed her seat and opened the folder of files they'd swiped from Philip's office.

He started to read.

In the kitchen, a coffee mug clattered against the stone countertops. She gripped the cup hard and winced. "Sorry."

He turned back to the computer and clicked on a file.

Another clang of sound rang out, followed by her quick apology.

"You're afraid of what we're going to find, aren't you?" He spoke without shifting his gaze from the computer screen.

The noises stopped.

"I'm worried, too," he admitted in a low voice. "I can do this alone. If you don't want to—"

"No." With a determined frown, she returned to the table. "I need to see whatever is in those files."

She moved to his shoulder and peered down at the computer. Her sweet scent tormented him as they scanned the file names. With her intimate knowledge of the business, they could decode Philip's naming system and map out the overall structure to the Hathaway Group's financial files.

Each project had its own folder and files containing monthly ledgers matched to invoices and receipts. Monthly expenses and projections rolled up into an annual reporting structure.

Aiden zeroed in on the files related to the riverfront development project.

"Did you work on the riverfront project?" he asked, careful to keep his tone conversational.

"A little. We were right in the middle of a massive renovation on the north side of town and I was constantly being pulled away. I jumped in when I could, but mostly just handled the design when it came time."

"So your dad managed all of it?"

"And Philip. And Jared."

His head whipped around. "Jared?"

When she nodded, the perfume of her scent teased his nostrils. "He's in real estate development, too, and he and my dad partnered on this project."

"How many other projects have they worked on together?"

"Quite a few by now."

Aiden's dread swarmed like insects when he turned back to the computer. Indeed, the emotions buzzing through him produced the distinct sensation that he'd just stuck his hand in a hornet's nest and given the hive a vicious rattle.

"Check out this one." She pointed to a name on the spreadsheet. "I've never heard of this company, but they accounted for—what is that? Nearly forty percent of the total project cost?"

"Hold on," he said and clicked out of the screen. "I saw something about them over here."

After a few more clicks, he'd opened a file of scanned receipts and started scrolling through the document.

"Wait, go back up. That one right there." Her hand touched his shoulder.

With her touch, a shock of heat and lust burned through his body.

"That can't be right," she murmured.

"What?"

"The cost for hardware. That's, like, a three thousand

percent markup on nails. I mean, prices for materials will fluctuate some, but not that much." Her soft gasp ruffled his hair near his ear. "Joey signed off on this invoice. He knows better than to pay those kinds of prices."

When she glanced at his face, her puzzled frown slipped into alarm. "What is it?"

"I didn't say a word?"

"But you're having thoughts." She shuffled around to sit beside him. "I can see them."

"What do my thoughts look like?"

She considered him for a moment. "They look... bad."

"They're only thoughts."

"Will you tell me what they are?" The hitch in her voice pinched his chest. "Please."

"I'm trying to think of all the reasons someone would knowingly pay inflated prices."

"And?"

"And, that's it." He carefully concealed his expression. "I'm thinking."

Her expression clouded. "Embezzlement?"

"That's one."

"What else?"

He hesitated, reluctant to add to the fear playing across her pretty features, but her light green eyes implored him. "Fraud. Theft. Money laundering."

She paled. "Please tell me you're joking."

His eyes held hers for several long heartbeats. "Let's keep looking."

CHAPTER 14

She tried to scream, but the large hand clamped around her throat squeezed tighter. With her arms and legs, she lashed out, clawing and thrashing.

"Brynn." Her name on his tongue loosened the hand. "Brynn, wake up."

Layers of the dream drew away slowly. She blinked, and a soft glow of dim lighting pierced the veil of darkness.

"Brynn." The familiar lilt rushed over her like a warm blanket. "Time to wake up now." An edge of worry rode his tone. "Brynn—"

"It's okay." On the sofa, she pushed up on her elbows. "I'm okay."

The silhouette of his form perched on the coffee table beside her. "You were dreaming."

"Yes." She sank back down into the cushions.

"Can I get you something? A glass of water—?"

"I'll be fine." A wave of nausea hit her, and she pressed her palm against her clammy forehead. "I just need a minute."

He sat quietly by her side while her breathing slowed and gradually slipped into a normal rhythm.

His voice reached out to her from the dark. "Do you have a lot of bad dreams?"

With difficulty, she swallowed. "Yes."

In the faint light from her laptop, she couldn't make out his features, but she detected the slight change in his breathing.

"Are they nightmares? Or memories?"

Fear marched through her veins with each beat of her suddenly pounding heart, now fully awake to the dangerous territory she'd wandered in to.

In her silence, his head dropped. "I see. I'm sorry."

She wanted to tell him the memories weren't all bad. Sometimes, they were softer. Golden-brown eyes. A lilting Irish brogue. The hint of a crooked smile.

But she couldn't tell him that.

His dark form rose and moved to the end of the couch. Light from the table lamp bathed the room in a golden glow when he switched it on.

His dark eyes glittered with pain. "I thought you might sleep better with the lights off. But you prefer to keep them on."

Her breath snagged in her throat. "How do you know that?"

With cautious steps, he returned to the coffee table and lowered his body back down on the wooden surface.

His cheek hollows were dark with shadows. "Because for the past two nights, I've slept in my car on the street outside."

Sitting, she swung her feet over the edge of the sofa. "But... why?"

"Because you'd never have let me inside."

Shock rendered her mute.

"Is it the accident?" His voice rasped with his emotion. "Does it scare you still?"

Suddenly, she craved the darkness.

She wanted to lie. So badly, she wished to utter the words that'd make him look away and forget what he'd seen.

But exhaustion sat as dark circles under his eyes, and deep lines of worry marred his face. He'd stayed up all night trying to help her figure out the mess at work, and now he asked about her fictional car accident with pained concern stamped on his features.

Tenderness ached in her chest.

Over the past year, there were so many times she'd yearned to talk to him. Times when the panic ravaged her, and she loathed every waking moment of every day almost as much as those rare hours when she lay vulnerable in sleep.

She missed him, because as much as she'd loved their physical relationship, his friendship had mattered the most.

A sigh pulled from her. "I wasn't in a car accident."

No flickers of surprise alighted on his face.

He'd already known that.

"You already knew that, didn't you?"

His eyes turned glassy with grief. "No, I didn't. Until now."

She ducked her chin.

"Brynn, I do not want to make guesses about what happened to you."

Before her eyes, the floorboards blurred. "I... can't talk about it. I've never told anyone."

"No one?"

She shook her head.

"How long have you lived with this alone?"

"It's been a year now."

"A year?" His hand trembled when he dragged it through his hair. "Why haven't you talked to anyone?"

"Who would I tell? For what purpose? It'd only hurt them, and there was nothing anyone could do about it, anyway."

In the quiet, he sat motionless. "If I'd been here, would you have told me?"

"I doubt I could've kept it from you," she admitted. "You've been here a few days and you've already figured it out. I can't keep anything from you." Her shoulders hitched. "I never could."

"If I had been here..." His throat worked. "What would you have told me?"

She squeezed her eyes shut against the surge of panic that rushed forward to drown her. But the blackness was worse. The world dipped in a nauseating swoop, and her eyes flew open once more. She gripped the edge of the sofa and she stared at the solid wood floors.

Before her eyes, his outstretched hand appeared.

Without considering it, she placed her hand in his, and his fingers closed tight around hers. Warmth and strength flowed through her.

"I would've told you... someone... hurt me." Her courage deserted her. "Before you say anything, I'd been working late staging a house. I—I was wearing sweatpants and a T-shirt. I was alone, but—"

"What? Jesus—"

"That's not why I didn't go to the police." She rushed to get the words out. "He threatened me and I—I didn't know what to do."

"Of course not—"

"I was scared and... I was weak—"

"You are not weak. God, Brynn. You were terrified. Traumatized. It's not your fault. None of it is your fault."

A sob wedged in her throat. Around it, she struggled to breathe while he repeated the words again and again. "I'm so sorry" and "It's not your fault."

His voice, roughened with an aching tenderness, swept

over her, through her, clearing away murky clouds of shame and chaos. All the while, she clutched his hand.

"Was it the man at the ball?" he asked. "The one with the tattoo?"

Fiery mortification scalded her face. "Was it that obvious?"

"No. But I know you." In his voice was the same dark devastation crushing her with its grotesque weight. "That night, you were upset. Your reaction was… telling."

She realized she shouldn't be shocked. She'd had a panic attack right in front of him. Of course, he was going to be curious about that.

"Who is he?"

"I don't know." Panic tightened her chest. "I made the guest list. I know everyone on it. But I—I don't know who he is or why he was there."

Air wheezed through her lungs, and he murmured more quiet words that calmed the rising terror.

"I wasn't here for you when you needed me. That's what you meant the other day, isn't it?" His tone held more heartbreak than accusation.

"What? No." She swiped at her cheeks with the back of her hand. "That's ridiculous."

He fell silent, but his eyes held hers and wouldn't let go, and as she looked closely into the face of the man she'd loved all of her life, the truth slammed into her.

With the pain that arrowed through her heart, tears squeezed her throat. "Yes."

His expression twisted with grief and pain.

"Yes, I did. I blamed you." Shame pressed down on her. "I'm sorry. That's not fair. I guess… I've been so angry with you for so long that I twisted it all around inside my mind."

He bent his head, and her hands shook with the urge to

push her fingers through his hair and drop kisses on his crown. But he wasn't hers to love anymore.

"You protected me once before. You probably don't remember—"

"I remember."

"I think I thought if you'd been here, maybe it wouldn't have happened. Or maybe you would've helped me afterwards, the way you did before. It's… crazy."

"It's not crazy." He lifted his head.

At his shattered expression, a tear slipped down her cheek. "I'm sorry. You didn't deserve that."

"It's okay." He caught her tear with the pad of his thumb. "I was mad at you, too."

The ache in her heart gave a sharp wrench. "For believing my dad over you?"

"That, and for not believing me when I told you I wasn't good enough for you." The shadow of a smile touched his lips. "You let me think I had a chance, then you proved me right when you rejected me."

"I didn't reject you." The vehement words spilled from her.

Flecks of gold and amber shimmered in his dark eyes. "I'm the son of a pathetic man. A bastard."

"You know I never cared about that." Her heart in her throat, she gulped. "Don't you?"

"I remember you said you didn't care." He spoke with gentle tenderness. "But sometimes it's hard to let go of the things we believe in our hearts are true."

Color rushed into her cheeks, and she dropped her chin. "Please, stop being so nice to me."

"I will not do that."

She lifted her head. "You have to."

"Why?"

"Because I hate you."

He flinched with the wince of his pain.

"I have to," she said softly. "If I don't hate you, I'll love you, and loving you never got me anything except a broken heart."

On his face, a tempest of emotion gathered. "I never stopped."

She frowned with her confusion. "You never stopped what?"

"You asked me when did I stop loving you?" The golden centers in his dark eyes burned with a fiery blaze. "I never did. Not once. In twelve fucking years."

She replayed the words in her mind, checking and rechecking them for accuracy.

He never stopped.

That's what he'd said. She hadn't dreamed his words or wished them into existence. He said them.

He never stopped loving her?

The words settled in her heart and pumped through her veins like a warm elixir.

If only their apologies could reverse the cold poison of their past. But had they inflicted too many hurts on each other? Had the wounds that wouldn't heal forever hardened them against one another?

Her world was upended, but all she could do was sit on the couch with her mouth hanging open. Through the windows, the first slivers of sunlight peeked over the horizon, and she stared at the awakening while exhaustion and joy and sorrow overwhelmed her.

Turning her face to his, her vision blurred. "I really wish you'd come home sooner than this."

"Me, too." His hand tightened around hers. "I thought I was helping you. I thought if I came back, I'd hurt you again."

"You stayed away, for me?"

"I didn't want to hurt you. And I didn't want you to hurt me. I didn't want us to hurt each other. Like we always do."

He dropped his head as he lifted her hand to his mouth. "I might've been wrong."

His lips brushed the skin on the back of her hand, and with that, all the anger and hurts of the past several weeks, several years, were suddenly, utterly spent.

She breathed in his scent. "I wish that night never happened. Not the part where we were together, but when my dad found us and everything that happened after. Aiden, I didn't know what to do. We were so young and… stupid."

"Speak for yourself."

Her watery laugh bubbled to the surface. "I don't know what I would've done differently, but I wish I'd been stronger. I wish I'd known what to say to you, but I could never find the words. I still can't."

"You don't have to say anything." His warm mouth brushed lightly across the sensitive spot on the inside of her wrist. "I understand. I really do."

When he raised his head, something in him had changed. Suddenly, he looked at her the way he used to when they were teenagers. Except differently.

In his eyes, all the lust and longing of their past mixed with the regret and sorrow of their present.

The world held its breath around them.

"Brynn." Slowly, he slanted closer.

Fiery longing blazed in his eyes, and she tilted forward, yearning to touch his stirring heat.

All her senses seemed to open at once.

Then the fear rushed in.

Not fear of him—for him, her heart leaped with wild wonderment—but fear of herself.

Fear of what she would do if he kissed her again.

Fear of what he would think of her when he knew the whole truth.

Fear of how he'd react the first time she shrank from his

touch. Would he be annoyed, the way Jared had constantly been? Would he consider her crazy and cold and a bunch of other ugly, hurtful things?

Mostly, she feared the hurt. She'd hurt so badly for so long she simply couldn't survive any more pain. The next wound to strike her would be the fatal blow.

Lurching to her feet, she climbed over his legs. Her foot caught on his knee, and she tripped but bounded up before she hit the ground.

"I have to go. I'm going to be late for work." She scrambled toward her bedroom door. "I—I'll—see you later. At the office."

Then she ducked inside her room and barred the door, leaving him with a puzzled frown on his beautiful face.

CHAPTER 15

The moment the door slammed shut, he reached for his cell phone. He didn't care that it was not yet seven o'clock in the morning or that he had no plan. He needed to do something, anything, to keep moving. Even if he was only treading water. If he stopped, he'd drown.

Cian's groggy voice came over the connection. "Yeah?"

"Can you meet me at Rory's?"

Maybe it was the time of day, or maybe it was the edge of panic riding just below the surface of his voice, but Cian didn't argue.

"When?" he asked.

"Now."

After a beat, Cian groaned as though rolling out of bed. "On my way."

Aiden disconnected, and as he scrolled through his call list, the sound of a shower running carried through the wall. He used the pad of his thumb to select the number.

Shea answered on the second ring. "Yeah?"

If it'd been almost any other moment in time, Aiden

might've laughed at the similarities between Shea's and Cian's greetings.

"Hey. It's me," he said.

"So eight o'clock in the morning is a good time for you?" Sarcasm, without a hint of sleepiness, shaded Shea's voice. "I'll make a note."

"Actually, it's 7:00 a.m. where I am."

"As a pub owner, I find this all very disturbing," Shea said.

Despite himself, soft laughter rumbled in Aiden's chest.

"What's going on?" Shea asked.

Aiden slid off the coffee table and onto the edge of an overstuffed armchair. "Do I remember it right that you have a law degree?"

"That's an alarming question to be asked at 7:00 a.m.," Shea said. "At 8:00 a.m. too."

"I'm not in jail, if that helps."

"In that case, yes," Shea said. "You remember right."

"What kind of law did you practice?" Aiden hoped his tone sounded casual.

"I was a civil rights attorney."

With a deflating twinge, Aiden scrubbed a hand over his face and reclined back in the chair.

Muffled sounds crackled through the phone speaker. "Not what you're looking for?"

"I don't need a lawyer. I was only curious."

"Are we bonding? At eight o'clock in the morning?" Incredulity put a hitch in Shea's voice. "Is that what this is?"

"Yeah," Aiden muttered. "Something like that."

"Then I should tell you I like to take long walks on the beach and read corporate law briefs in my spare time."

Aiden sat upright in the chair. He'd already known Shea was a good business owner, but he was a corporate law junkie, too?

"I also like to travel," Shea said. "I hear Chicago's lovely this time of year."

Aiden fumbled for a reply. "Uh… now's not a good time."

"Why not?"

"It's complicated."

"I get that. I do," Shea said. "But you're my brother. I want to know you."

A stab of guilt pierced Aiden in the chest. "Work is busy. In a couple of months, when things slow down might be better."

"I thought you were a bartender."

"Only when I'm spying on my siblings who aren't aware of my existence."

Shea made a noise, like a grunt and a chuckle mashed together. "Fair enough. What do you do the rest of the time?"

While his mind churned, Aiden chewed the side of his thumb. "Freelance."

"How very millennial of you."

On his feet, Aiden paced Brynn's living room. "I'm working with a business owner right now, and their books are a mess."

"A mess how?"

Words formed on Aiden's tongue, but he quickly discarded them.

"Let me guess," Shea said. "It's complicated?"

Aiden's gaze slid to Brynn's bedroom door. "Yeah, you could say that."

"If you want me to look at anything, let me know."

"To be honest, I could use your help." Aiden considered his next words. "But depending what we find, I'm not sure I'll be in a position to resolve any issues."

The quiet on the other end of the connection told Aiden that Shea had picked up on his subtle cues.

"I offer my opinion only. Off the record." The gravel in

Shea's timbre grew heavy. "Whatever you choose to do with the information is up to you."

"I appreciate that. Can you text me an email where I can send you some files?"

"Will do," Shea said. "Next time we talk, can we do it after I've had my coffee?"

When he disconnected with Shea, Aiden removed the external drive from Brynn's laptop and retrieved his suit coat, which he'd slung over the back of a dining chair. At the door, he glanced back at her bedroom door.

After all that she'd told him, he didn't want to leave her. He wanted to stay. He wanted to be with her. But given her hasty retreat and dismissal, he suspected she wanted him gone. Perhaps she only needed a little space, or possibly she'd never forgive him for not being here when she needed him.

As he'd never forgive himself.

Helplessness and grief pelted him, but while the grief would ravage him until the end of his days, in this moment, he was not helpless.

First thing yesterday morning, he'd asked Erin, the staffer that had helped Brynn organize the ball, to comb the guest and donor lists for anyone that fit the description of the man with the bushy red beard and a snake tattooed on his right forearm, or for any other man's name she didn't recognize. She'd given him a list of eight names.

Eight men who may or may not be the one he sought.

He had serious doubts they'd find the piece of shit that had Brynn so rattled on the guest list for a swanky charity ball, so from Erin, he'd also gotten the name and contact information of the event photographer.

After that fiasco of a board meeting, he'd called the photographer and fed her a story about an assailant and the need to urgently identify him. She'd promised to upload all the photos she'd taken at the ball to an online storage site and send him the link where he could access it.

And while Brynn slept, he'd received an email with the link to the online gallery, where she had uploaded over one thousand photos taken at the ball. Aiden had combed through every one of them, and sometime near dawn, his efforts had paid off.

In one picture, he spotted the son of a bitch lurking in the background.

Now, he fled Brynn's building and climbed into his car parked on the street out front.

On the drive to Rory's loft on the south end, the city whirred past in a blur of steel and concrete. Ribbons of orange cast out by the rising sun pushed through the cracks between skyscrapers, banishing the long shadows of darkness to the deepest, darkest corners.

When he reached Rory's brick row house, he parked in the empty lot of the gothic-style Catholic church across the street. The thunder of traffic from the nearby interstate pursued him as he shuffled across Rory's desolated street and ducked down the alleyway behind the long line of three-story homes.

As he approached Rory's unit, the lower-level garage door stood open and the high-pitched wail of a table saw spilled out into the alley.

While he waited for Rory to finish, Aiden paced the pavement in front of the garage door, the coil of dread in his gut winding tighter with each turn.

The screeching noise receded, and Rory straightened.

With a glance at Aiden, he tugged the safety glasses from his face. "Where were you last night?"

Aiden's aversion to making long-term commitments extended to signing permanent housing contracts, and he'd been crashing at Rory's while he figured things out.

He dragged a hand through his hair. "I stayed at Brynn's."

"Ah." Rory stuck the clear glasses on top of his head. "Does her boyfriend know?"

A bite of cold fury nipped Aiden in the chest. "He's not her boyfriend anymore."

"Isn't he?" Rory lifted the piece of wood off the table and examined the cut. "That's interesting."

"What are you working on?"

"Brynn needed some custom cabinets built." Rory filched another piece of lumber from a pile at the end of his table.

"You never told me you do work with her," Aiden said.

"You told us not to talk to you about her."

The knife lodged in his chest twisted with terrible regret. "I was wrong."

"In that case, yeah, I do a lot of work for her." With his amiable smile, two dimples dented Rory's cheeks. "We have a symbiotic working relationship."

"How's that?"

"I put up with her perfectionism and insane workload, and she keeps me from having to get a real job."

At the mouth of the alley, Cian's silver SUV appeared and turned up the lane. Bits of gravel crunched and popped beneath the vehicle's tires as he sidled up alongside the building.

Rory's playful expression fell as Cian's lanky frame emerged from behind the steering wheel.

Cian took one look at Aiden and cursed. "Now what?" He slammed the car door shut.

"You're not gonna believe this." Rory slid his glasses back on. "We found them. Three more long-lost siblings. Sisters this time."

Cian pulled up, then relaxed suddenly.

His head shake didn't quite hide his smile. "When are we going to meet these siblings? The real ones, that is."

Aiden frowned. "Do you want to meet them?"

Cian hitched one shoulder. "Of course."

Aiden's gaze shifted to Rory. "You?"

"They're our brothers," Rory said, lining up the wood beneath the saw blade. "Yeah, I want to meet them."

Aiden raked his fingernails across his jawline. "I'll, uh, see what they want to do."

Cian leaned against the hood of his vehicle and folded his arms over his chest. "I assume you have a damn good reason for waking my ass up at this godless hour."

Aiden peered down the empty alleyway. "Either of you know Manny Moretti?"

Rory shoved the safety glasses through his dark hair once more. "He's a board member at Hathaway Group, isn't he?"

"Yeah. You know him?"

Rory's shoulders moved. "I know of him."

"What can you tell me about him?" Aiden asked.

"Big money. Big ego. Same ol' bullshit," Rory said. "Why do you ask?"

Picking his words carefully, Aiden filled them in on what happened at the board meeting. While he spoke, pensive frowns settled over their features.

"What do you need from us?" Cian asked when Aiden had finished.

"Information."

Cian's eyebrows knitted tightly together. "Information on Moretti?"

"For starters."

"What else?"

"Brynn's uncle and her cousin."

Rory moved to the end of the large stainless steel table. "Anything specific?"

"I want all of it." Aiden's voice dropped with his growing vengeance. "Hobbies. Relationships. Money. Vices."

With a laugh, Rory wiped his face on the sleeve of his T-shirt. "How we supposed to get all that? Unless we ask Xavier."

"No cops."

Aiden's swift dismissal drew a startled look from Rory.

"No cops," Aiden repeated. "Not right now. We need to find another way."

"I don't know—"

"I know how," Cian cut in.

Rory's head swiveled to him. "You do?"

"I know some guys who specialize in collecting that kind of information."

Rory's frown turned skeptical. "Who?"

With a grimace, Cian shrugged. "A couple of guys from the gym."

A MMA fighter until last year, Cian had trained at a local gym owned by his coach.

"Oh, yeah?" Disbelief saturated Rory's voice. "A lot of gym rats have a pressing need for dirt on wealthy businessmen?"

"You'd be surprised," Cian muttered. "Organized fighting draws a lot of bad elements. That kind of stuff was everywhere."

"What kind of stuff are we talking about?" Aiden asked.

After a beat, Cian said, "Organized crime."

"The *mob* hung around your gym?"

While Rory got hung up on that tidbit, Aiden jumped ahead. "Trying to rig matches?"

"Rigging matches, collecting gambling debts, looking to recruit body men. You name it."

"They get to you?" Aiden asked quietly.

Cian's features hardened. "They tried."

"How?" Rory asked.

"First, they straight-up offered cash. When I didn't bite, they tried other methods."

Unease crept up Aiden's spine. "What methods?"

"The usual. Bribery, blackmail, extortion." A humorless smile touched Cian's mouth. "But you can't squeeze someone who doesn't give a fuck. I'd committed no crimes I needed to hide, and I kept my private life private, so they couldn't threaten my family. I quit before they really dug in." He pushed away from the car. "But I can get us information."

Aiden didn't like the use of the word us. "This isn't your problem. It's mine."

"I got nothing else occupying my time."

"You have plenty to deal with right now," Aiden said.

Cian's lean face grew suddenly serious. "I need something to think about. Other than dying, that is."

For a moment, Aiden stared into his brother's face. Then he pulled his phone from his hip pocket. "I need help finding someone." His fingers flew over the phone's screen. "I have a picture. It's not great, but you can see his face."

The soft buzz of cell phones sounded, and Cian and Rory both reached for their devices to open the picture Aiden had just sent them.

"Who is he?"

Aiden pulled out a folded paper, which he handed to Cian.

"What's this?" Cian asked.

"Probably nothing," Aiden said. "But there's a slim chance his name is on this list." He waited while they brought up the images. "He's the one with the beard."

Rory peered at his phone screen. "Why are we looking for him?"

Aiden's gut churned. "I cannot say. But it's important."

Cian watched his face closely. "What are you going to do when you find him?"

"I'm going to kill him."

CHAPTER 16

*S*he was crazy.

There was no other way to describe the frenzied state of her inner world while she sat calmly at her desk and pretended to work. One moment, she was dizzy and buoyant with hope, and the next, the darts of doubt deflated her and she sank into despair.

And whenever she pondered what Aiden, who sat only a few feet away in his office on the other side of the wall, must be thinking about all that'd transpired in the twilight of dawn, she didn't know whether to laugh or rage or weep.

Between the board meeting, the messy financial records, and her panic attacks and nightmares, he had to be itching to flee Chicago and, this time, never look back.

But because of the machinations of her dad and Manny Moretti, he couldn't leave. He was trapped.

As if conjured by her frantic thoughts, Aiden appeared in the doorway.

A troubled frown etched his striking features. Evidence of the sleep she knew he hadn't gotten the night before showed in the bruises under his tired eyes.

She wanted to go to him. She wished to pull him into her arms and apologize for everything.

But of course, she didn't do that.

"Everything okay?" she asked.

"I talked to Philip. He's packing his office."

Her stomach twisted into a tight knot. "What did you tell him was the reason you were letting him go?"

"I told him we were going to be doing things a little differently going forward." His cool tone sent a chill racing through her. "He took it as a personal attack."

"He was angry?"

Aiden inclined his head. "I'll let you know when he's left the building."

"Thank you for dealing with that. Hopefully, Jacklyn knows what she's doing?"

"I think I'll find us someone from the outside. We could use a fresh perspective." His warm gaze probed her face and chased the chilliness from her body.

The air in the room grew suddenly charged.

"What are you doing today?" he asked.

She looked down at the blueprint in her hands, her task momentarily forgotten. "I'm going to head over to the Ukrainian Village project and meet with the superintendent about the report from the landmark office. They sent back sixty-five comments."

"Sounds like a lot."

She smiled at his intentional understatement. "It is. We can't move ahead with our work until we've convinced them we have a plan that takes all sixty-five of their concerns into account."

"Need any help?" The gold flecks in his dark eyes heated.

"I'm sure you have enough to do without helping me too."

"I will always make time for you." The way he said the

words made her insides soft and squishy and a delicious hunger that tightened her belly.

With her body's reaction to him, warmth flushed her skin, and memories flooded her mind.

The best, most wonderful memories.

Though twelve years had passed, the emotions overwhelmed her as powerfully as if she experienced it all again for the first time.

Her first taste of the insatiable desire. The first time she took a man inside her body. Her first rush of all-consuming pleasure.

Watching her, the color on his cheeks heightened, and his eyes narrowed.

She visibly startled, and instinctively, her hand shot to the high collar of her blouse. Through the flimsy fabric, the weight of her hand pressed against her ravaged skin, and the other memories returned.

Grief sucked all the joy and pleasure from her. They weren't teenagers anymore. She was no longer a curious, openhearted young woman.

She was older now. Guarded.

Scarred.

They couldn't have what they once had, not without him seeing the changes in her.

Did he still want her? Would he be able to love her body the way he once had, even with the observable, unalterable evidence of her ugliness? Would her scars only remind him of her taint? Every time?

Talk about a mood killer.

Mortification swamped her. She was doing it again. She was freaking out at the mere thought of being with a man.

Her mind was attacking itself. Again. Because she was going crazy.

As she fumbled through her desk drawer for her purse,

her hands shook. "I have to get going if I'm going to meet Travis on time."

She yanked her jacket off the back of her chair, but the collar caught on the armrest, and she gave several short tugs before it jostled free.

As she slipped past him, she risked a fleeting glance at his face, so she glimpsed his solemn expression up close.

What she saw stole her breath.

There was none of the annoyance or anger Jared might've shown and that she'd expected. Instead, if she hadn't known better, she might've believed she'd broken his heart rather than her own.

She fled.

Shame pursued her the rest of the day while she avoided returning to the office, and the next day as well. At home after a full day of work and some intensely vigorous shame avoidance, she changed into a pair of stretchy pants and poured a glass of wine.

But as she lifted the wineglass to her lips, her cell phone vibrated.

She tilted the device, and Joey's name flashed on the screen. She hadn't spoken to him since the board meeting, and a punch of dread struck her.

"We got a problem at the Wicker Park house," he said the moment she answered.

"What kind of problem?"

"They hit a water line in the basement."

Brynn groaned.

"It took two hours to get the city to turn it off." Joey's harried tone passed through the phone. "We're completely flooded."

"How deep?" she asked, stepping into her sneakers.

"Deep." His voice became muffled, then he cursed. "I'd say it's at least six inches."

"I'm on my way."

Thirty minutes later, Brynn pulled up to the curb in front of the brick workers' cottage. Chaos reigned inside the house. In the basement, loud voices carried over the low roar of pumps set up in the small space to remove the water, which rose high enough to submerge the lowest stair step.

The next several hours passed in a blur of frantic activity mixed with long periods of helpless idleness, during which times her mind chewed over the potential costs of repairing the damage. Midnight came and went before they'd removed enough water and could drag in large box fans to dry out the waterlogged space.

A full assessment of the destruction would have to wait until the morning.

It was nearly two in the morning when the three crew members who'd stayed to help scooted out, leaving her and Joey to lock up the house.

On the front stoop, Brynn tucked her arms inside her jacket and pulled the coat tight around her against the cool night air.

Joey rocketed down the steps after her and careened down the walkway toward the street.

Every muscle in her body ached with exhaustion, tempting her to let him go. But he'd been avoiding her all evening, and she knew from her own expertise in games of evasion that, with time, the tension between them would only grow more distressing.

Plus, she needed some answers.

She scrambled to catch up to him. "Hey, can I talk to you for a second?"

"I'm kind of tired." His long strides devoured the ground.

Her breaths came harder as she struggled to stay in step with him. "I'll keep it brief."

At his truck, he drew open the heavy tailgate.

She slid out of the way before the sharp corner struck her hip. "What was that at the board meeting?"

"What do you mean?" He tossed a wound-up hose into the truck bed.

"I mean, why did you side with Manny about changing the bylaws?"

"I didn't think it was a big deal." He slammed the gate shut and went around to the driver's side.

"Not a big deal?" She followed him into the street. "It opened a path for him to gain more shares in the company. If Aiden had quit, he'd have gained those shares, and now, when your dad retires in a few years, he'll get a chunk. I thought we agreed to keep his investment to a minimum."

His hand on the car door, he shot her an annoyed look. "What do you want me to say?"

At the snap in his tone, she blinked at him.

Not only were they cousins, but she and Joey had been friends for years, and that friendship had translated into a great working relationship, one with very few disagreements or outbursts despite the high-pressure nature of their jobs. During that time, they had crafted a plan to take over Hathaway Group when their dads retired and run the business together. As partners.

She'd been a bridesmaid in his wedding, and for the past three years, babysat his young daughters at least once a month so he and his wife could enjoy the rare date night.

And he dared to look at her like that? Like she didn't have a right to know what the hell had changed all that?

"Why did you do it?" she asked. "Why didn't you defend us?"

He had the decency to look abashed, but slowly, his expression changed until dark fear riddled his features. "I had to."

"Why?"

In the void left by his silence, her mind grasped onto a memory. That odd moment during the meeting when Manny had mentioned Joey's wife.

"Because he knows." Fear shuddered in his voice.

The warmth of her blood seemed to steal away. "He knows what?"

"Last year…" He stared at his hand on the car door. "Michelle and I… we were fighting all the time and… I met someone—"

At Brynn's gasp, his head snapped around. "I didn't mean to do it. It just happened."

She recoiled. "You cheated on Michelle? Oh, Joey."

"If he tells her, she'll leave me." His eyes glinted with his desperation. "I can't lose her or the girls."

"But…? Has he…? Is he… blackmailing you?"

With a vicious yank, he wrenched open the car door and ducked inside the cab. "I'm sorry."

He hauled the door shut on his mumbled apology, then the car's engine fired and propelled the vehicle through the dark night.

Suddenly alone on the quiet, dimly lit street, she scurried to her car and dove inside. Her hands were ice cold and trembling when she jammed the key into the ignition and eased the SUV away from the curb.

While she drove through the maze of deserted side streets on her way back to the main road, her thoughts careened out of control, jumping from one terrible worry to the next as she grappled with all that Joey had revealed.

Lost in her churning thoughts, she didn't notice the car behind her until its bright headlights beamed in her rearview mirror.

At the next stop sign, she planned to turn, preferring to drive around the block rather than lead the car with the glaring lights.

But when she turned, so did the car.

She turned again at the next stop sign, and again, so did the car.

When they passed beneath a streetlamp, the light briefly glided over the faces of two men in the car's front seats. At the next crossroad, she executed another turn, leading them back toward the street she'd been on when they'd emerged behind her.

The car followed her.

Her heart kicked.

At the very next stop sign, she turned, completing the circle, and the car turned behind her.

She stabbed the button to lock all the doors and continued on to the main road, where she made a rolling stop, then whipped her car out into traffic. The truck she cut off blared its horn.

Undeterred, she weaved around and snuck between several more vehicles as she made her to the highway junction. Blessedly, she hit the wave of traffic lights and slipped under three green lights before easing onto the interstate ramp. Sliding into traffic, she headed north toward home.

With frantic glances, she kept watch in her rearview mirror. Just when she'd begun to hope she'd shaken the car, it sidled up behind her.

Her heart tried to pound its way out of her chest as she dropped her speed in the feeble hope that they'd get annoyed and pass her.

While other cars zipped by her in the left lane, the car remained close on her tail with their high beams on.

She punched the accelerator, pushing down on the pedal until the needle on the speedometer hovered over a dangerously high number.

The car stayed close.

Though she slowed to a safer speed, her thoughts raced

ahead with terrifying scenarios. The long, dark tunnel of panic dragged her downward.

Her heart thumping in her ears, she grasped in the dark for her cell phone. Should she call 911? What would she tell them? That someone was flashing their high beams at her?

She returned her phone to the center console. Sucking big gulps of air into her lungs, she scolded herself. Once again, she was letting the fear win. She was tired and over-reacting.

The exit to her condo neared, and she peered hard into the rearview mirror when she edged onto the off-ramp.

The car followed her.

Fear knocked a panicked cry from her, and she cranked the steering wheel and careened over the gravel shoulder and back onto the highway.

As she knew it would, the car mimicked her erratic driving.

She snatched up her phone, and her fingers flew over the screen.

"Hello?" Aiden's voice was gruff with sleep.

"I'm sorry to wake you—"

"What's wrong?" he asked, his voice instantly alert.

"The basement flooded at the Wicker Park project and I was there all night bailing water and I just left and—and there's a car following me and—and—and I tried to lose them, but no matter what I do, they keep following me and—and I don't know what to do."

"Where are you?"

"On the highway. I just passed my exit. I was afraid... if they followed me home...." Fear squeezed her throat.

"Good. That's good."

"Aiden, what are they going to do to me?" Her words leaked out in a ragged whisper.

"Nothing, *a stór*. They will get nowhere near you." The

sound of his voice pushed her creeping terror back into the shadows. "You're going to drive to me. I'm at Rory's. Drive to me. Stay on the main roads."

"Okay." She gulped heavily. "I'll call when I'm close—"

"No. Don't hang up. Stay on the phone," he said. "If you have to set me down to drive, that's fine, but don't hang up. Keep talking. Tell me what's happening."

At the next exit, she left the highway, only to get right back on the southbound ramp.

"Did you do it?" Aiden asked.

"Yes. They did, too. Aiden—" Her voice climbed with her rising hysteria.

"You're doing great, sweetheart. Are your doors locked?"

"Yes," she squeaked and stabbed the automatic lock button several more times.

The drive to Rory's house on the south side of the city seemed to pass in a time warp. At Aiden's instance, she read aloud each road sign as it whizzed past her car window. In between markers, she heard Aiden's low voice and the muffled replies of someone in the background, but she couldn't make out their words through the phone's speaker.

When she read the road sign for Rory's exit, Aiden came back on the line. "Come down Twenty-Fifth to the alley. You're going to pull into Rory's garage. We're outside waiting for you."

The menacing car exited the highway behind her.

"Oh, no," she whispered. Terror stole her voice.

"What is it?"

"I have to stop for a red light."

"Do you see any other cars?"

Her gaze darted left and right and back again. "No. Can I run it?"

"Do it."

As the car approached the stoplight, she jammed the

accelerator and burst through the empty intersection. She repeated the crime at the next traffic light, then turned onto Rory's street.

"I see you." Near the mouth of the alley, Aiden's silhouette emerged from the dark and he stepped into the spill of light under a streetlamp.

Braking only enough to allow her to make the tight turn, she hit the curb with a jolt, then sped up the narrow alley. In her rearview, the shapes of three more men detached from the shadows and moved to block the alley's entry point.

She pulled into Rory's garage and silenced the car engine. In the piercing quiet, her heartbeat echoed in her ears while through the phone, the rustle of noises coming tightened the coil of panic constricting around her.

She pressed her forehead against the steering wheel and squeezed her eyes shut. And listened.

Muffled voices.

Quick, sharp breaths.

A shout.

Then Aiden's voice crackled over the connection. "They're gone. I'm headed your way."

Unwilling to part with her lifeline, she retrieved her phone from the cradle and eased open the car door. She slid from the vehicle, but when her feet hit the ground, her knees buckled, and she fell back against the car door.

He appeared at the rear of her car, and at the sight of him, emotion swamped her. The panic and fear fractured apart inside her, making room for relief and embarrassment and a myriad of other sentiments.

His dark eyes peered into her face as his long strides carried him to her side. "Are you all right?"

"I'm okay." But her hands shook so badly, she lost her grip on her cell phone, and it clattered to the pavement. "Did you see who it was?"

He crouched down and plucked the phone off the ground. Straightening, he handed it to her. "I didn't recognize them. But I got their plate numbers."

"I'm s-sorry." Teeth chattering, her whole body trembled as the panic dissolved.

"You're shivering." He looped an arm around her shoulders and tugged her against his chest.

Wrapped in the warm cocoon of his arms, the tension drained from her in a rush. She clung to him, burrowing into his heat and clean, spicy scent.

"Are you sure you're all right?"

Unable to speak, she nodded.

His fingers kneaded the base of her neck until her breathing slowed and evened out.

The three other men strode down the alley toward them. She picked out Cian's long, lanky stride and Rory's graceful gait, but the third man's walk she didn't recognize.

When the men neared, she turned her head. "I'm sorry I woke you."

"Are you kidding?" said the man with the unfamiliar walk. "Did you see us? Standing all together like a bunch of tough guys? We looked cool, right?"

Unbelievably, laughter bubbled in her throat.

"Yes, you're very cool." The words rumbled in Aiden's chest, where her head lay.

"And we didn't even have to break a sweat." He smacked Cian on the arm. "How about that, Captain Badass?"

"It was all you," Cian said. "Everyone fears Benjamin Walker."

A goofy grin spread across Ben's face, and he raised the baseball bat in his hand. "Don't forget, my trusty sidekick."

Ben gave the bat a whirl, and with a sharp curse, Rory ducked as it whizzed past his head.

Slowly, he straightened. "Step away from the bat, Benji."

A comical grimace contorted Ben's features. "My bad." He leaned the bat against the garage wall and backed away.

As the trio slipped by and filed through the backdoor and into the house, their voices echoed around the cramped garage. When they'd faded completely, she moved to extract herself from Aiden's embrace.

But she couldn't will her weak limbs to obey. "I'm sorry," she repeated. "I d-don't know why I called you."

Of course she knew. She hadn't been thinking clearly, or she would've stopped herself, but as it was, instinct had kicked in and overruled reason. Without layers of doubt or overthinking to obscure the truth, she'd made her choice. Reflexively, he was the comfort she sought whenever she was hurt or afraid.

Above all others, he was the one she wanted.

He was the one she trusted.

He was the one.

He always had been.

He always would be.

"I'm glad you did." His mouth brushed over her forehead.

With the tender kiss, she sagged more heavily against his solid chest. The thundering of his heart echoed through her bones, and though she knew she should move away, she craved his warmth and strength more than she wished to spare herself another broken heart.

Indeed, a moment in his arms just might be worth a lifetime of heartbreak.

CHAPTER 17

$\mathcal{T}$error had drained the color from her cheeks, and she was shaking so hard, her tremors reverberated through him. He was certain if he let her go, she'd crumble into a pile at his feet.

If he let her go, so would he.

"Do you want to sleep here tonight?" He rubbed a hand up and down her back, as if the friction might manufacture some warmth. "Or would you like me to take you home?"

Her wide eyes slid to the mouth of the alley. "Do you think they'll come back?"

"And face the wrath of Ben's bat? Nah, they won't be back. But we may have trouble finding you a bed if we stay here. Why don't I drive you home?"

Without argument, she handed him her car keys and shuffled around to the passenger side door.

Still a couple of hours from the morning rush, the streets were nearly empty as he maneuvered her vehicle through the city and the northern neighborhoods. As he drove, the shallow, erratic cadence of her breathing evened out, then fell into a slow, steady rhythm.

She laid her head against the seat back. When a yawn pulled from her, her chin quivered.

Her head rolled in his direction. "I really am sorry I woke you up in the middle of the night."

He stole a quick glance at her. "You have nothing to apologize for. I wasn't even asleep."

After a beat, she turned her face to the window. "Liar."

A thump of quiet laughter hit him in the chest. "I'll be the first to let you know when you owe me an apology."

Watching her profile, he caught the small smile that teased her lips.

It evaporated all too quickly.

"I talked to Joey tonight," she said.

By the time she'd finished relaying the details of what she'd learned about her cousin, a dark shadow of confused dread clung to Aiden. "Moretti's blackmailing him?"

"That's what it sounds like."

His grip on the steering wheel tightened. "I wonder who else he's blackmailing?"

"I wondered that, too." The shadow expanded to fill her voice.

At her condo, he slid the SUV into her leased parking spot, then walked with her up the dark path to the building's front entrance. The cool night air held a crisp fall chill, and beyond the Greystone's massive silhouette, Lake Michigan groused and grumbled.

Inside the old structure's art-deco styled foyer, they moved to the shiny steel elevator. With a soft ping, the doors slid closed, and the lift carried them to the top floor.

In the hall outside her door, she made quick work of the lock and crossed the threshold.

She turned back. "Did you want me to call you a cab? Or… you can stay…."

"I want to sleep with you." The words were out of his mouth before he'd considered them.

Her eyebrows lifted.

"Oh, c'mon, get your mind out of the gutter," he said. "I'm your boss, for crying out loud."

Rather than roll her eyes at him or fire off a sharp retort, or even give him a begrudging smile, she stared. Her green eyes appeared huge in her pale face.

A lump lodged in his throat, and he swallowed it with an audible gulp. "I want to stay. Here. With you. I want to sleep here with you. In case you need me. Or if you want to talk." *The way we used to.* "If you'll let me in, I'd like to stay. Please."

While he'd rambled, she'd conducted an open study of him, and when he fell silent, she took only a moment to decide.

She stepped back and opened the door wide.

He passed through the archway and closed the door, plunging them into darkness a moment before she switched on a lamp and soft light bathed the room in its warm glow.

With harried steps, she went to the patio doors and flung them open. Cool air rushed inside along with the lulling roar of the lake. Today, the waters churned and frothed, like a snarling beast prowling at the gates.

Unfazed, Brynn closed her eyes and dragged in a deep, deliberate breath. It was not the first time he'd witnessed her purposeful, meditative attempts to draw air. While she stood before the open door, Romeo crept close, then squeezed around her legs and out into the night.

"The water helps," she said when she detected him behind her. "I don't know why."

He angled his shoulders sideways and slipped by her. The large patio had been constructed as part of the building's architecture, and the heavy, rough-cut stones wrapped them in a protective fortress high above the waves crashing to shore down below.

The chill night air nipped at him, and he shoved his hands into the pockets of his blue jeans as he took in the view. To the south, the lights of the downtown cityscape twinkled like a cluster of fireflies. The steel monoliths and majestic towers seemed dwarfed by the immense Great Lake lapping at its shores, as though keen to devour the mighty metropolis.

He inhaled deeply, as she had, hauling the smell of fresh water and earth into his nostrils.

"It's calming up here." In the dim light that reached them from indoors, his gaze sought her face. "I see why you like it."

Her white teeth flashed in the soft darkness. "There's a rooftop deck."

He craned his neck and peered up into the black sky. "How do you get up there?"

"This way."

He followed her around the corner of the building where the terrace wrapped the home's structure. When she started to climb, he hesitated, unable at first to see the pressed metal staircase fastened to the wall. In the building's shadow, he reached out, and his hand grasped the thin metal railing.

An already impressive view, the sight from the roof stole his breath. Moonlight gleamed on the water's rolling surface and the wet rocks that lined the beach. He propped his elbows on the deck railing and bore witness to the amazing spectacle.

Behind him, she grappled in the dark, and a strand of patio lights strung from one end of a wooden pergola to the other winked on.

At his side, she mimicked his stance. When she lifted her arms over the rail, a gap formed above the zipper of her hooded sweatshirt, and the ragged edges of her scar peeked out.

She caught his gaze on the wound, and her hand shot to the gap. But in the end, she didn't adjust the fabric and let her hand fell away.

He wanted to know how it'd happened. The words gathered on his tongue, but he left them there, unspoken. His wish to know what she'd gone through couldn't outweigh her safety. He knew enough to surmise how it'd happened, and the details would only reinjure in the telling.

Besides, he supposed what he really wanted was for her to want to tell him how it'd happened.

He studied her profile, admiring her small nose and the soft curve of her cheek. "I haven't seen you at the office much this week. Where have you been?"

A breeze lifted the ends of her hair, and the light strands danced around her face. "Avoiding you."

His chest cavity constricted. "I'm sorry."

"That's my line," she said with a fragile smile. Then her brow crinkled. "Why are you sorry?"

The pang in his chest gave an unbearable wrench. "I'm sorry I wasn't here when you needed me."

Something on the black horizon captured her attention. "That wasn't me who felt that way. It was the hurt." She snuck a glance at him. "That's definitely not why I've been avoiding you."

"Why, then?"

He held his breath through the long, quiet moment.

"I haven't been with a man since… it happened, and… I haven't missed it." She heaved a sigh into the lake. "You make me miss it."

The breath left his body in a rush.

Huge, hope-filled eyes landed on his face. Then a sudden turmoil kicked up in their green depths and she looked away.

"I miss it with you, too." A husky rasp filled his voice.

She squeezed her eyes shut.

"Does that scare you?"

"It terrifies me," she whispered. "Not the thought of being with you, but… I'm afraid it'd be different. That you'd be disappointed."

"That's not possible." Certainty clipped his tone.

"I made a decade-long career out of disappointing you. Besides, I'm…" Grief ravaged her expression, and she ducked her chin. "…different now."

Pain stabbed him in the center of his chest.

"You're right," he said. "You are different. It's been twelve years. We're both different, and that's as it should be. Back then, you were pretty amazing, but now, you're so much more. You're smart and strong, and so talented."

"I don't feel strong." She kept her face angled away from him. "I think I might be hopeless."

"Are we still talking about sex? Because I know better."

She tossed him a look. "That was a long time ago."

"You're frightened. Rightly so." He choked down the surge of raw anguish. "But I want you to know you don't have to be afraid. Not with me."

Her gaze darted sideways to him and then quickly away. "Of all the men I know, I think you're the one I'm most afraid of."

The wound in his chest gave a gutting wrench.

She kept her lashes lowered when her fingers brushed her collarbone. "It's not the only one. I…. There are others. H-he had a knife, and I fought him…."

A thousand earthquakes rumbled and wrecked inside him. His hand shook when he dragged it over his mouth.

"They're scars," he croaked. "They don't change who you are."

Her lashes swept up, and he nearly stumbled back with the force of the pain in her eyes. "These did."

"They don't change who you are to me." Devastating

aftershocks reverberated through him. "They don't change how I feel about you."

Pink flushed her cheeks. "What if we do it and it's not like it was before? What if we aren't good together now?"

"I've waited for you all my life." Emotion shredded his voice. "It'll be good."

Doubt demolished the smile that tried to form on her lips. "You haven't even seen them. When you do…."

"When I do, it'll be hard. I hate what happened to you, but nothing can change how I feel about you. Not the years we spent apart. Not the angry words. Not scars. Not even death. After all this time, you're still the one I want. The only one."

A softness came into her tired, puffy eyes.

He brushed a strand of hair off her forehead, eager to sink into that softness.

She yawned.

He held out his hand to her. "C'mon, let's get you to bed."

Big green eyes flew to his face. "To bed, to sleep?"

"Yes, to sleep. It's five o'clock in the morning."

Her smile did form then.

"We're going to get used to each other again," he said. "And when you're ready—*if* you decide you want more—we might even kiss."

The smile lingered on her lips when she placed her hand in his, and he clasped it tight.

WITH THE MORNING SUN, he slipped from her bed. His low voice near her ear, assuring her he'd handle things at the office, pulled the veil of sleep over her once more.

At her bedroom door, he glanced back at her, and a crooked smile touched his soft mouth. That smile coaxed a contented sigh from her as she burrowed deeper into the bed linens. Bed sheets that smelled like him.

She breathed him into her body—*Aiden*. Finally, he'd come home. Through the drowsy haze of her slumber, she wondered if he was real or merely a dream.

It was well past noon before she arrived at work, and when she checked her calendar for that afternoon, a gang of leaden butterflies banged to life in her stomach.

In less than an hour, she had a meeting scheduled with Jared—a meeting that'd been placed on her calendar weeks ago by her dad—to discuss opportunities to deepen the partnership between their two companies.

Her stomach curling into knots, she collected her laptop and prepared to head to the conference room. But just then, Aiden appeared in the doorway.

The black suit he wore hugged his lean frame and failed to conceal the solid strength of his chest and thighs. Her heart leapt to her throat.

"Hi," she said stupidly.

Dark eyes touched her face. "Hi."

His questing gaze lit a trail of fire across her skin. "Are you waiting for me? I was on my way."

"There is no meeting."

"What?" She reached for her computer mouse to recheck her calendar. "Was it cancelled?"

"It's already over."

Butterflies dipped and swerved. Straightening, she studied his inscrutable expression. "I didn't mean for my personal life to interfere with business."

Sudden anger animated his features. "*Your* personal life has nothing to do with it. His does. He's the one who acted like an ass, and he's the one who'll pay the consequences for it."

Aiden's words smacked into her like a breaking wave crashing to shore. He was right.

Of course, he was right.

Why hadn't she seen that? Why had she been so quick to assign blame to herself?

His fury cooling, he adjusted the collar of his skull-white dress shirt. "We will not be working with him in the future, and I'm checking with legal about dissolving our existing contracts. Turns out, his personal and moral failings carried over to his business. You were right to question his practices."

"Me?" She dropped heavily into her chair. "What did I do?"

"You tipped me off when you mentioned those property appraisals. I wanted to see if you were right that they were too high, and what I found was a big scam." As he spoke, he moved deeper into her office. "He's been inflating home prices to secure massive loans—I do not know what he's been doing with all that money—and now he's about to default on a fifteen-million-dollar loan. He's done, and so are this company's business dealings with him."

He came to a stop in front of her desk. "You okay? You look a little pale."

Stunned to speechlessness, she stared up at him for a moment. "How could I have been so wrong about him?"

"Do not be too hard on yourself. He's a con man. A good one. He preys on kind hearts." The gentle slide of his voice wrung a pang from her heart. "The shame is his, not yours."

With a sigh, she pushed up from the chair and rounded the desk. "Still, I feel like an idiot."

"You are not an idiot." Golden-brown eyes soothed over her.

At his lingering gaze, a twinge of insecurity struck her. She tucked a loose strand of hair behind her ear.

"You look beautiful today," he said, his voice low and heated.

Bemused laughter spilled out of her. After sleeping through the morning, she'd taken an abbreviated shower, then tossed on a blouse and a pair of slacks, skipping makeup and bothering only to yank a comb through her wet, tangled hair.

"You're a terrible liar. I'm a mess."

"That's how I like you looking."

Once-leaden butterflies took carefree flight. "Like a mess?"

"Like you just rolled out of bed after a night of marathon sex."

She shot a quick glance at the doorway to make certain no one lurked nearby. "If memory serves, not so much a marathon as a sequence of consecutive sprints."

"Are you doubting my stamina?" He swayed slightly forward on his feet.

"Not at all." She slanted toward him.

When their bodies touched, a jolt of electricity sparked between them, and they drew apart.

"Will I see you later?" he asked.

A flare of warning niggled in the back of her mind. The last time she played with her passionate, fiery stepbrother, she'd gotten burned.

But she couldn't make herself stop, any more than she could smother her smile. "I'd like that."

With another long look that all but singed her clothing, he was gone.

Before settling down to work, she snagged her coffee cup off the desk and went to check the coffeepot.

After claiming the last splashes of coffee leftover from that morning, she turned, and collided with a male body.

Coffee sloshed over the brim of her cup, and she gasped when the hot liquid seared her skin.

The man cursed and shook his arm, spraying brown droplets over the white wall and the recently replaced carpeting.

Annoyed, she glared up at him, and another gasp erupted from her when she looked into Jared's bloody face.

CHAPTER 18

The skin surrounding his left eye was red and seemed to swell as she stared, while a trickle of bright blood oozed from a crack in the skin in the center of his bottom lip.

She openly gaped at him. "What happened to your face?"

"Why don't you ask your brother?" He used the pad of his thumb to wipe at the blood on his lip. "You fuck him yet?"

With his crudeness, she gasped. "You have no right to ask me that."

His smirk made him resemble the serial killer revealed at the end of every prime-time crime drama. "Maybe he'll have better luck thawing you out than I did."

Brynn swallowed her outrage with a sip from her coffee mug, then shrugged. "Maybe he already has."

Jared's smug smirk crumbled, and he brushed past her. While he stalked to the elevator, she used a paper towel to blot at the coffee splatters on the sleeve of her blouse.

When the elevator doors drew closed and she knew him to be beyond the point where he could hurt her, she expelled a prolonged breath.

Then she tossed the soiled paper towel in the trash and set out for the corner office.

Aiden stood behind the massive black desk, his head bent as he searched the cluttered surface.

She leaned against the doorjamb and folded her arms in front of her. "Were you going to tell me?"

He glanced up and made a quick assessment of her face. "Your ass looks incredible in those pants. There, I said it."

"Nice try."

Casually, he selected a folder from the pile on his desk. "You'll have to be more specific."

"You did a bit more than end our business with Jared."

He cracked open the folder.

She tipped her chin to gesture toward the hallway over her shoulder. "I just ran into him—"

Aiden's head snapped up, and he flung the folder aside as he rounded the desk. "Did he lay a hand on you? If he so much as—"

"He didn't touch me." She held up her hands to ward off his charge. "Did you do that to his face?"

A satisfied smirk tried to claim his mouth and won.

"Aiden!"

"I am not admitting anything."

"Do you deny it?"

The faintest shadow of regret shaded his features. "I do not."

Her heart battered her breastbone. "I don't need you to fight my battles for me."

"I know that."

"And I certainly don't want you beating people up for me."

"I know that, too." He peeked at her from beneath the long sweep of his eyelashes. "I didn't do it for you. That was for my own personal gratification."

A laugh spilled from her before she reined it in. "What if he presses charges?"

"I would gladly pay my debt to society ten times over for the chance to do it again."

While her laughter fizzled, she rubbed the ache forming between her eyebrows.

He inched closer, and like a flower tilting toward the sun, she moved to close the small space between them as his radiance drew her to him.

When he peered into her face, the heat became too intense, and she ducked her chin. "Just... be careful with him."

"He's a weak man."

"Is that what he is?" she asked dryly.

With the tip of his finger, he traced the curve of her still-tender cheek. "I'm not saying he isn't dangerous. I'm saying he's a fraud as a man, and deep down, he knows it. That's why he lashes out."

Into the whisper of space between them, she confessed her fear. "I was an easy target for him."

"You are not weak," he said, his voice fierce and gentle at once. "You're one of the strongest people I know, and trust me, I know a lot of badasses."

Pleasure warmed her cheeks. "You're only saying that to get me into bed."

He didn't laugh along with her joke. "I know you don't need me, Brynn. The ugly truth is, I need you."

Among the fiery flecks of gold in his eyes, vulnerability shimmered. She marveled at it for a moment until his gaze latched on to her mouth.

"I also need to eat." He leaned close and braced his forearm against the door above her head. "What do you say? Do want to knock off early and go to dinner with me?"

He smelled of citrus, and clean man, and her head spun

with giddy delight. She gripped the doorframe behind her. "I just got here."

"Yes, but I'm starving."

Hunger filled his voice, and a flutter of yearning whispered low in her belly. "Do you want to grab something from the food truck?"

"I don't want to go to the food truck." His husky tone matched the promise in his eyes. "I want a proper meal."

"It's only two o'clock," she breathed. "I haven't done any work yet."

"I'll give you a couple of hours to get your work done, then we'll go to dinner."

"I should stop by the house in Lincoln Park…."

He pinned her with his steady gaze. "Brynn, I'm trying to ask you out on a proper date."

Her heart stuttered. "A date?"

"Yes, a date." His expression softened. "We've lived in the same house, worked in the same office, slept in the same bed, and experienced the best sex of our lives with each other, but we've never actually gone on a date like two normal, unrelated people."

She bit down on her bottom lip to stifle a smile. "The best sex of our lives?"

"You admitted as much to me last night."

Heat swept over her skin, and her breath snagged in her throat. "I don't think that's true."

His dark eyes gleamed in his handsome face. "It is."

"Okay, well, I might've said something along those lines, but *you* didn't."

He grew suddenly serious. "Sex with you wasn't only the best sex of my life, it was the best experience of my life. You are the best thing that's ever happened to me."

Her heart tripped clumsily along behind her faltering

lungs. She'd never been openly pursued by him before, and she hadn't expected to enjoy it quite so much.

"Yes," she said. "I'll have dinner with you tonight."

But back in her office, the wicked barbs of doubt prodded and poked. A few even pierced.

She'd never seen Aiden with a woman who was less than stunningly perfect. The supermodel, Samantha Whitaker, and her best friend, Molly, possessed charms far beyond Brynn's small, plain looks.

Indeed, Brynn seemed to be the singular exception to Aiden's preference for perfection. And if they continued down this path they were on, he'd soon get a very real, very ugly look at just how imperfect she really was now.

Despite what he'd said last night, despite what he may even believe, the reality of her marred flesh would test his tolerance for physical imperfection.

By the time the end of the workday drew near, her self-doubts had poisoned the well of her happiness. With hope had come fear. With her memories, grief.

As had always been the way, Aiden existed in her heart as joy and sorrow, side by side. Inseparable.

A little after quitting time, he appeared at her door.

She hedged. "Should we be doing this? If anyone sees us...?"

His gaze sharpened on her face. "We'll say it's a business meeting."

The last time she and Aiden started a relationship, fear of what their parents would do if they'd found out had hung over them, and in the end, that fear was warranted. Now they were adults, and while no one could forbid them or punish them, a range of unforeseen consequences seemed suddenly possible, from shifting family dynamics to the risk to their professional reputations.

"We can be discreet." The vulnerability had returned to his eyes. "If that's what you prefer."

At his concern for her, even when his own insecurities hounded him, caused all the threatening scenarios her mind tried to conjure to evaporate in a puff of smoke.

Not one of them was worth giving him up.

With a nod, she retrieved her purse from her desk drawer and went to him.

Out front, a car waited for them, and Aiden held the door open while she piled into the back seat. When he slid in behind her, his broad shoulders filled the small space, and when he settled in the seat beside her, the length of his thigh pressed against hers.

She froze, anticipating the wrench of nausea. She'd grown so accustomed to it that she swallowed thickly out of habit.

But it didn't come.

She experienced no queasy panic or dizzying dread, and instead, she leaned into his warm strength despite her request for discretion only moments earlier.

In the car's cramped interior, she grew acutely, wonderfully aware of him. The soft rise and fall of his breathing. The size and power of his hands as they rested on his thighs. His scent, his heat, his intensity, all mixed to form a potent cocktail of an arousing man.

While she watched the city roll past through the car's window, a smile flirted with forming on her lips.

At the gentle clasp of his fingers around hers, her breath caught.

When the driver pulled up to the curb and she peered outside at their destination, a laugh burst from her.

She turned to him. "A business meeting at Navy Pier?"

His crooked smile clutched at her heart. "You can't call yourself a Chicagoan if you've never been to Navy Pier."

As they made their way out onto the large pier, a gusting

breeze that held the sun's warmth pushed away the cooler fall temperature that'd moved into the city. Her heart stirred with excitement. She didn't even care about the tourist attraction, but that he thought to bring her.

They ate dinner on the patio of a restaurant lining the pier. Sunlight reflected off the crests on the waves and shattered into crystal sparks while they lingered over their meal and after-dinner drinks, talking about his years overseas at university and his experience working with small businesses and large corporations alike.

The entire time, she fought the urge to reach across the table and brush his hand with her fingers, or push her hand through his thick hair, or gaze at his beautiful face like a lovesick schoolgirl.

By the time they left the restaurant and strolled along the pier, the sun had set and lights from the Ferris wheel and other carnival rides illuminated the night sky. She decided then that even if it was a tourist trap, it was a magical place. Or it might've been her date that gave the evening its enchanting feel.

When their driver delivered them back to the Hathaway Group offices, they took their time walking to their cars in the parking garage.

At her car door, she rummaged through her purse for her keys.

Clutching them in her hand, she pushed her hair off her forehead. "Thank you for dinner."

"You're welcome," he said, and the heat in his voice spread a lick of fire through her.

Her body was slanting toward his again. "Do you want to stay at my place again tonight?"

"I thought you'd never ask." His hand between their bodies lightly gripped her waist. "I'll meet you there. I'm going to stop at Rory's for a couple of things."

They stood so close that when she nodded, his mouth brushed her temple. The rasp of stubble on his jaw scraped her skin and sent an arrow of desire firing through her.

"Brynn." He said her name as though he were tasting it on his tongue.

She lifted her chin, bringing her mouth within a whisper of his. In the air between them, their shortened, shallow breaths mingled.

His fingers danced along her the side of her neck. "I can't tell you how many times I imagined being like this with you."

"I thought about you, too."

He closed his eyes as if experiencing a slash of pain. "What did you think about?"

"All of it." The words gushed from her heart. "All the times we were together, all our talks in the middle of the night. I wanted to remember everything. I was afraid I would forget you."

When he looked at her, his dark eyes glittered with emotion. "I was afraid I'd been forgotten."

"Never," she whispered.

"I'm sorry for all that happened." His hands cupped her face. "But I'm not sorry to hear you didn't let me go so easily."

Then his mouth brushed against hers. His tongue peeked out to take a soft taste of her, and the slow lick fluttered low in her belly, like warm fingers teasing between her legs. A moan vibrated in the back of her throat, and he pushed his hands beneath the curtain of her hair.

She was at the spinning center of a kiss that could demolish her life—again—but she didn't care. Proof of his arousal pressed against her abdomen, and need pulsed between her thighs.

She'd never been able to resist him for long, and in that moment, she didn't want to resist him. She wanted to open for him. No matter that she was making herself vulnerable to the one man who could destroy her with a word or a look.

Just then, a bright light flashed near her face. She blinked open her eyes, then squeezed them shut again when another flare popped off.

Aiden cursed and angled his body in front of Brynn.

The man with the camera took one look at Aiden's thunderous expression and scurried away, darting through the parking garage and out into the city streets.

Her heart pounding against her breastbone, Brynn pressed her palm to his shoulder. "It's okay. It's just the tabloid."

Another curse dropped from his lips. "Aren't there any celebrities in this town they can harass?"

A sardonic frown touched her features. There were few celebrities in town as handsome as Aiden, and certainly none offered as scandalous a story as conducting an affair with their stepsister.

"So much for discretion," she said.

HE'D SLEPT in her bed every night for the past two weeks.

Only sleep.

And though they hadn't found time to sneak away for many more dates, it'd been the best two weeks of his life.

Which was exactly what he'd told her three nights earlier when he'd looked up from reading one of her books to find her hovering at the foot of the bed.

At her expression, he'd sat and swung his legs over the side of the bed. "What is it?"

"I'm sorry," she'd said. "I know I should be ready for more by now."

Reaching out, he'd grasped a fistful of her nightshirt and

gently tugged her to him. "Hey, no. There's no time limit here. That's not how it works."

"I don't know how it works." Watery tears had mixed with her frustration. "What if it takes another year? What if I never get over it?"

"Don't do that to yourself," he'd said. "It's not something you have to get over. It's something we have to learn to move forward with. Together. We have time."

She sniffled. "I just… I want you to know it's not you."

With both of his hands, he pulled her face down to his. "I've waited for you for twelve years, and I'll happily wait twelve more if that's how long you need."

A tear had rolled down her cheek, and he'd caught it with his finger.

The vibration of his cell phone on his desk drew him back to the present. With a grimace, he answered the call from Shea.

"You weren't kidding when you said the books were a bit of a mess." Shea's gravelly voice sounded like he'd eaten a bag of rocks.

"What'd you find?"

"I'm not done yet, but I think you were right to be suspicious."

Dread snaked through his gut. "How bad is it?"

But Aiden knew the answer before Shea uttered the words.

Money laundering.

When Aiden fired Philip, the devious accountant had indeed absconded with many of the files, as Aiden had predicted he would. But the deception proved useful, as those missing files were the very ones Aiden had focused in on to untangle the maze of dubious activity.

The deeper Aiden had dug into the records, the wider the web of nonsensical transactions seemed to grow.

"Leo got wind of what we were up to, which means his wife found out, and well, that was that," Shea said.

Dread coiled into alarm. "What was that?"

"Man, I got flow charts and graphs and… I don't even know what some of this stuff is." The sound of shuffling papers carried through the phone. "I can tell you the point where the money is entering the company and when it leaves again, but I can't tell you where it came from or where it's going. That's the million-dollar question—whose money it is?"

Aiden cursed. He shoved a hand through his hair. "Just send me everything, will you?"

"It's on its way," Shea said easily. "Now about that visit…."

"Uh, I gotta go."

"I'm gonna keep bugging you about this."

"Thanks for your help." Aiden ignored the pang of guilt that struck him in the center of his chest. "I really appreciate it."

No sooner had he disconnected with Shea than Donna buzzed him.

"Mr. Morris is here to see you."

"What the hell does he want?" Aiden snapped.

But Jared strolled into his office before Donna had time to reply.

"I want to talk to my good friend, Mr. Nolan." Aiden's name on his tongue dripped with disgust.

He closed the door behind him, and Aiden took immediate satisfaction in seeing that the shadow of the shiner still lingered around his left eye.

"Get out," Aiden said.

In response, Jared tossed a tabloid newspaper onto the desk.

Slowly, Aiden dragged his gaze from the bastard's annoying face to the paper.

Taking up the entire front page was a picture of him and Brynn kissing in the parking garage. Inset with the photo were several smaller images, including one of him and Clarissa, the supermodel he'd dated briefly, and several of him and Molly the night of the ball.

Among the montage was a photo of him dancing with Molly alongside another, taken when he'd dropped her off at her home after they'd left Brynn's condo. In it, they stood on her front porch and her expression as she smiled up at him was one of pure seduction.

"Drop the lawsuit," Jared said, referring to the breach of contract suit Hathaway Group had filed earlier that week. "Or everyone in Chicago will see this."

Relief rushed through him that Jared cared only about the lawsuit. For a moment, he'd feared the money Hathaway Group appeared to be laundering belonged to Brynn's ex.

Aiden pretended indifference. "You own the *Daily Sun*?"

"It's good to have well-connected friends."

"You call a tabloid owner well-connected?" Aiden tossed the paper at him. "You need to get out more."

Rage colored Jared's face with splotches of red when he caught the newspaper. "And you need to do what I say."

"Is this supposed to be funny?"

"Do I look like I'm joking?"

Aiden shrugged. "Looking at you makes me laugh."

Jared crumpled the tabloid in his fist. "I'm sure Brynn will find this funny."

Right away, Aiden understood Jared's ploy was intended to hurt Brynn. Unbeknownst to Jared, making their affair public would hurt her beyond the obvious reasons. She wanted to be respected. She'd *earned* respect, and if the entire city thought she was sleeping with the boss, her reputation would be tarnished.

Cian's words floated through Aiden's mind. *You can't blackmail someone who doesn't give a fuck.*

Problem was, he did give a fuck. A big, massive one.

He could imagine her reading that trash article. He could imagine what she'd think seeing him with those other women. It didn't matter that nothing had happened between him and Molly. It didn't matter that he hadn't spoken to Clarissa since the handful of dates they'd gone on over a year ago.

Aiden and Brynn had been in this exact place once before. Twelve years ago.

And that time, she'd believed the lies. She'd believed that he'd knocked up Samantha Whitaker. She'd believed her dad over him.

Jared slammed the tabloid back down on Aiden's desk. "Let me answer that for you. She'll be pissed off and humiliated."

"I don't know how it embarrasses her," Aiden said. "You're the one whose girlfriend dumped you for a younger, richer, better-looking man."

Red with fury, Jared fumed.

"If this is all you got, it's pathetic. Truly." With swift steps, Aiden moved to the door and yanked it open. "Get out."

Jared walked slowly toward him. At the door, he stopped. Facing Aiden, he puffed up his scrawny chest and stared Aiden down with a comically non-menacing scowl.

Aiden made a sudden movement.

Jared flinched and scurried through the door.

Aiden swung the door shut with a resounding bang and dove for his cell phone. With unsteady hands, he typed a text to Brynn, who had spent the afternoon out of the office.

Where are you? he typed.

Her reply came quick. *I'm heading home now. Meet you there?*

On his race to beat her to her condo, he broke several traffic rules. He couldn't explain the urgency that drove him, except to acknowledge that the ghosts of their past still haunted him every now and again.

He hoped this time would be different from the last, but forces outside their relationship always seemed to get in their way. With a curse, he pushed the thoughts away and tried to focus. He needed to get to her. It was the only thing that mattered right now. He had to reach her so that he could try to explain before Jared sprang his miserable little trap.

But rush hour congestion waylaid him, and her SUV was already parked in her spot when he arrived at her condo. His feet pounded the pavement as he sprinted from his car to her building. Upstairs, he burst through the front door.

She sat on the sofa with her head bent as she looked down at Jared's tabloid resting on her lap.

Horror gripped him as the memories of that predawn morning twelve years ago flooded his mind. If not for the terrorizing flashbacks, he might've wondered how she'd come to possess the paper so quickly. She didn't even read tabloids, and somehow this exact issue had reached her in a matter of hours.

Her head came up, and she stared at him with huge, questioning eyes.

"I can explain." His voice rasped with his desperation.

"No." As he watched, her light green eyes darkened with anger. "Do not say a word."

CHAPTER 19

"Brynn, please—"

She held up her hand. "You don't have to explain."

His expression twisted with pain, and she stilled.

She stared as, for just a moment, they might've been transported to another time, twelve years ago, when he wore that same expression as he'd pleaded with her to believe him.

And she hadn't.

Her heart squeezed.

"It's not what it looks like." Emotion grated his voice.

"I know it's not," she said softly.

The heavy line of his eyelashes went down and up several times as he blinked at her. "You do?"

"Of course I do." She stood, then flung the tabloid onto the coffee table. "This garbage isn't worth a minute of our time. Seriously, how stupid do they think we are? The paper owned by Jared's buddy just so happens to show up in the hallway outside my door." An inelegant snort escaped her. "Give me a break. I don't know what their game is, but they suck at it."

He gaped at her in silence.

"Did you read the story?" she asked. "They painted me as some kind of femme fatale who set my dad up and seduced my stepbrother in an evil plot to steal the company from both of you. It made me sound like a vicious bitch."

"Why are you smiling?"

"I just told you." She pointed at the newspaper. "It made me sound like a vicious bitch. Me." She pressed her hand to her chest. "I'd just been thinking that I'm too nice. Too gutless, especially with people like Jared Morris. But this chick?" She pointed at the paper once more. "I like her. She's a fighter."

Aiden's laugh rang with his incredulity.

But the terror still clung to his face and shoulders, so she crossed to him. "I'm sorry. This is all my fault."

Confusion twisted his features. "How is this your fault?"

"When I bumped into Jared that day, he was acting like such an arrogant jerk that I couldn't resist trying to put him in his place."

"What did you do?"

"I might've let him think we were," she waved her hand between their bodies, "you know, sleeping together. For real. After I refused to sleep with him for the last year." Her shoulders hitched with her guilt. "I couldn't help myself."

The smile worked its way across his face in slow, steady increments.

She rose up on her tiptoes and dropped a soft kiss on his cheek, near the corner of his mouth. "I'm so glad you were smart enough not to fall for his crap."

His arms came around her. He held her tight against him and buried his face in her hair. "Thank you. I... I'm..." He swallowed heavily. "I was so scared."

"Scared that'd I see those pictures and believe them and not you?"

His arms squeezed her tighter, and a rush of love poured from her.

"I'm so sorry." She pressed her mouth to the warm skin on his neck. "For everything."

A shudder racked his shoulders, and she pulled his scent into her body with a deep, prolonged inhale.

When she stepped out from his arms, the invisible cord of heat and hunger refused to release them. They stared at each other while the longing that'd drawn them to one another since the first moment they'd met in a crowded airport over twelve years ago spun and tangled around them.

She wanted to be with him again. It was no longer a matter of *if* she wanted to be with him, but when, and how often they could do it, and would he still want her after they were together again? The way they once were?

"Aiden…."

But she didn't know how to tell him she was tired of giving the fear all her power. That she wanted that power for herself. That she wanted to claim it and wield it for her own purposes.

Like the fictional woman in that ridiculous tabloid, she wanted to take for herself, and what the real Brynn wanted most was love.

And pleasure. She expelled a shaky sigh. She was long overdue for some pleasure.

She wanted him. She wanted to give him all that was in her heart. Every part of her.

Unable to find the words, she used her body.

She reached out and pressed her palm flat against his chest while, with her other hand, she gripped his nape and pulled him down to her.

With the gentle brush of her mouth over his, every nerve in her body came alive. His lips tasted like sugar, and she licked, tasting him with small, greedy nips. A moan gathered in his throat, and she slipped her tongue inside his mouth to steal it from him.

He thrust his hands into her hair, and his heart beat wildly against her. She clutched a fistful of his shirt, then her fingers were working clumsily at the buttons.

Large hands closed around her wrists, stopping her from popping the next button.

She broke off their kiss and pulled back enough to peer into his face. The hammer of doubt struck her beneath the breastbone.

"Is it my scars? If you don't want to see them, we can turn off all the lights—" She was moving to flip off the switch on the wall beside the gaslit fireplace, the only source of light in the slowly darkening room, when he tugged her to him.

He buried curses in her hair. "No, Jesus, no."

"Then what is it?" She pressed her forehead to his shoulder. "You're unsure about something."

"I'm not unsure about anything," he said, drawing breath like a winded athlete. "It's what I know for certain that makes this so hard."

She eased from his arms.

His dark eyes glimmered. "If we do this, I won't be able to go back to the way things were before. I won't be able to leave you again." He delivered the words as a threat, and it took her mind a moment to absorb their meaning.

"Say it again," she whispered.

"This time, it's forever."

Hope filled her heart. "Promise me, Aiden."

"I will never let you go, Brynn."

As if falling into a dream, she slipped into his arms.

Beneath the tender assault of his mouth, her head spun, and a lick of fire lashed from her belly to the aching center between her thighs. When he took her hand in his and led her down the short hallway, she floated along behind him, every step that drew them closer to her bedroom like a walk through a warm pool of desire.

In her room, he lowered his body onto her bed. Sitting on the edge of the mattress, he pulled her between his thighs. She bent her head to reclaim his mouth, and her hair fell forward around their faces with a billow of her flowery shampoo.

He reached for the hem of her blouse.

Her hand shot out to grasp his wrist. "Wait."

Suddenly, her heart thrashed, not with her aching need, but with fear.

His eyes held hers as he lifted his hand and pressed a kiss to her fingers. "I love you. All of you."

She squeezed her eyes shut.

"Do you trust me?"

"Yes," she said, with no hesitation.

"Then do not be frightened with me," he said, his voice thick. "I will not do anything you don't want me to do."

She swallowed the sharp taste of terror in her mouth and slowly drew her hand away.

"Trust me," came his husky whisper.

Then he whisked her blouse away from her skin.

Beneath the shadow of his heavy lashes, his dark gaze moved over her body, touching on the large, ropy welt slicing from her collarbone to her shoulder and the smaller inflamed ridges on her rib cage and down her side.

Half-turning, she hooked her long hair over one shoulder and unfastened her bra in the back. The material gave way to a cluster of ravaged skin, left red and angry most days by the constant rubbing of her bra's wide band.

Her eyes clamped on his face she held her breath until her lungs burned.

He lifted his hand, and the tips of his fingers grazed across the scars on her back.

She sucked in a hiss of air.

When his gaze swung to her face, a primitive, guttural pain filled his dark eyes. As though her injuries had wounded him, too.

"Does it hurt?"

"N-no." Still clutching her bra to her body, she toyed with the ends of her hair. "Some places are numb, and others are overly sensitive."

Pain riddled his expression as he continued his careful exploration.

"There's one more"—a gleam of sweat beaded across her face and neck—"b-between my legs."

His eyes blazed in his suddenly pale face when his hands moved to her waistband. He popped the button and eased the slacks down over her hips. She stepped free of them and stood before him in her panties with her arms hugging her bra to her body. The trembling in her heart reached her limbs.

Apprehension narrowed her movements when she shifted her stance. Gently, his hand slipped behind her knee and lifted it to the mattress beside him.

With the pad of his thumb, he brushed over the raised wound that ran along the inside of her thigh. Like the damaged skin on her back, the persistent rub of her thighs often inflamed the welt.

Tension overloaded his shoulders. Reaching up, he cupped her face in both his hands and dropped a kiss on her mouth that was lacked the commanding heat and hunger of moments ago. It was gentle, almost chaste, and delivered with such tenderness that tears tightened her throat.

Then his fingers trailed down the side of her neck and danced across her collarbone before he hooked them under the straps of her bra. He drew the scrap of material away from her body.

Slowly, she lowered her arms.

His large hands moved to her waist and inched upward. With the pad of his thumb, he brushed the scar over her rib, then his mouth dropped a kiss where his thumb had been.

He repeated the motion, his thumb edging higher to sweep the underside of her breast, followed by the warm caress of his mouth.

Need arrowed from her breasts to her core.

His mouth played servant to his roaming hands as they explored the dips and valleys of her body, finding every place she craved his touch. Fire flowed from his fingers to soothe her aching bones and awaken the parts of her soul she'd neglected for too long.

He lifted tendrils of her hair off her neck so that his mouth might find the secret hollows at the base of her throat and behind her ears. His teeth grazed an earlobe, and a pleasant shiver chased through her. Her head lolled back, and she closed her eyes.

When his warm palms cupped the heavy weight of her breasts, a moan piled in her throat. The smooth slide of his hands down her sides to her hips released the lusty groan.

He hooked his thumbs inside the waistband of her underwear, then dragged the white cotton down.

Naked before him, her rapid breathing became ragged.

He remained fully clothed in his crisp white dress shirt and black pants, and she fumbled with the buttons on his shirt while his palms smoothed over the swells of her bare bottom.

With one hand on her backside, he gripped her nape with his other and pulled her down onto the bed, rolling her to the side so that she lay beside him.

The decadent journey of his hands resumed, and she relaxed into the mattress as he his fingers relearned the curves of her body. With wicked swirls, he circled first one nipple, then the other.

Desire pooled between her legs.

She arched her back, chasing his fleeting touches, but his fingers skated back down her body to dance along her hip bone.

Eager to surrender, she parted her legs for his touch. His fingers danced over the scar and then pushed through her soft, springy hairs.

The first fiery stroke ricocheted through her, and she sucked in a sharp breath. But the next delicious slide sent voluptuous waves radiating from her core outward. His clever fingers searched out her most sensitive nerve endings, and the coil in her belly clenched tighter and tighter until she rocked her hips, pushing her heels into the mattress to lift her body toward his touch.

When she dared to peek at him, she found he watched her with hooded eyes. Her lust surged, and carnal, primal need consumed her.

Her veins throbbed and her heart lurched with erratic beats.

Her lungs burned from her labored breathing as she rocked her hips.

Still, he remained fully dressed.

"I want to touch you, too," she rasped in his ear. "Aiden, please...."

He rose off the bed, his golden-brown eyes devouring her body as he unfastened the buttons on each of his cuffs, then moved to his shirt front. He tossed the white dress shirt into a heap in the room's corner and reached behind him to tug the undershirt over his head.

His lean torso rippled with muscle when he shucked the T-shirt and set to work on the button of his pants.

She bit down on her bottom lip as he peeled away the last

barrier between them. Freed from the restraints of his boxer briefs, his hard shaft stood flat against his abdomen.

A sudden rush of emotion closed the back of her throat.

She'd wanted this for so long, but had been too scared and hurt to admit it, even to herself. But somehow, someway, he was standing in her bedroom, beautiful and naked, and a tornado of emotion whirled through her. Tears ached in the back of her throat.

All her life, she'd waited for him.

He knelt between her thighs and pressed his palm flat on her stomach. With his other hand, he trailed a finger along her sensitive folds, then pushed inside her hungry opening. She turned her face into the pillow to bury her desperate gasps.

When her hips swiveled, lapping up the pleasure from his talented fingers, he lowered his body between her thighs.

His broad shoulders pressed her wide when he dropped his head.

Her head came up off the pillow. "You don't have to—"

He licked inside her.

With a gasp that slid into a moan, her head fell back.

The stubble on his jaw abraded her skin and sent coils of pleasure spiraling downward. Then his tongue parted her, warm and wet. With naughty kisses and decadent licks, he rekindled the molten fire.

Waves of ecstasy rippled out from her core, but he withdrew his fingers, and she pulled back from the edge. Her cry of frustration prompted a deep rumble of naughty laughter in his chest.

She buried her hands in his thick, soft hair, and soon the long, languid glide of his fingers stirred the warm flutters low in her belly.

But again, his touch retreated.

He kept her there, poised on the brink of bliss. Tumbling,

peaking, easing, and cresting again, and again. Her thighs trembled, but he was relentless, not allowing her pleasure to peak until she quivered all over.

Sensation exploded, and she threw her head back as wave after wave of torturous pleasure surged through her.

"I've been waiting twelve years to do that," he said as he crawled over her.

The weight of his body on top of her was exquisite.

His hard length nudged at her opening as he reached over her head to rummage through the nightstand he'd been using for his belongings.

Between their bodies, he rolled on a condom.

When finally—*finally!*—he wedged between her legs, he gripped her bottom in both of his hands and raised her up to him, as though she were a sacred offering. But he didn't sink home as she yearned for him to do.

The tip of his erection teased at her entrance, dipping into her slippery heat, then retreating. The need to be filled throbbed between her legs, but he kept up the delicious torment until she clasped her legs around his waist and her hungry core pulled him deep.

He filled her in a long, slow plunge.

Finally, he was part of her again.

She wrapped her arms around him and, drawing him deep, held on with every part of herself.

A shaky breath shuddered through him.

In the back of her mind, she waited anxiously for the freezing panic she could not control to arise, but it didn't come.

In this moment, with him, fear was an impossibility. She knew only hunger and want and greedy need.

And love.

Together, they moved.

Then suddenly, he stopped. He lifted his head, and a

frown stirred between his eyebrows. His hand prowled beneath her pillow, and when he tugged his arm out from under her, he held a long strand of dark beads.

The rosary that'd once belonged to him dangled between their faces.

"Is this…?"

She watched the thoughts play across his features to find the rosary here, now.

"I didn't steal it. Y-you left it behind."

His eyes shifted from the rosary to her face. "You kept it? All these years? Why?"

"It… calms me. When I…."

An aching tenderness touched his features. "When you have a panic attack?"

Fear pinched her chest, and she nodded. "Are you going to take it back?"

With the strand wrapped around his palm, his fingers brushed her cheek. "No, *mo chroí*. It's yours now."

The rosary grazed her neck when his hand moved to her throat, and when he cupped her bare breast, the cool beads hooked on the pebbled peak of her nipple. The skin around her nipples puckered with the light tease of his fingers and the cool smoothness of the beads.

His tongue lapped at her as his hips moved inside her once more.

At first, they were slow and careful, but soon the cautious dance of their bodies wasn't enough. Slow became urgent. Gentle became desperate.

Memories of who and what they had been, of past hurts and agonized longing, were consumed by the roar of their passion.

She was made for this moment, and her heart gloried to love him openly. Freely.

Forever.

When the first delicious spasms crashed over her, she stared into the golden fire blazing in his dark eyes.

"Promise me," she whispered.

"I won't leave you," he said. "I promise."

He called out her name, and his lusty croak brought about the climax of her own need.

Her moans turned into cries that sounded like anguish but felt like ecstasy as the fire claimed them.

CHAPTER 20

The next thirty-six hours passed in a haze of hedonistic pleasure-taking and giving. Too absorbed in each other, they left Brynn's bed only long enough to shower or gather food from the kitchen.

Too eager to fuck the hell out of one another, they returned swiftly and often. By comparison, the outrageous debauchery of his teenage wet dreams seemed virginal.

He wanted to turn off all the clocks, to freeze time and stay with her like this forever. Hidden away from the world. Lost in their own private, sex-fueled reality.

Which was why, when his cell phone buzzed with an incoming call late Sunday afternoon, he ignored it.

Brynn stopped in the middle of telling him about her winding path through several college majors. "That's your phone."

He wanted to smash the device with his fist for interrupting her, but he lifted his head off the pillow and glanced at the phone's display.

Then he let his head drop.

For a moment, he'd forgotten what awaited him out there

in the real world, and the phone's reminder relit the spark of fear in his chest.

The sound of her soft, husky voice stirred the tiny spark into flame. "Aren't you going to answer it?"

His hand found her hip.

She shot a look at him over her shoulder. "Was it one of your half brothers?"

He would have to tell her what he'd learned from Shea, but his mouth went dry with the thought. The truth was going to crush her, so he swept her hair aside and buried his face in the crook of her neck, searching out the sweetest of her intoxicating scents.

With his deceit, he experienced a gnashing pang of regret. He didn't want to lie to her, especially not now, after they'd finally moved past their anger and wariness with each other, but neither could he bear to break her heart.

Maybe he could figure out a way on his own to fix the mess her dad had left behind. If he could spare her the pain of learning the full truth, he would do so.

With a soft sigh, she laid her head on her arm. "Why don't you want to talk to them?"

He took a nip at her earlobe. "One thing I don't need is more family."

She rolled onto her back and gazed up at him. Questions filled her eyes, but she didn't ask any of them.

Instead, she reached up, and her palm cupped his cheek.

He closed his eyes, then spoke the only truth he could give her in that moment. "One family rejected me already. Isn't that enough?"

"Your family didn't reject you." The softness in her voice soothed the ache inside him. "After you left, everything changed without you."

He fell back into the pillows and stared up at the soaring ceiling. "You became millionaires."

"Cian and Rory didn't. They've... had their struggles without you. Your mom, she hasn't been the same since. She's missed you terribly."

In the pillows, he turned his head. "Did she say that?"

"She didn't have to. She's your mom."

He found the ceiling once more. "Yeah, well, you assume she's like other moms. But she isn't."

"I don't know much about other moms, but I know yours misses her sons when they're not around. She missed you so much."

"If you say so."

"I do," she said with a quiet resolve that pinched his heart. "Sometimes, the look on her face... it's like looking into a mirror."

When he swallowed, his throat strained with tightness. Then he twisted onto his side and claimed her mouth. The kiss started hot and possessive, but her succulent softness soon captured control of him. He gentled, melting into her heat.

"Are you going to call him back?" she murmured against his mouth.

Beneath the sheets, he smoothed his hand up her thigh. "Later."

FRAGMENTS OF DAWN sunlight punctured the darkness when his cell phone buzzed on the nightstand. Aiden cracked open one eye to Cian's number flashing on the screen.

Slipping from the bed, he accepted the call.

"Yeah." His dry throat grated like sandpaper as he stole through the bedroom door and pulled it closed behind him.

"Where are you?" Cian asked.

"It's six o'clock in the morning." Aiden shoved a hand

through his rumpled hair and moved down the hall. "Is this payback for the other day?"

"I wish. We need to talk."

Unease crawled up his spine. "I'm at Brynn's."

"Give me twenty minutes," Cian said. "I'm on my way."

"Everything all right?" Aiden asked, but Cian had already disconnected.

While he showered, shaved, and dressed for work, Brynn continued to sleep, and the sound of her soft snores soothed the rough edges around his heart as he crept quietly through the room.

When he returned to the living room, he stood gazing out at the lake for only a few minutes before a terse knock struck the door.

Cian strolled into the condo, his hazel-green gaze darting around the open space. "Where's Brynn?"

"She's sleeping."

Cian's dark eyebrows climbed.

"I'm sorry if it bothers you." Aiden's tone held no apology. "But that's the way it's going to be from now on."

At the patio door, Cian's mouth curled into a sardonic frown. "What bothers me is how damn long it took you two to figure this out." He twisted the lock, and the latch released with a dull thud. "And that you haven't turned on your phone for two fucking days."

When Aiden followed him out onto the terrace, the chill air of early morning nipped at his skin. They moved to the half-wall railing high above the lake's agitated churn.

Cian squinted against the sunlight and shoved his hands into his coat pockets. "You want the bad news, or the shit news?"

Though he'd been expecting more bad news, Aiden experienced a wince of dread. "What is it?"

"I found him."

Wild fury kicked in Aiden's veins when his gaze fastened on Cian's face. "Who is he?"

"Devin McInnes. Seems like a massive piece of work. Been arrested a half-dozen times for everything from drug possession to assault and battery. Did fifteen months in Jacksonville for stabbing someone with a broken beer bottle in a bar fight."

The lake's agitation roiled in Aiden's gut. "How did you find him?"

"Funny story, actually," Cian deadpanned. "I was following Moretti."

"Moretti?"

"McInnes seems to be some kind of body man or bodyguard for Moretti."

The air wheezed from Aiden's lungs. "Moretti has a bodyguard?"

"An entire squadron of them, from what I can tell."

Down below, waves crashed ashore, and Aiden gripped the terrace wall to keep from being pulled under. "Why does a businessman need bodyguards?"

"I was wondering the same thing." Cian peered out across the lake a moment, then glanced back at Aiden. "You ready for the shit part of all this?"

A preemptive curse broke from Aiden.

"I talked to X."

Aiden had sent Xavier the plate number of the car that'd followed Brynn and asked him to run it through the state's registration system.

"Did he get us a name?"

"He did," Cian said with a slow nod. "Devin Gerald McInnes."

Another breaker crashed over Aiden's head.

"What are you going to do?" Cian asked quietly.

Beneath the relentless pounding, Aiden thrashed for air. He couldn't answer.

"Should we tell Brynn?"

With a wrench of pain, Aiden shoved away from the wall. "No. Not yet."

"She could be in danger."

He was drowning. "Stay with her. Don't let her out of your sight."

"Where are you going?" Cian asked as Aiden careened toward the door.

"To get some damn answers."

AIDEN STABBED the tiny black button, holding down the security gate doorbell to send the strident buzzer ricocheting through the opulent home. When the gate eventually drew open, he stomped on the car's accelerator and roared up the short driveway.

His long strides devoured the front steps. At the top, he raised his fist, but the door swung open before he pounded on it.

Alan, dressed in work slacks and a white undershirt, appeared red-faced and winded. "You're going to wake up the entire house."

Aiden pushed inside. "I'm confident that is the least of your worries right now."

Alan took one look at his stepson and then shuffled across the grand foyer. With a nervous glance at the staircase, he crooked his head. "C'mon. We can talk in here."

Aiden followed Alan into the dark wood-paneled study where this nightmare had begun only a few weeks ago.

The moment Alan slid the pocket doors closed, Aiden exploded. "What the hell have you done?"

Alan took another anxious appraisal of Aiden's expression and paced to the large liquor cabinet. Pressed against the wall between two windows overlooking the courtyard, he drew open the heavy doors, and though it was not yet eight o'clock in the morning, plucked a decanter from the array of spirits. He yanked out the stopper and flipped over a glass tumbler.

"Money laundering is a federal crime," Aiden said. "You could spend years in prison."

"You're not going to send me to prison." Bourbon flowed into Alan's glass. "Brynn would never forgive you."

"Where did you get the money? Is the artwork stolen? Is that it?"

"It's not my money." Alan cradled the tumbler in his palm when he turned. "They just park it with us for a while until they need to move it again."

"Who? Whose money is it?"

Alan lifted the tumbler to his lips and gulped down a healthy swallow. "It comes from different places. There are so many, I can't even tell you all of them."

"If you don't know where it's coming from, how does it get to you?"

"Moretti. He gets it to Philip, and Philip…" Alan swirled the tumbler and the amber liquid sloshed. "…makes it disappear."

"Moretti?" Submerged by the nightmare unfolding around him, Aiden's lungs spasmed for air. "You make him sound like a mob bag man or something."

Alan tossed back the last of the bourbon.

Slowly, Aiden realized his stepdad's lack of response was an admission.

A sharp curse erupted from Aiden.

Alan held up both his hands. "Calm down."

"Don't tell me to calm down." Fury shook Aiden's voice. "You put a target on my back for the fucking mob."

"I took the target off Brynn." A bead of sweat broke out on Alan's forehead.

"You're laundering the mob's money." Icy terror tried to claim Aiden. "You put every single one of us in their sights. What the hell were you thinking?"

"I had no choice."

"Bullshit."

"I was going to lose everything," Alan hissed. "Your mother was going to leave me. Brynn would've lost everything. She never would've forgiven me. When Moretti approached with an offer, what was I supposed to do?"

"Tell him no." Aiden's bellow echoed around the room. "Don't commit crimes."

"It was just a loan."

"Banks give loans, Al. You don't go to the fucking mob."

"No bank would loan to me. Moretti made sure of it. It wasn't even a lot of money."

Aiden gaped at the older man. "It's the fucking mob. You don't play footsy with the mob without them sticking their tongue down your throat."

"You think I don't know that now?" Alan slammed the empty tumbler down on the cabinet shelf. "I thought he was a businessman. I—I tried to get out."

"Did you?"

"Yes!" Alan snatched up the decanter of bourbon. "I thought if I started a new business where they could get the same thing from me, they'd leave Hathaway Group alone."

"You knew they wouldn't, or you would've given the business to Brynn." Aiden clenched his fists against the rush of his fury. "Instead, you pulled me into this mess. I knew you hated me, but I'll admit, I underestimated just how much."

"I don't hate you." Amber liquid streamed into Alan's glass. "I love my daughter."

"If that were true, you never would've let this happen."

Derision clustered on Alan's features. "You think you know so much. Moretti and his ilk are bad men. Very powerful, very bad men."

"And you put your family right in their path." Aiden's anger lashed like a whip. "The family you swore to protect. That you took an oath to protect."

"That's right. I took an oath." Alan crammed the stopper in the decanter's wide mouth. "I took an oath to honor my wife. How does losing everything do that? How does me getting gunned down help your mother or Brie? How does Brynn stay safe if the business folds and she loses everything? Her home? Her livelihood?"

"Believe it or not, Al, being broke isn't the worse fate in the world."

"Yes, but your mother…," Alan raised his glass, "she likes nice things."

"Don't you dare blame this on her."

While Alan sipped his drink, Aiden stared him down.

"What would you have me do?" Alan snapped when the tension became too much for him. "Write a breakup note to Moretti?"

"Fix it. Go to the police. Come clean."

With a wave of his hand, Alan dismissed the suggestion like it was nothing more than a pesky gnat. "I tried that. But Moretti found out. They have people everywhere. At the banks, in the police departments. All I did was piss him off."

In his veins, Aiden's blood turned cold. "What do you mean? What did he do?"

The color on Alan's cheeks rose.

"Tell me." The words squeezed out through the crack in Aiden's clenched jaw.

"He—" Alan's head moved with a sharp shake, as if to dislodge an unpleasant thought. "He sent someone after Brynn."

Drowning, Aiden gasped for air.

"It was just a scare tactic," Alan croaked. "But it worked."

Water rushed over Aiden, pulling him down, down.

Brynn's soft features, twisted with pain as she confessed it all to him, flashed before through Aiden's mind. Wishing to protect them, she'd kept her secret. She'd taken it all on by herself—the shame, the fear, the silence. She'd pulled it inside her until it warped and distorted everything. She'd carried it alone.

And the entire time, her dad knew.

"You knew?" Disgust riddled Aiden's words. "You knew what they did to her, and you did nothing?"

"They roughed her up a little, scared her pretty good, but she's okay."

Behind Aiden's eyes, white-hot fury exploded. "She is not okay, you son of a bitch."

"What was I supposed to do?"

"Go to the fucking police," Aiden roared. "Lock him up. He's still out there. He could do it again, to her or someone else. What the fuck is wrong with you? He could've killed her."

Tumbler in hand, Alan shot forward, pointing his index finger at Aiden. "Yes, but he didn't. She's alive. Right now. And you need to make sure she stays that way."

With a surge of rage, Aiden struck Alan's hand, and the glass tumbler clattered to the floor.

Eyes wide, Alan stumbled back.

Aiden stalked him.

Alan's foot caught on the corner of the plush oriental rug and he slumped into an armchair.

Aiden loomed over the older man. "Do not ever go near her again."

"She's okay." Alan's words rang with familiarity, as though he'd repeated them many times. "Just do what they say, and she'll be okay."

Wave after wave of terror pelted Aiden. "God damn you."

The fiery flame of fear in Alan's eyes cooled. His shoulders slumped. "God has nothing to do with this."

Aiden drove a hand through his hair and tugged on the ends. Fear pummeled him and his hands shook with the terror that gripped him.

"Keep them happy and they won't touch her." A bleak despair weighed down Alan's words. "It's the only way."

CHAPTER 21

When Brynn stepped into the living room, she drew up in surprise to find Cian hunched on a stool at her kitchen bar, eating a bowl of cereal.

"What are you doing here?"

Discomfort packed his shoulders. "I came to talk to Aiden."

She glanced around the living area. "Where is he?"

"He… had somewhere to go."

He wore an odd expression, and she narrowed her eyes at him. "Okay, well, I'm late for work—"

"Great." He bounded out of the chair and carried his bowl to the kitchen sink. "I'll come with you."

After a beat of confused silence, she said, "You'll come with me? To work?"

"Yeah, why not?" he said, shrugging into his jacket.

She blinked at him. "Because I have to work."

"I won't get in your way." He stepped around her on his way to the foyer.

"But…" She turned with him. "Why?"

With an awkward yank, he hauled open the door. "I'm curious about what you do."

"You've never been curious before." She approached the door with caution.

"That's not true." He plucked her coat off a wall hook by the door and shoved it at her. "I was busy before. Now I'm not."

The entire day, he trailed her like a shadow. He rode with her downtown and, except for the brief sound of his soft snores drifting across the conference table, he sat quietly in the corner during her staff meetings.

In the afternoon, he tagged along with her to two project sites. There, he appeared slightly more interested, but he didn't ask questions or snoop around the worksites, the way Aiden did whenever he tagged along.

Aiden, who was, in fact, curious.

Cian, not so much.

After work, he tailed her to her front door, then remained hovering in her foyer with his coat on.

"Are you coming in?" She plopped her purse on the dining table. "Or are you just going to stand there?"

Before he could answer, there was a swift knock on the door. The gathering frown swept from his face. "You're right. I should probably get going."

He swung the door open, and Rory slipped inside while Cian shuffled out. The brothers exchanged a look, but no words. Then the door fell closed and Rory shrugged out of his jacket.

He dumped his coat over the back of a dining chair, then shuffled over to the couch and plopped down. He stretched across the table for the remote and switched on the TV.

"What is going on?" she demanded.

Rory reclined into the cushions. "Aiden asked me to stay until he gets here."

"Where is he?"

He hadn't been at the office that morning, and he hadn't yet responded to the text she'd sent him around lunchtime.

"I don't know," Rory said, his attention riveted to the television screen.

Worrying thoughts poked holes in the euphoric hangover still hovering around her after the weekend spent with Aiden.

She dug her cell phone out of her purse and sent him another text. *Where are you?*

His reply came before she'd finished pouring a glass of wine. *Something came up. Rory is going to stay until I can get there.*

Why? When will that be?

Soon, was all he typed in answer.

But he didn't come home soon.

She occupied herself with laundry and other tasks, but whenever she passed by the front window, she searched the quiet street for signs of him. What was he busy doing? Had something come up at work? Why wouldn't he tell her what it was? Why was he being so secretive?

By eleven o'clock, she'd given up pretending to be busy and simply stood staring out the window at the traffic trickling by in a steadily weakening stream. While she waited, her worries ballooned into doubt-filled bubbles of fear and anxiety.

Had she done or said something to upset him? Had her scars bothered him more than he'd let on? Was he having second thoughts?

At midnight, she abandoned her watch and went to bed.

But her doubts continued to torment her, and she struggled to fall asleep. It wasn't until her exhausted mind latched onto the memory of his crooked smile that she calmed enough to sleep.

He hadn't changed his mind. He wouldn't leave her again. He'd promised.

~

WITH EVERY HOUR THAT PASSED, the pounding beat of fear banged faster and louder against Aiden's skull. He thrust a hand through his hair and blinked several times, trying to clear the haze of panic narrowing his vision.

Holed up at Rory's, he'd taken a deep dive into the trove of documents Shea had sent him, only to sink to the bottom of the cold, dark seafloor as if he were a bag full of coins. Dirty, filthy coins.

Helpless terror spiraled through Aiden as he stared at the computer screen.

Alan and his coconspirators had mixed a cocktail of crimes, including fraud and money laundering. By using several loopholes unique to real estate that allowed them to operate behind a murky veil of LLCs and corporate partnerships, their identities remained obscured from banks and regulators. Unless or until someone went looking for them.

Leo's wife had sliced through the shadowy web of transactions and loan transfers to trace the winding flow of their dirty money in and out of Hathaway Group. The only thing she hadn't uncovered were the names behind the corporate ownerships.

But Aiden didn't need to know their names, because Alan had already told him what he'd find if he went tumbling down that rabbit hole.

The mob's money flowed through Hathaway Group.

Every question that sprang to his mind prompted the same short, devastating answer.

How had this happened? Mob.

How had it gone so far, so quickly? Mob.

How had Alan let his own daughter become a victim of their cruelty? Mob.

Falling ever farther, faster, down the tunnel of clawing desperation, Aiden grabbed his cell phone. With no plan, no clue what to do, he started dialing.

The hand he'd thrust through his hair pulled at the dark strands while the call rang.

"Hey, it's me," he said at the sound of Shea's raspy voice.

"I was beginning to think you didn't like me like that."

Silence crackled over the connection when the terror stole Aiden's voice.

Through the phone, Shea's shuddering breath reverberated. "Look, none of us asked for this," he said. "But it doesn't have to be weird. We're brothers. That's really the start and the end of the story."

"I'm in trouble." The words left Aiden's mouth as a ragged plea. "The files you sent…."

"What about them?"

Aiden confessed it all. That the business belonged to his stepfamily and that he suspected the worst about the source of the money. He couldn't withhold his darkest fear. That if he made one misstep, someone would hurt Brynn. When he'd finished, Shea remained quiet so long Aiden worried their connection had failed.

"I'm not trying to pull you into anything," Aiden said into the void. "But… can I send Brynn to stay with you for a while? Until I figure out what to do?"

"Let me get back to you," came Shea's clipped reply. "Hold tight for a few days. And send Brynn to me. She'll be safe here."

By the time he let himself into Brynn's condo with the key she'd had made for him, it was well past midnight.

It might as well have been years instead of hours since

he'd left her bed that morning. They lived in a new world now, one with no morning or afternoon, but only dark night.

On the sofa, Rory pushed upright. "What the hell is going on?"

For now, for Rory's sake, Aiden refused to expand the circle of people who knew the answer to that question.

"It's almost two o'clock in the morning," he said. "Let's talk later."

Rory dragged the sleep from his eyes as he pushed to his feet. "I've got to be up early, so I'll let it go this once. But the next time you call me for a favor that involves not letting someone out of my sight for a single second, I'm going to need an explanation."

Aiden agreed to the demand while Rory shrugged into his jacket. When Rory slipped through the front door, Aiden locked it behind him.

Down the hall, he crept quietly into Brynn's bedroom.

Her deep, rhythmic breathing reached him in the dark, and he followed it to the edge of her bed. As quietly as possible, he stripped out of his clothes. Then he slid beneath the covers and curled his bigger body around hers from behind.

He wrapped an arm around her waist and tugged her close.

She stirred. "Where have you been?"

"I'm sorry," he whispered next to her ear. "I'll explain later. Sleep now."

But she didn't sleep.

She snuggled closer so that his chest pressed against her back and his hips cupped her lush bottom. With a wriggle, she cradled his swelling sex.

His lust building, he found the side of her neck with his mouth and nuzzled until a moan vibrated in her throat. He abraded her soft skin with his teeth, but near the scar on her shoulder, he gentled his touch. The need to please her, to make her happy and keep her safe, burned through him.

"I've never done it like this before." Her husky voice clenched his insides.

Emotion wrenched his chest. Her sweet uncertainty combined with her fearless resolve to give all of herself to him, despite everything, shattered his heart.

He whispered instructions to her as his palm smoothed down her thigh and at her knee, lifted gently. She hooked her leg over his hip, opening her heart to him.

From behind, his hands glided up the front of her body, caressing her thighs, hips, and breasts. She trembled, and so did his hands. She was a precious gift he didn't deserve. How would he ever be worthy of her?

She arched her back, and he explored down her body, over her quivering stomach, to the aching peak of her sex. With the tip of his finger, he circled and teased, but he withheld the contact she craved most.

He stroked her silken flesh until the moisture from her body made his fingers slippery and her hips writhed with her desperate search for his elusive touch.

Her breaths came in harsh rushes when she reached behind her and clasped the back of his neck. "Aiden, please."

He denied her pleas and worked her body, building the exquisite tension higher and higher. She bit down on her lip to stop the needy screams from bursting from her.

"Tell me what you want, Brynn."

"Please," she panted. "Touch me."

He tortured her some more.

Her hand on his nape tightened, while with her other hand, she clutched at the bedsheets. When she lost the battle and cried out his name, he slid two fingers into her warm, wet heat. Her hips swirled and bucked.

When the head of his shaft nudged the damp furrow

between her thighs, a gutting wrench pulled from him and he withdrew from the crook of her body to fumble through his nightstand for a condom.

She reached back and toyed with his balls while he sheathed his hard length. The groan that tore from his chest came from the deepest place of his darkest need.

Then he positioned himself behind her once more. She flung her leg over his thigh and he bent his knee, parting her wide. Her hungry flesh grasped at his thickness and he slid deep in one long, liquid glide.

When her lush flesh surrounded him tightly, his breathing turned ragged, as though he'd suffered a crushing blow.

How had he survived so long without her? Without her, he was starving and empty.

She was life to him. If he lost her now, again, it'd be the end of him.

Whatever evil lurked in the shadows, he had to beat it back and keep her safe.

He moved inside her, urgent and desperate, and though he was buried deep, she begged him for more. She begged him to give her everything.

He curled his arm around her waist and held her tight against him as, together, they climbed.

Higher and higher they soared until the pleasure became aching and their need for release overwhelming.

Love, his and hers, tangled and knotted to form a tapestry of warmth and light around them. Neither Aiden nor Brynn, but them.

Us.

He would forever remember that night, when her soft pants and lusty moans tightened his balls and squeezed his heart with unbearable pain. When she was fierce and sheltered in his arms. When he didn't know if they'd be free in a week, a month, a year.

Free or alive.

"Promise me," she gasped.

"Brynn." He knew what she wanted him to say, but he had to tell her the truth. "I love you. I will always love you."

Fire consumed him when her body clamped around his shaft.

In the aftermath, he stumbled from the bed on legs weakened by the force of their joining and disappeared into the bathroom. Exhausted and eager to return to her bed, he made quick work of things.

When he slid under the covers, he reached for her, but she slipped from his arms before he could haul her against him. The fingers of his outstretched arm brushed over something cool and he lifted the rosary, which had once again been tucked beneath her pillow.

Wrapped in the sheets, she struggled to her feet. Seeing the strand in his hand, a worried frown touched her features.

His chest ached. He hated that frown. Born of terror and smoothed over with sheepish insecurity and even, at the last, a self-mocking smile. That she had hidden all her pain and fear at the price of her self-confidence tore him apart.

Before he could offer her the talisman, she plucked something off the floor and flung it at him. When he moved to block the flying object with one hand, she snatched the rosary from his other and scurried away.

He filched the black ski mask off his abdomen where it had landed. While his mind churned with his troubled thoughts, he fingered the knitted threads of yarn. When he looked up, spiraling fear gripped.

At the bathroom door, she'd stopped and glanced back.

While she watched him, her smile fell. "Everything all right?"

The question froze him. Unable to speak, he gave his head a slow shake.

Her head tipped to one side, then slowly, she walked back to the bed. Perched on the edge of the mattress, she reached out and smoothed her hand across his brow.

"What is it?" she murmured. "What's happened?"

He pushed his hand beneath her hair and pulled her face down to his. His kiss caught the corner of her plump mouth.

"Nothing," he said. "I'm just tired."

She drew back and searched his eyes. "These past few weeks, you've listened to me and loved me through all of my pain. I want to do the same for you."

His throat tightened. "I don't want to hurt you."

She considered that, then a soft sadness glimmered in her eyes. "Keep your secrets and we'll both know pain. The hurt is only different, but not less. Or tell me the truth and be the one to help me heal."

He stared into her light green eyes while his mind floundered for a way out of this moment.

But there was none.

The deep breath he dragged into his lungs racked his body as a shudder.

CHAPTER 22

"What did you do?" she teased. "Beat up one of my ex-boyfriends?"

He didn't smile, but only gazed at her with dark eyes that gleamed in the shadows of his face.

Unease chased up her spine. "It can't be that bad, can it?"

Her fingers swept the hair off his forehead, and a soft purr rumbled in his chest.

Then he started to talk, and with each of his carefully chosen words, he tore her world apart.

Her heart thumped painfully against her chest cavity. Denials burned in her throat.

"Are you saying my dad has been working for the mob?"

It was too unbelievable. How could such a thing be true? How could it have happened?

But as she stared into his dark eyes, a thousand truths flickered, and bit by bit, all the little, unexplainable things began shifting into a tidy row.

The changes in her dad's temperament. His unusual demand to give Manny Moretti a stake in the company. The board meeting. Joey's talk of blackmail.

Her dad's decision to hand the company over to Aiden without warning. Without discussion. Without consideration beyond a seemingly impulsive desperation.

Suddenly, it all made sense. The truth echoed in her bones.

"He gave you the business so he could escape?" she asked. "Is that it?"

The line of Aiden's mouth thinned. "He says he wanted to protect you."

"Protect me?" Outrage drove her to her feet. "He brought the mob into our lives. How was that protecting me?"

"I won't defend him."

Her stomach roiled, and she careened toward the bathroom, but her feet tangled in the bedsheets and she tripped.

She righted herself, then whirled on him. "Why? Why did he do it?"

Aiden dropped his legs over the edge of the bed. "He was in financial trouble and thought he was going to lose everything."

"Money? He was worried about money?" She was going to throw up.

"Like I said, I won't defend him. He might've been easily corrupted, or he may have come to it with great difficulty." His voice gentled. "But whether he means it when he says he was trying to protect you or not is irrelevant. He belongs to them now, not us."

She lost her stomach then, making it into the bathroom just in time.

When the retching eased, she flushed and dropped the lid shut. Sweat clung to her brow, and she sagged against the cool veneer of the tub.

Aiden appeared in his boxers and wet a warm washcloth in the sink. He passed it to her, then his hand found the back of her neck and he rubbed.

Through her tears and nausea, he continued to massage her nape.

"What are we going to do?" she whispered.

He moved to sit beside her on the cold, hard bathroom floor. "We don't have a lot of options."

She hated the twinge of defeat in his voice. "Tell them to me, anyway. Please."

"We could try to give back the money, but I don't think we can come up with all of it. I'm not even sure they'd let us walk away if we somehow found the cash."

Terror wrapped around her throat.

"We could fall in line," he said, his tone as cold and hard as the tile flooring beneath them. "Everything goes on the way it is now, except…"

"Except we'd be working for the mob."

He dipped his head. "We do what they say, when they say it, or else."

"Or else what?" When she glanced at him, the naked fear in his eyes knocked a breath from her lungs. "What if we go to the police?"

Shadow darkened his face. "It's possible, if we cooperate, we might stay out of jail. Others may not. Your dad. Your cousin and uncle. Any staff who knew what they were doing and helped."

She propped her elbows on her knees and scrubbed her face with both her hands. "I should've known what was happening."

"Don't even go there. These crooks take deception to levels decent people could hardly imagine." He folded his arms over his bare torso. "I suspect a big part of Philip's job was keeping the honest people like you from figuring out the truth."

She peeked at him through her fingers. "So either way, we lose everything?"

"If we're lucky, we get to start over."

Her heart gave a painful wrench, and she dropped her hands. "I'll go by myself and say I did it. All of it. Maybe that way, they'd let you keep the business."

He silenced her with a look. "I won't let you do that."

"And I won't let you be pulled any deeper into this mess."

"They will not just take your word for it." In his tone, frustration hovered just below the surface. "They'll need evidence, and the evidence will show it wasn't all you."

"Yes, but if I confess—"

"We're not going to the police," he snapped. Then, with a sudden flash of motion, he bounded up and strode from the room.

Slowly, she climbed to her feet.

The bedroom was dark except for the stream of light from the bathroom that filtered across the space. Before the glass wall, he stood with his hands on his hips, gazing out at the black sky.

When her reflection appeared in the glass behind him, he spoke to it in a quiet voice. "It's too dangerous."

"More dangerous than falling in with the mob?"

He turned, and she glimpsed the fear that ravaged his expression. "If they found out… we'd never be safe in Chicago again. We'd have to leave."

"There are protection programs, aren't there? We might—"

He gave his head a sharp shake. "I won't risk it."

"I don't think we have a choice."

While he didn't argue, he didn't relent, and defiance clung to his rigid spine. His dark eyes glittered in his pale face.

Between her breasts, she clutched the sheet tight in her fist. "What aren't you telling me?"

"The man who attacked you—" His voice faltered. "He's one of them."

The blood left her head in a nauseating rush. "How do you know that?"

A muscle ticked along his jawline. "Your dad…."

His words hit her like a bucket of ice water, and she gasped with the cruel shock.

He was moving toward her.

"Wait, what?" She stumbled back. "Do you mean h-he knows?"

Aiden drew up, as though peppered with pain. "He… he knows they sent someone after you, yes. And that they hurt you."

"No, he can't," she said. But the denial held no power.

With every sickening thud of her heartbeat, the poisonous truth marched through her veins, invading every vessel, every cell with the awful truth.

"He never said anything. He knew, and he never told me… he cared… or was sorry… or…." Her anguish spilled over and streamed down her cheeks. "He never tried to help me."

His arms came around her, and she burrowed into his warmth and strength as the grief poured out of her. Grief for losing the man she'd once thought her father to be, and grief for the little girl who believed such a weak, unscrupulous person was the only one who could ever love her.

Grief for the girl who'd chosen him over the only other man she'd ever loved. Aiden deserved so much better than this.

"Run away with me." Her words sounded muffled against his warm skin and she pulled back to look up into his startled face. "Right now. Let's leave all this behind us and—and —go overseas. Just the two of us. The way we should have done twelve years ago."

He brushed the backs of his fingers across her cheek. The

tender regret in his eyes took a notch out of her heart. "Brynn—"

"Don't—" A watery hiccup cut off her plea. "You're going to say no, I can tell. But please, I'm begging you, just… don't say no."

"We cannot outrun this." His fingers slipped into her hair.

She closed her hand around his wrist. "We can try. We have to try. We can't give up."

"I'm not giving up, but neither can I allow them to hurt you again." With his thumb, he caressed her jawline. "We need to get you somewhere safe. I'm sending you to stay with my brother for a while."

"What? No." Panic closed her throat. "I'm not leaving you."

"I insist."

"And I refuse." She grasped his wrist so tight that the bite of her fingers left white marks on his skin. "You once asked me to run away with you, and I said no."

"Brynn—"

"I thought I was protecting you, but really, I was protecting myself. I was a coward. It was easier to send you away than risk being abandoned again. I picked safe over my happiness. I picked my dad over you." The tremor in her heart filled her voice. "Aiden, I picked wrong, and I've regretted it every day since. Now I'm asking you, please, pick me."

With gentle pressure, he drew her to him and pressed a kiss to her forehead. Then he released her.

"I cannot." He dropped his gaze, seeing in her face, perhaps, the anguish in her heart. "I need to know you're safe while I figure out what to do."

"Aiden, please don't do this." Her head ached along with her heart, and she rubbed her forehead. "We've been here before."

"It's not the same."

"It *is* the same." She stomped a foot with her frustration. "It's the exact same if ten years from now we're standing here wondering what could've been."

"I will come for you when I can."

"When will that be? A week from now? A year? Another decade?"

His features hardened like cold steel. "I'll give you tomorrow to pack and make arrangements, but then you must go. This isn't open for debate."

"Why isn't it open for debate? It's my life. They've taken far more from me than they have from you. I get to have a say in how this ends, don't I?" On the tail of her fury, sudden despair pounced. "Aiden, please, I can't lose you."

"And I can't lose you." The words erupted from him. "These men—"

"I know." Her fierce whisper silenced him. "I know what they are. I know what they're capable of."

At his sides, his fists clenched and unclenched. "I will not sit by and let them destroy our lives. I see what they've done to you. I see the fear you live with every day. I feel it, too." His voice broke when his palm struck his chest. "I won't stand for it any longer."

"As long as I'm with you, no one and nothing can destroy my life."

"I will not let them hurt you." Dark eyes caressed her face. "Even if that means I have to let you go."

With that, silent tears rolled down her cheeks. "You said forever. That's wh-what you said. You p-promised."

"We will be together, Brynn. One day. One way or another."

One day. One way or another.

Of all the awful, ugly words they'd spoken that night, she hated those words the most.

"When? How?"
"Soon," he said. "But not yet."

CHAPTER 23

They woke to an overcast sky.

At Aiden's insistence, they rode to the office together in his car. Headlights from passing vehicles dissected the steely gloom as he steered them through the maze of big, black monoliths puncturing the heavy gray clouds.

In the seat beside him, she kept her face turned to the window. She'd pulled her hair back at the temples and twisted the toasted honey strands into a thick braid.

She appeared young and vulnerable, and suddenly, he was hurtling back in time to a different place, when they'd secreted away in her teenage bedroom and imagined being exposed as lovers was the worst thing that could happen to them.

Before their naivete had been burned away by deceit and treachery.

He swallowed the painful lump in his throat. "When you're away from the city and safe, I'll go to the police and come clean."

And hope that asset forfeiture and bankruptcy were the worst of it.

She pretended not to hear him.

"I don't know what will happen when I do."

But mob retaliation and a lifetime in witness protection seemed very real possibilities.

Her silence endured.

"I am sorry, Brynn. Please believe me."

With one hand, she reached up and made a small swipe across her cheek.

The enormity of it all sat heavily on his chest, and his voice grated when he said, "I love you."

Her whispered reply came only when he'd eased into his parking spot and cut off the engine. "I love you, too."

When they stepped off the elevator and moved toward their offices, Donna waited for him at his office door.

"Good morning, sir," she said. "Your eight o'clock has arrived. I've shown him in."

Alarm screeched through Aiden.

He hooked a hand under Brynn's elbow and gently drew her behind his body. "I don't have a meeting scheduled this morning."

"Right this way. Please." With serious brown eyes, Donna gestured for him to step through the office door. "Ms. Hathaway, you may wish to join the meeting."

The fear he felt reflected in Brynn's light green eyes. He reached for her hand and clasped it tight in his. Then, with the inescapable certainty that everything was about to change churning in the pit of his stomach, they stepped through the door.

A man with auburn hair and massive shoulders that strained the fabric of his navy suit coat pushed to his feet. "Mr. Nolan?"

The door clicked shut behind them when Donna exited.

"I'm Agent Kendrick." The towering redhead flipped open a black billfold to reveal a gold badge and identification card stamped with the letters F.B.I in bold black across the top. "I'm a friend of your brother's."

Her hand still tucked inside his, Brynn squeezed his fingers tight.

"You know Shea?" Aiden asked, his heart thrashing against his breastbone.

"Not very well, no." A smile touched Agent Kendrick's wide mouth. "I was referring to Leo. He and I served in the military together. He and Prue gave me the thirty-thousand-foot view of what's gone on, but there wasn't time to dig into the gritty details. I wanted to contact you as quickly as possible."

"Prue?" Brynn asked.

"Leo's wife." Aiden gripped the edge of his desk for balance.

Agent Kendrick lowered his colossal frame into the chair. "Would you and Ms. Hathaway be willing to speak with me for a few minutes?"

The heavy beat of silence thundered in his ears.

"I did it," Brynn burst out.

"Brynn—"

She laid her hand on his chest, over his heart. "Aiden, I've got this. Just go sit down over there and look pretty." With a pat and a soft push, she turned to Agent Kendrick. "He did nothing wrong. It was all me. Well, not me personally, but me, my family. My dad, actually. Aiden was only trying to help—no, not help. He was trying to make sure we didn't get away with it."

"Brynn—"

"He has no clue about any of this. But I do. I know every-thing. You can talk to me."

Agent Kendrick's whiskey-colored eyes gleamed. "I like

you."

"I didn't mean for any of this to happen." With wide, guileless eyes, she glanced at Aiden over her shoulder. "And I'll do whatever I have to, to make it right."

His heart wedged in his throat, or else he would've demanded she stop trying to throw herself in front of the runaway freight train that'd become their lives. Nobody had ever risked so much to protect him.

Agent Kendrick's sharp gaze shifted between Brynn and Aiden. "I'm glad to hear that, because our Chicago field office has been dealing with this crowd for a while now, and to be honest with you, they needed a lucky break. I think you two could be it."

Aiden's frown deepened. "How do you figure that?"

Kendrick balanced his ankle on his knee. "You have access to the type of evidence they need."

"You want access to our files?"

"I'd love access to your files, if you're willing to share them with me." Kendrick's index finger tapped frantically against the sole of his shoe. "But chances are we won't find their fingerprints on any of it. These guys know what they're doing, unfortunately, and they cover their tracks well."

Brynn sank slowly into a chair. "They?"

"Manuel Moretti works for the Cerone crime family. He and his nephew, Jared Morris, oversee several rackets involving a dozen or more businesses throughout the city." Kendrick's serious gaze shifted back and forth between them. "Your former accountant is an associate of theirs."

Brynn's mouth, which had dropped open, suddenly snapped shut with an audible clack. "That little son of a—" She bit back the curse.

Leaning forward, Kendrick propped his elbows on his knees. "How do you feel about wearing a wire?"

"Isn't that dangerous?" Brynn asked.

"All you have to do is get one of them talking," Kendrick said. "If we snag him conspiring to commit crimes, or bribing or coercing you to commit crimes for him, we can end this quickly."

Behind his desk, Aiden paced. "Couldn't an undercover agent do that?"

Kendrick tracked Aiden's agitated movements. "They won't talk to anyone they don't know, and we haven't been able to infiltrate their ring on our own."

Brynn scooted to the edge of her chair. "I could call him and ask to reschedule our meeting."

"Absolutely not." Aiden's tone lashed with his terror. "If anyone's going to do it, it'll be me."

"He won't talk to you." She waved off his words. "If I grovel, he won't be able to resist the opportunity to rub it in my face."

A roguish smile touched Kendrick's mouth. "I really like you."

"She's leaving town first thing in the morning," Aiden ground out through clenched teeth.

"Now I don't have to." She rose slowly to her feet. "Aiden, this is exactly the help we need."

He steeled himself against the soft catch of her vulnerability. "This only makes me more certain that you cannot stay. If Moretti finds out we're talking to the FBI, I don't want you anywhere near this town."

"We can help protect you both," Kendrick said. "Wherever you choose to be."

Aiden's stomach heaved. God, he hated this. He hated that she was in danger and he couldn't protect her. He hated that he was the one who'd put that pained expression on her face. He really hated not knowing what to do or who to trust.

"I won't lie to you," Kendrick said. "You're in a no-win situation. You've been dealt a shit hand, but I want to help you get out with your lives and a chance to make a future for yourselves."

"But what we I can't get him to say anything incriminating?" Brynn asked. "Then what do we do?"

"Then we're no worse off than we are now." Kendrick's massive shoulders lifted, then dropped heavily. "We regroup and try again."

Aiden narrowed his eyes. "That sounds like it could take a while."

"There's no limit to the crimes and criminals in this cesspool." Gravity haunted Kendrick's voice. "With a little time and effort, you might gain the access we need to bring the whole thing crashing down."

Brynn openly gaped at him. "Are we talking about becoming informants?"

"What if you could help put them out of business for good and behind bars where they belong?" Kendrick asked. "What if you could stop them from ruining the lives of everyone who has the misfortune of crossing their paths? What if you could put an end to the misery they spread everywhere they go?"

Light green eyes clamped on Aiden's face. While his mind grappled with Agent Kendrick's words, he stared into her eyes. His entire world existed in those eyes.

"What do you say?" Agent Kendrick held out his hands, palms facing up. "Want to help us take these bastards down for good?"

～

THE LOW HISS of the zipper as she dragged the pull tab around the black suitcase echoed with finality.

Uncertain how to pack for an indefinite stay on a remote island while hiding out from the mob, she'd filled two hefty pieces of luggage with her belongings, then hoisted both bags off the bed and wheeled them into the front hall.

The town where Aiden's half brothers lived was only five hours away, and she and Rory planned to make the drive first thing in the morning, leaving by seven to slip out of town ahead of the morning traffic.

In the living room, Aiden paced before the fireplace, but drew up when he saw her.

Worry ravaged his features, and she wanted to go to him, apologize for all he'd suffered because of her dad, then haul him into her arms and tell him everything would be okay. Somehow.

But she didn't do that. Because although her mind understood why he was sending her away, understanding didn't melt the knot in her stomach or fill the gaping hole in her heart.

All her life, she'd felt this way. First, after her mom left and never, not once in nearly twenty years, tried to contact the daughter she'd abandoned, and then again after Aiden had gone.

Now her dad had orchestrated a new refrain of her misery. Same song, different verse.

Love meant betrayal.

She dropped her luggage by the front door. "I want to go see my dad."

Alarm stole across his beautiful face, but he moved to collect his car keys from the table near the front door. "I'll drive you."

"I want to talk to him alone," she said as she pushed her arms through the sleeves of her jacket.

His spine rigid, he yanked open the door. "I'll wait for you outside."

On the drive, she picked through the jumble of hurts and

grievances she wished to fling at her dad's feet that she could then point to and demand… what, exactly?

An apology? An explanation?

After entering the security gate code Brynn recited to him, Aiden parked at the base of the stone porch steps and climbed from the vehicle.

But Brynn didn't reach for her car door latch.

She stared up at the stately house, so unlike the home where she'd grown up. Now she knew tainted money had bought the opulent mansion. How many people had been hurt so that her dad could afford to live with his family in a home like this?

Her door opened, and the crisp fall air swept inside the car.

Aiden crouched before her. "You don't have to do this. You don't owe him anything."

When she looked into his golden-brown eyes, pain surged, raw and aching, to consider all that her dad had taken from them, twelve years ago and again now.

"You're right. I don't owe him anything." She stepped from the vehicle. "But he owes me."

Her anger carried her to the front door and inside the sprawling estate.

"Dad?" Her voice echoed around the soaring ceilings and through the quiet house.

Siobhan would be with Brie at soccer practice, but her dad's Lexus was parked in the driveway, so Brynn moved down the hall toward his study.

At the heavy pocket door, she didn't bother to knock and dragged it open.

Slouched in the chair behind his desk, her dad stared through the windows at the courtyard behind the house, clutching a bottle of liquor to his chest.

"Dad?"

He looked at her with red-rimmed, bleary eyes.

The pungent smell of whiskey burned her nostrils as she approached. When she stood before for the ornate mahogany desk, she stared down at the surface littered with hundreds of photographs. The old photos were faded, and a few had curled edges.

She peered close and a harsh gasp pulled from her. With a shaking hand, she picked up a photo and peered into a face similar to her own.

In the picture, Brynn's mom wore a paper birthday hat and looked on while Brynn attempted to blow out all twelve candles on her birthday cake. Her mother appeared relaxed and happy, and not at all as though she would abandon her daughter and husband within the year.

Brynn plucked another photograph off the desk, and another.

"Why didn't you ever show these to me?" she asked, her voice filled with the emotion she thought she'd exhausted in the aftermath of all his other lies and manipulations.

Rather than answer her, her dad lifted the bottle to his lips and drank.

"I know what you've done." She hated the waver in her words. "I don't know what's going to happen from here, but I wanted you to know that I know, and I won't ever forgive you."

He took another swig from the bottle.

"You should go to the police." Tears burned the backs of her eyes as she traced the outline of her mom's face with her finger. "Maybe they'll show you some mercy."

"But you won't?"

"No, I won't." She picked up another photograph. "I was wrong about you."

"I didn't mean for any of this to happen." The whiskey in

the bottle sloshed when he gestured. "Things… got out of hand."

"If that's true, then you'll do what you must do to put an end to this." She reached for another photo, and another, and stuffed them inside her coat pocket.

"I'm your father. It's my job to protect you."

"You failed." The words stuck in her throat and she choked on them. "More than you'll ever know."

With desperate urgency, she plucked up more photographs, until suddenly, she stilled.

Her fingers brushed the raised, circular seal when she lifted the paper off the desk. Her eyes moved over the small typeface several times before her brain deciphered the meaning of the words.

Certificate of Death. Diana Jane Hathaway.

Certificate of Death.

Diana Jane Hathaway.

Cause of death: intentional self-harm.

The last pillar of Brynn's carefully constructed world crumbled beneath her.

Her mother was dead?

Her mother was dead.

Her dad knew and had let Brynn believe she was alive. Alive and unable or unwilling to love her own daughter.

As Brynn stared at that piece of paper, the last fiction fell away. Her whole life was a house of mirrors. Lies and deceptions and little else.

Poisonous lies seeped through her, making her ill.

"Everything I did," her dad's voice reached her from far away, "I did to keep your name off one of those."

A sob built in her throat, but she swallowed it down with a ruthless gulp. She wouldn't shed one tear in her dad's presence. She would save every one of them for later. She would save her tears for her mom.

Turning blindly, she strode from the room. He called out her name, but she didn't turn back. She wouldn't turn back for him.

All her life, she'd believed her dad had loved her the way her mom never could, and because of that lie, she'd chosen him, over and over again. She picked him over her friends. Over her career.

Over Aiden.

Aiden, who waited for her outside.

The sob tore from her throat, and then she was running. Behind her, her dad bellowed her name, but she didn't stop. Tears and treachery blinded her as she fled, desperate to outrun the pain.

She burst outdoors and slammed hard into his chest.

"Hey, hey." Aiden's strong arms closed around her. "What is it? What's happened?"

She clutched his arms, and her mom's death certificate crumpled in her hand.

Air wheezed through the tight passage of her throat, and the words leaked out of her. "Please. Get me out of here."

She had no memory of the ride home.

Hours later, the curtain of darkness had fallen across the windows when she lay in her bed staring at the flames dancing in the small gas fireplace. She'd slept some, but the crushing sorrow frequently punctured her slumber.

Aiden lay beside her in the dark, and the shallow rise and fall of his breathing told her he was awake.

She reached for his hand, and his fingers clamped tight around hers.

"What do you remember?" His voice found her in the dark. "What was she like?"

Her exhausted mind rooted at the memories, but they'd faded long ago. "I've tried to forget her for so long that now I can't remember."

The tears came then.

"They'll come back to you." He slipped his arm around her waist. "When you're ready."

Sometime later, her nightmare woke them both. While her thundering heart slowed to its normal rhythm, he held her hand, and she rubbed her thumb back and forth over the knuckle of his index finger.

When she'd calmed enough that the first talons of sleep tried to claim her, a memory floated through her mind. "I remember her reading to me, and singing. She loved music. She would sing while she cooked."

"You do that, too."

A lightness touched her heart, which a pang of sorrow quickly snuffed out. "I want to stay here with you."

He released her hand and rolled away from her. The sound of him rummaging through the drawer of his nightstand persisted a moment before he lay back on the mattress.

His hand appeared before her face. She reached out and lifted the brass house key from his palm.

While she gazed at it, her fingertips brushed the cool metal, then she gasped and bolted upright in the bed.

"Where did you get this?" she asked. "I thought I threw it away."

The key to the house where Brynn had grown up once belonged to her mother, and after she'd left, Brynn had held on to the key in the silly hope that her mom would one day return and need it.

"I made Rory dig it out of the garbage for me," Aiden said.

She craned her neck and gazed down at him. "Why?"

"I couldn't let it go." His fingers toyed with a lock of hair on her shoulder. "I wanted to keep a piece of your heart with me always."

She closed her hand around the key.

"When this is all over, I will come for you, and I will

replace that key with a ring." His words blazed with the intensity of a fierce fire. "I will make you mine, Brynn."

With the key clasped tight in her palm, she pressed her fist against her heart.

"I've always been yours, Aiden."

CHAPTER 24

While she waited for Rory, Brynn sat perched on the edge of the sofa and stared down at the brass key in her hand.

She swept the pad of her thumb over the metal, warmed by her unbroken grip.

Though everything felt awful, she had her mom's key.

And she had Aiden's heart.

In the armchair across from her, his knee bounced with agitation, and a dark scowl touched his features.

Love squeezed her heart.

His demand that she leave town hurt and had made her angry. But she realized now she'd been looking at the present through the prism of their past. He wasn't rejecting her or trying to control her.

He was trying to protect her. Not with lies and manipulation, but with truth and love.

She could see that now, and though they'd never get back the years wasted to pride and hurt and anger, she wouldn't regret their ugly past. The darkness had shown the stars to them.

So while she still hated to leave him alone to deal with the mob on his own, the terror in his golden-brown eyes kept her from arguing with him anymore about it.

She would go. She would do it for him.

But watching his scowl darken with each passing second, she would hate everything about what was happening to them.

"He's only a few minutes late," she said.

He'd balanced his cell phone on his unmoving knee and pressed the power button to check the time once more.

She worried her bottom lip. "When are you meeting Agent Kendrick?"

"I'm supposed to be there at eight."

Aiden planned to meet with the FBI that morning to discuss the details of a sting operation designed to snare Jared and Moretti.

Beyond sharing the hope that it wouldn't be necessary, Aiden and Brynn had not discussed Agent Kendrick's proposition that they become informants in a larger operation. If one well-designed sting could solve the immediate danger, the temptation to walk away would be overwhelming.

Just then, Aiden's cell phone vibrated, and he swiped to accept the incoming call.

"Where are you?" he snapped. After a beat, he cursed. "All right. See you when you get here." When he'd disconnected, he shot her a look. "Rory's stuck in traffic about ten minutes out."

"You should go."

"I'm not leaving you."

"You can't miss this meeting." She pushed up off the couch. "I'll lock all the doors and windows. I'll be fine for ten minutes until Rory gets here."

Scowl in place, he remained firmly planted in the chair.

"Go. Please." Her desperation painted her words with

quiet urgency. "Get us out of this mess so we can be together."

With a resigned sigh, he stood.

They moved through the condo, checking the locks on all the windows and both patio doors, but at the front door, he hesitated.

On impulse, she rose onto her toes and brushed her lips over his mouth.

After a beat of surprise, his hands cupped her face and held her there.

"I love you," he murmured against her mouth. "I'll see you soon."

Then he was gone.

Twenty minutes later, her cell phone buzzed, and Rory's number flashed on the screen.

"I cannot find a parking spot," he said when she answered.

"I'll come down." She began searching the room. "I've got to get Romeo in his carrier, then I'll be right there."

"I'll circle the block until I see you."

She found Romeo curled up on the end of her bed, and a small tussle took place before she'd secured him inside his cramped plastic kennel. She balanced the carrier on top of her largest suitcase, then dragged both pieces of her luggage out into the hall and across to the elevator.

A sound might've reached her ears a split second before she turned back to close and lock her door, but the hard metal gun barrel pressed against her temple before she detected the man to her right.

Icy terror froze her, then a flash of movement from the left caught her eye a fraction of a second before his flying fist crashed into her face.

Pain shattered, then her world went black.

AIDEN'S MEETING with the FBI lasted all morning, and by the time he arrived at Hathaway Group, exhaustion dragged on him.

The meeting had gone well, and only ended once they'd agreed on a solid plan and two agents had coached him on how best to execute it. Now, all he needed to do was confirm that Brynn had arrived at Shea's. Then he could set the plan in motion and, hopefully, put an end to this nightmare.

Six hours had passed since he left Brynn at her condo, and depending exactly what time she and Rory had hit the road, they should be near their destination by now.

He sent her a text for an update on their whereabouts, but when he didn't get an immediate reply, he shot a text to Rory as well. Impatience had him sending one more text to Shea in case they'd already arrived and were with him.

Unable to focus his mind on work, he instead paced a well-worn path across the floor of the spacious corner office.

The first response came from Shea. *Waiting for them at the dock. Will let you know when they're here.*

With every minute that passed without a reply from Brynn, the dread snaking through his gut coiled tighter and tighter. As another half hour passed with no texts from either her or Rory, the path he stalked around his office wound faster and faster.

He texted Shea again. *Anything?*

No, came the quick reply.

Aiden called Rory's cell but got no answer.

When he was about to dial Brynn's number, his phone buzzed.

"I've been waiting at the dock for an hour now." Shea's clipped words crackled over the connection. "She's not here."

Panic swarmed Aiden. "What do you mean, she's not there? Where is she?"

"I was hoping you could tell me," Shea bit out.

"They left before eight o'clock this morning." Aiden thrust a hand through his hair. "They should be there by now."

Shea wrestled with that for a moment. "Maybe they… ran into some traffic?"

"Let me call you right back." Aiden dropped the call with Shea and dialed Brynn's number.

Fuck.

The call rang once in his ear.

Fuck fuck fuck.

The second ring cut off midway.

"Mr. Nolan." A man's voice rustled over the connection. "I've been expecting your call."

"Moretti, you son of a—"

Moretti chuckled. "Now, now. Let's not end our negotiations before they've even started."

"Where is she? If you lay a finger on her, you're dead."

"Ms. Hathaway is enjoying my hospitality until you can join us. How about dinner?"

"Where are you?"

"I'll send someone to collect you. Don't even think about playing the hero, or she will find my generosity has limits."

The connection died.

Aiden's palms smacked the table when he bent over, gasping for breath. She must be so scared. What if she panicked? What if they hurt her—?

What was he going to do?

What the fuck was he going to do?

With a growl of fear and frustration, he swung his arms across the desk's surface, hurling papers and file folders and pen holders through the air. He shoved both hands into his hair and tried to think through the black haze of his terror.

What was Moretti after? What did he hope to gain?

Control. He wanted to control Aiden. But if he killed Brynn, he lost his bargaining chip. He had to know that. He might be a piece of shit human being, but he wasn't stupid enough to throw away his leverage.

At least, that's what Aiden prayed.

Rory could be another matter altogether. Where was he? Had Moretti taken him, too? Did he know who Rory was?

Though it seemed unlikely he wouldn't know, Aiden hoped to hell he did not.

His hands shaking, he snatched up his phone. Should he call Kendrick? Did he dare?

Did Moretti know Aiden had been having conversations with the FBI? Is that what led him to kidnap Brynn? As he'd done with Brynn's father, was this Moretti's play to keep Aiden in line?

Against his will, his fingers flew over the phone's screen.

When Cian answered, Aiden spat the vile words. "Moretti took Brynn."

A curse exploded through the phone.

"Rory was with her," Aiden said. "I don't know where he is. He's not answering his phone."

"Do we know where he's taken Brynn?"

"No," Aiden choked out. "He's sending one of his goons to collect me later."

"How long do we have?"

"I don't know. A few hours maybe." Bile rose in Aiden's throat.

How could he leave her with that bastard for hours? He knew Moretti's delay was intended to torment him, and dammit, it would work.

"What do you need?" Cian interrupted the nightmare unraveling in Aiden's mind.

"Guns," he said. "I need weapons. And armor. A bullet-proof vest, if we can get it. And a phone. A clean phone."

"Right. Where should I meet you?"

"At Brynn's."

Aiden broke several laws on his race back to Brynn's condo. Her car remained parked in her leased spot, and after finding a space for his vehicle, Aiden made a quick search on foot of all the lots and street parking available within several blocks of her condo.

Rory's car was nowhere in the vicinity.

Returning to her condo, he kept his head up and his eyes moving in case Moretti had set a trap for him. When he stepped off the elevator at her door, a chaotic scene greeted him. Brynn's two bulking suitcases littered the hall, as did Romeo's carrier, which had been tipped on its side.

The cat's feeble meow set Aiden in motion. He righted the carrier, then made a sweep of the condo.

No signs of a struggle existed inside the unit, and slowly Aiden came to believe that they'd ambushed her when she stepped out the front door.

Sick with his terror, he hauled Romeo inside and released him from his crate, then collected Brynn's luggage from the hall.

Then he waited.

Every few minutes, he tried Rory's phone again in case he was unconscious in a ditch somewhere and the sound of his ringing phone might rouse him. If Moretti had taken Rory, too, would he have told Aiden? Or would he have kept that card close to his vest in case he needed to play it later?

The curtain of nightfall had dropped when a light knock sounded on the door. Aiden crept up to the door and peered through the peephole.

Cian stood in the hall, an oversized black duffel bag slung over his shoulder.

Aiden swung open the door, and Cian hustled inside.

"You hear from Rory?" He hoisted the bag onto the dining table with a hard thud.

Aiden shook his head. "Nothing."

Cian dragged the bag's zipper open and lifted out a Kevlar vest, which he hooked over one of the dining chairs. Then he lifted out one black object, and another, and another.

When he'd finished unpacking the bag, a small horde of firearms lined up in a neat row from one end of the table to the other.

Standing shoulder to shoulder, they studied the various-sized weapons.

"There's no way they're going to let you walk in there with any of these." A dark foreboding accompanied Cian's words.

"I have to get her out of there." Fear and helplessness choked Aiden. "If they hurt her again…."

At the flash in Cian's eyes, Aiden trailed off.

Damn.

"When?" Cian's tone was low and lethal.

"Last year."

In his hazel-green eyes, turmoil swirled.

"We need to bring her home." An explosive mix of anger and devastation shredded Aiden's voice.

The light in Cian's eyes shifted with the determined set of his chin. "What time is your date picking you up?"

"Dinner was all he said." With the wrench in his gut, Aiden winced. "I suspect he'll let me squirm for a while."

With a defiant scowl, Cian locked eyes with Aiden. "You know I'm going with you, right?"

The possibility of having a trained fighter by his side when he walked into Moretti's trap sent a surge of hope through Aiden, but as he looked into Cian's red-rimmed eyes and noted the pallid color of his skin and the hungry leanness of his large frame, a resigned sigh escaped him.

"I cannot allow you to do that," Aiden said. "They won't stop until they've squeezed me or killed me, and I refuse to let them use you to get to me."

"So, we agree."

A curse slipped out of Aiden's mouth. "These men are ruthless. I don't believe they'd hesitate to kill either of us. Right now, it's me they want. Let's keep it at that."

"They can't kill me." The shrug lifted Cian's bony shoulders. "I'm already dead."

The words slashed at Aiden.

"If the cancer's not gone, they'll start me on a different chemo cocktail. But who knows what will happen?"

The words hung in the air, heavy and rancid.

"Whatever we need to do to get Brynn and Rory out of there, I can do it." Steel wrapped around Cian's hard tone. "They can't put me away in the Supermax for decades, because I won't be alive that long. They can't torture me, because I no longer feel pain. They can't kill me because I'm already dead. I'm invincible. I know it sucks, but let's face it. You need me."

The sharp rap on the front door made both men jolt.

Adrenaline kicked through Aiden's veins, and he approached the door with swift, silent footsteps. Nearly twelve hours after Moretti had taken Brynn, Aiden was desperate to reach her.

He gazed through the peephole.

With a curse, he dropped his forehead against the door with a soft thump.

After a beat, he yanked open the door. "What the hell are you doing here?"

One by one, men filed into Brynn's condo.

Five men.

Shea's broad shoulders moved. "You never called me back."

"I've been busy," Aiden said. "No offense, but now is not a good time."

One of Shea's dark eyebrows inched skyward. "Is there ever a good time for your girlfriend to go missing?"

"I thought she was his sister?" Jack, the pro hockey player, rivaled Cian in size.

"Stepsister," Aiden ground out.

"Ah. I see how it is." Luke's lips curled into a slow smile—or was he Leo? "Very cool."

At Cian's muted snort, Aiden slid him a dark look. "Cian, this is Shea, Noah…" It took him a moment to recall which name belonged to which face. "…Jack, Leo, and Luke."

"I'm Luke, he's Leo."

"I'm sorry." Aiden tracked Leo's movements as he wandered toward the dining table. "But I don't have time for a family reunion right now."

"We're one brother short anyway, aren't we?" Noah's gaze scanned the room as he pushed deeper into the condo.

"Rory was with Brynn when she went missing." That draped a heavy disquiet over the men. "So while I appreciate you all showing up here, I need you to get out so I can find our brother and bring him home."

"You must be the oldest." Noah glanced at the others. "He thinks he doesn't need our help."

"Must be an older brother thing," Cian mused.

Shea bristled. "So now it's a character flaw to want to make things better for your family?"

"Not a flaw," Jack said. "Just an annoying quirk."

Leo lifted the M16 off the table and tilted it to the left and right, inspecting the weapon.

Aiden experienced a stab of helpless anger. "It's not that I don't need help. I'm in way over my head here and I well know it. But I won't drag all of you down with me. I need to do this alone."

"But that's the point," Shea said smoothly. "You're not alone."

Cian folded his arms over his too-thin torso and leaned back against the table. "Didn't you say one of them is a Marine?"

"Ooh-ra," Leo murmured.

"And one's a cop," Aiden shot back, drawing a grimace from Cian.

Luke, testing the grip on a handgun, bared his teeth. "I'm on hiatus."

Cian slanted forward. "They sound like a handy bunch of guys to have around."

"Here's another fun fact—our dad was a mob goon." Shea's proclamation landed at their feet like a grenade with the firing pin pulled. "He spent time in prison for carrying out a political hit."

The bomb's destruction was devastating. In the aftermath, a soul-crushing silence hung over the group.

Aiden struggled to catch his breath. "So, what are you saying? The mob is in our blood?"

"I am not saying that," Shea said. "Our dad's failures aren't ours."

"We weren't born into the mob," Noah said. "Our dad was radicalized and, I think he found them to be convenient bedfellows."

"Oh, well, that's a relief." Sarcasm dripped from Luke's tongue. "For a minute there, I thought you were trying to say it's our birthright."

"More like… a family tradition." The flicker of amusement in Shea's bright eyes quickly extinguished. "I've thought a lot about what kind of life we might've had if we'd stayed in Ireland. Our dad's failures might not be ours, but we can certainly learn from his fuckups. If we can help get you out of this, let us. Please."

Aiden stared hard at the floor for a long moment. "It's me they want. Not any of you."

"For now," Cian argued.

"Exactly." Aiden's head came up. "If that changes, they won't come for you alone. They'll come for your wives and your children." He jerked his chin at Noah. "You have any kids?"

Something flared in his dark eyes. "One on the way."

"Then, go," Aiden pleaded. "While there's still time."

"You could die." Cian pressed the heels of his palms to the edge of the table beneath him. "Without us, you almost certainly will. That doesn't bother you?"

"Of course it does." Aiden held Cian's gaze. "But if the price for Brynn's life is mine, I'm strangely comfortable with the idea. I'll have known and served my purpose. That's more than most people can say before their time is up."

Resignation settled as a bleak silence over the room.

Until Leo lifted the rifle and checked its sights. "At least let me show you how to use this thing."

With the tip of his finger, Jack nudged the gun barrel aside, then he twisted toward Aiden. "You don't have a hockey stick, do you?"

CHAPTER 25

She blinked, but the darkness remained.

Pain split inside her skull, and a moan escaped her with the wave of nausea.

Oblivion reached out to her. Her eyelids grew heavy, and she welcomed the escape from the pounding in her head.

When she woke next, she blinked into the inky dark.

Memories splintered across her mind—

—the aching in her heart.

—the man she sensed a moment too late.

—the terror and pain that exploded with the crash of his fist into her cheek.

Everything after that remained obscured behind a murky veil.

Beneath her, the floor was cold and hard. She tried to move, but her limbs were leaden. With her weak tug, something cut into her wrist.

She struggled against the confines, but her fight was short-lived as another wave of nausea pummeled her. With a sharp gasp for air, she rolled onto her back.

She might've slept, or slipped back into unconsciousness, but when she next woke, fear jolted her fully awake in the blackness.

Shudders from the cold besieged her body. The spasms racked her with enough force that her teeth chattered and her head struck the hard floor. Everything ached.

Lying in the dark, she listened. Was there anyone else in this place with her?

"Hello," she whispered, but there was no reply.

No sounds reached her at all. If she screamed, would anyone hear her?

Fractured glimpses continued to flash through her fuzzy mind.

The wounded glimmer in Aiden's dark eyes when she'd said goodbye.

Voices of two men arguing.

Those men, they'd taken her.

Her mind grasped at the memory of a face, but it was blank.

Who were they? Where was she? Why had they brought her here?

What did they intend to do with her?

Somewhere in the back of her sluggish, jumbled mind, an answer materialized.

Moretti. It had to be him.

She dropped in and out of consciousness. Her frightened thoughts awakened her often, and each time, a fresh terror pelted her.

Rory! Where was he? Had they hurt him when they'd taken her? Or had he'd gotten away? Had he warned Aiden?

Was Aiden looking for her right now? Or had they gotten to him, too?

She struggled against her restraints. She needed to find him, either to warn him or to help him.

Nausea gripped her, and she swallowed bile.

She pressed her cheek against the cold floor and dragged deep breaths into her lungs while her queasy stomach churned.

The last time she saw him, she'd been hurting. Had she told him she loved him? What if it'd been her last chance to say those words to him? If she never saw him again, would he know the truth? Would he know she loved him?

Noise split the darkness, and she jolted. Her breath froze in her lungs as her body went still.

A low creak spilled a slice of light across her prison.

Terror constricted her throat, then suddenly, the snarling blackness became a brutal brightness.

She squeezed her eyes shut against the cruel glare of the overhead lighting. The weighty fall of footsteps sounded, then two feet scuffed the ground before her face.

The toe of one shoe nudged her stomach, but she lay paralyzed with fear, afraid to move. Afraid to breathe.

One foot pulled back, and with a swift kick, struck her in the ribs. Pain shot through her, and she gasped for air. Coughs racked her body.

Then man placed his hands and his knees and crouched down. "Wakey, wakey."

Her eyes cracked open, and the sudden stab of desperate terror pummeled her when she stared at the coiling snake tattooed on his forearm.

"Hey." In the doorway, another man appeared. He said nothing and didn't come inside the room, but jerked his head toward the hall.

"What?" The man with the snake tattoo retreated. "I was just looking at her."

The light switched off again, plunging her into darkness once more.

"Boss said none of that." The door creaked as it edged shut. "Not right now."

"Who's gonna tell him?"

In the pitch-blackness, her mind conjured terrors from the shadows.

She tried to beat them back, but her head throbbed, and the panic choked her.

Aiden. She would focus on him.

But she couldn't focus.

Except to replay his name on a perpetual loop.

Aiden. Aiden. Aiden.

The litany brought fire to her heart and strength to her limbs.

He would come for her. If he could.

He would find her, and when he arrived, she would be alive.

The truth echoed in her bones.

After his brothers had gone, Aiden dressed and rechecked the weapons he'd strapped on his body, then he sat in the dark and waited.

Frantic terror whipped through him, and he closed his eyes. With every thought that floated up and every scenario that played out in his mind, he pushed them aside.

In the silence, only the essential existed.

Brynn.

When the knock finally sounded on the door, it shattered the quiet inside the condo.

Moretti sent two men. One kept watch while the other swept his hands over Aiden's torso and legs, plucking the handguns from his waistband and ankle holster.

They flanked him as they moved through the building

and out into the cool, moonless night, where a sleek black sedan idled at the curb.

The men moved Aiden toward it and steered him into the backseat. One man settled in the front with the driver while the other climbed into the back beside Aiden, then the driver navigated away from Brynn's street and moved through the black night toward the interstate.

In the distance, the cityscape rose like a beast, and they careened toward it while his heart thundered inside his skull. Minutes later, skyscrapers gave way to smaller dwellings as they rolled through one of Chicago's most affluent neighborhoods.

Sprawling estates receded behind manicured lawns and tall fences as they wound closer to Lake Michigan's shoreline. Shadows on the home's exteriors crouched like demons before a fire.

The driver eased the car through the gate and parked in front of the French style stone mansion, aglow with lights buried in the landscaping. From the outside, it appeared like a traditional, upscale home featured in one of Brynn's design magazines. It was hard to believe that a psychopath lived within.

Indoors, the opulence became outrageous. Extravagant furnishings, priceless artifacts, and more original paintings cluttered the spacious home as the men led Aiden toward the back of the house.

Adrenaline burned through his veins, and he held his body tense, on alert for any sound, scent, or sight of Brynn.

They arrived at a door tucked away in some far-off corner of the estate. One man rapped his knuckles on a wood-paneled barrier. It opened a crack, and after a brief conversation, the door swung wide. But rather than let them in, a woman stepped out.

Tall and dark-haired, she offered the men a coy smile as

she slipped past, except for one fleeting moment when her gaze locked with Aiden's. Whether it was her alluring smile or the skintight white dress she wore, his guards lingered in the hall while they watched her saunter away.

The man at the door smacked one guard on the chest to snap his attention back to the task at hand, and they shuffled Aiden into the room.

While another thick-necked goon patted him down, Aiden's gaze swept swiftly around the space. He counted seven men, including his two escorts, the two doormen, Moretti and Jared, plus a man clinging to the shadows at the back of the room, two escape routes in the door and a window in the far corner, and many weapons.

If he wanted to walk out of here alive and with Brynn, he'd have to be smart, and he'd have to be prepared to give Moretti everything he wanted.

Aiden repressed his reaction when the goon found the knife he'd hidden inside his coat, and with a pointed look at Aiden's escorts, filched it from his pocket.

From behind the massive ebony desk, Moretti grinned. "Mr. Nolan, how nice of you to join us. Come, let's talk." He gestured to the empty chair beside Jared.

Every muscle in Aiden's body was lit with fire as he moved toward the desk.

His gaze flitted to Jared, who slumped in the overstuffed armchair and with a petulant frown in place of his usual smirk. A fresh wound on top of the one Aiden had given him swelled his right eye shut.

At the empty chair, Aiden stopped. "Where is she?"

"Have a seat," Moretti said.

"I'll stand."

Moretti frowned, and his gaze shifted to something behind Aiden, then strong hands pressed down on Aiden's shoulders until he sank into the leather chair.

Like a flipped light switch, Moretti's fake smile returned. "There. Now we can talk."

"Where is she?" His voice tight, the words leaked from Aiden like the slow hiss of air from a balloon.

"You just got here. Have a drink." Moretti wiggled his fingers at Jared. "Get him a drink."

While Jared climbed out of his chair and hustled over to the bar in the corner, Aiden never took his eyes off Moretti. He was a small man with big goons, bigger guns, and a vindictive streak he'd be stupid to underestimate.

"I assured you Ms. Hathaway would be safe in my home." A dangerous edge crept into Moretti's tone. "I gave you my word. You're not doubting my word, are you?"

"Not at all," Aiden lied. "I'm Irish. It's in my blood not to believe anything unless I can see it for myself."

A deep chuckle shook Moretti's chest as raised voices sprang up from the corner of the room. Jared settled the dispute with a nasty snarl for the man in the shadows, then walked back to the desk with a glass of whiskey cradled in his palm.

He handed it to Aiden, who set it on the edge of Moretti's desk. "Tell me what you want."

Moretti eyed the tumbler of whiskey, and Jared jumped up to slide a coaster beneath the glass.

Moretti's chair groaned when he leaned back. "I want everything, of course. Hathaway Group will work with Mr. Morris on the downtown development project, and any other projects we decide to pursue in the future. You will continue finding our clients the best deals to suit their needs, and you will continue to reap the benefits of doing business with us. Oh, and Philip will have his job back."

"Is that all?" Aiden quipped.

"That's all." Moretti held out his hands. "See? I'm a perfectly reasonable person. This didn't have to be so hard."

"Where is she?"

The line of Moretti's mouth thinned. "I'm trying to help you. Show a little gratitude. Because of me, you'll be able to keep living this lifestyle. You can buy yourself fancy houses, nice cars. You can travel anywhere in the world you want. Most people would kill to have these things."

Aiden curled his lip in a sneer. "After a while, I won't even remember what it felt like to have a soul."

With an amused smile, Moretti shook his head. "You are so refreshing." He shifted his gaze to Jared. "Are you watching? This is the best part." Then his cold eyes snapped back to Aiden. "Do we have an agreement?"

"You know we do." The thrashing of his heart echoed in his ears. "Where is she?"

"And that is how you do it," Moretti said to Jared. "Not with that ridiculous tabloid. You must take away every other option available to them before they're yours. They're far more agreeable when their choice is you or nothing." For Aiden, a cruel smile twisted his mouth. "Now, ask me nicely."

"Bring Brynn to me now. Please." Each word lashed from Aiden's tongue. "Or I will fucking kill you."

Red mottled Moretti's face, but then a howl of laughter burst from him. "You got balls. I'll give you that. Too bad you're Irish. Are you sure your father wasn't Italian? I've met your mother. Something tells me she could handle an Italian lover."

Aiden shoved down the surge of rage. Moretti was trying to goad him, but there was nothing the man could do or say that would provoke Aiden to put Brynn in greater danger.

"Brynn," he said through clenched teeth. "Now."

"Remember, you brought this on yourself. It didn't have to be this way." Dark malice laced Moretti's tone, and then he tipped his chin at the man in the shadows. "Get the girl."

When the man stepped from the dimly lit corner of the

room, Aiden got a look at him for the first time, and for a moment, the chill black rage blinded him.

With a soft shake of his head, the clouds cleared away, and his gaze locked on the man with the bushy red beard and the tattoo of a snake wrapping around his right forearm.

CHAPTER 26

He had come for her.

She could feel him. She could feel his heart. It burned like an ember and lightened the darkness.

Aiden. Aiden. Aiden.

"Here." The word was nothing more than a faint croak. She swallowed painfully. "I'm here."

She gritted her teeth against the pain and struggled to edge her body upright against the wall. A plunge of dizziness roiled her.

He had come.

The lock turned over in the door, and glaring lights struck her.

She blinked, her eyes adjusting, while his heavy footsteps drew near.

His rough grip clamped around her arm, and he yanked her to her feet. "C'mon, princess, time to go."

At her back, he fiddled with her restraints a moment before the ties fell away. She rubbed her sore wrists, but with a shove between her shoulder blades, he pushed her toward the door and she lurched forward on shaky legs.

A cloud of fogginess filled her head as they moved down a long hall, up a flight of stairs, and through another spacious hallway to an interior door.

Her stomach clenched with her fear, and she shrank back, but the door drew open, and her captor delivered another hard push in her back to send her stumbling into the room.

Then he was there.

In his guarded eyes, the terror in her bones mirrored back, but her heart sang at the sight of him. Then her feet were moving under her and she was falling into his arms.

He hauled her against his chest, and his mouth brushed her temple and her forehead. "Where are you hurt?"

"I'm okay," she said. "I'm not hurt."

He was here. He was alive, and they were together. Nothing could harm her.

"Mr. Nolan, Ms. Hathaway, thank you for your visit." From behind a large desk, Manny Moretti watched them with cold eyes that sent a shiver running through her. "Next time, I won't be so hospitable. George will see you home now."

They turned toward the door, but Jared blocked their path.

"Such a touching scene," he sneered. "And here I thought you were a frigid bitch."

"Jared, that's enough," Moretti warned.

The arm with the snake tattoo gave Jared a playful slap on the chest. "You just needed to get rough with her. That's how she likes it." With an ugly leer, the man pursed his lips at Brynn. "Isn't that right, sweetheart?"

The growl deep in Aiden's chest vibrated against her ear when she burrowed closer to him.

A strange keening noise arose, like the howl of a wounded animal.

Aiden's arms tightened around her.

"You... you touched her?" Fury contorted Jared's face.

Her attacker grinned, revealing a mouth full of crooked teeth. "Nah, I just fucked her. She cried a lot less than you do."

A strangled sound erupted from Jared when he hurled himself at the man, and with a jarring tackle, slammed him to the floor.

Behind them, Moretti bellowed, and the other men in the room rushed forward.

Just then, the fiery crack of a bullet firing from its chamber pierced the sound barrier, shattering her eardrums.

Aiden shoved her to the floor and flung his body over her. He covered their heads with his arms, and she pressed flat against the cold marble.

A scream died in her throat as more gunfire exploded, each crack a fresh horror that choked her.

Then, a foot from her face, her attacker's body convulsed on the ground. As she watched, he went still, lifeless, though his expression held onto his surprise at the bullet lodged between his eyes.

Men shouted in English and another language she didn't recognize, and their pounding feet raced past her face. Her ears ringing, it took her a moment to realize the gunfire had stopped.

She lifted her head, but Aiden didn't move. "Aiden?"

He lay motionless on top of her.

Frantic fear clawed at her when she slid out from under him. He let out a soft groan, but remained still on the ground.

"Aiden?" Pushing to her knees, she rolled him onto his back.

Terror seized her heart.

Blood covered his face. Red pooled rapidly on the floor beneath him, crimson wet seeping over snow-white marble.

She used the sleeve of her shirt to wipe it away, but more took its place.

Her fingers trembled as she searched the side of his neck, desperate to find his pulse. Around them, men were running and barking orders.

With her shirt, she wiped at the blood around his eye. His name burned her throat with her desperate screams.

His eyes fluttered.

She gasped as though life returned to her body in a rush. "Baby?"

His eyes blinked open, and she gazed into the fiery flecks of gold that were life to her.

"Brynn...?"

She bent over him, and her hair fell around them, block out the smells of gunfire and death. Her tears dampened his face as she dropped kisses on his mouth and cheeks, eyes, and forehead.

"We have to get out of here." The stench of violence permeated. "Can you sit?"

"Brynn..." Reaching up, he brushed her hair back from her face. "Go. Leave me."

"No." She was shaking her head. "I won't leave you here."

Not in this ugly place.

"Brynn...."

"No." Her denial was a sob and a plea.

"It's okay." He smoothed his palm across her cheek. "You were never meant to be mine for long."

"Aiden, please get up." She slid an arm under him and tugged on his shoulders. "You have to get up. I won't leave you."

"Should we burn it?" she heard someone ask.

Though the movement was slight, Aiden raised a tiny fraction off the floor.

Hope kicked through her.

"Let me help you," she murmured, slipping her arm around his torso.

He was heavy, and weak from loss of blood, but adrenaline gave her more strength than she could've mustered on her own, and together, they got him to his feet.

They shuffled to the door, but there, Jared's body stretched across their path, staring up at them with dead eyes.

She yanked on Aiden's pant legs to help him lift his feet as they stepped over him.

In the hall, she turned, but Aiden grumbled. "Other way."

Her limbs ached as she hauled him through the enormous house. A man ran past them, but in the chaos, no one stopped them, and soon, they staggered out into the chilly night.

"Do you have your phone?" she asked as they teetered on the porch steps.

On the bottom stair, his knees buckled, and she stiffened her spine to hold him upright.

His grunt knocked loose. "Moretti took it."

Darkness engulfed them, and with it, the terror climbed in her throat. She had no clue where they were, and no way to get Aiden the medical help he urgently needed.

At that moment, a low whistle floated on the air.

Aiden's head came up.

The whistle warbled again, and her heart lurched.

She turned them toward the sound.

They stumbled across the front lawn, and as they neared the edge of the house, a dark-haired man she didn't know emerged from the shadows.

His sharp curse pierced the quiet night, and he darted to Aiden's other side to help hoist him. "What happened?"

"They shot him." Terror shook her words. "He's losing blood."

The man carried most of Aiden's weight as they tore across the side yard.

In the distance, the sound of a police siren wailed.

"Who are you?" she huffed, running to keep up with him.

"Leo."

At the walled fence, another dark-haired man she didn't know caught up with them. "What the hell happened?"

"He's been shot," Leo said as together, they lifted Aiden and propelled him over the top of the stone barricade.

Leo followed Aiden over. Then the unknown man reached for Brynn and shoved her to the top of the wall. She swung her legs around, and when she started to tumble, firm hands on the other side of the fence caught her and hauled her safely to the ground.

"What the hell happened?"

Brynn looked up at a third unknown man who had lighter hair than others.

"He was shot." With a grunt, the dark-haired man bounded over the wall.

Leo had lugged Aiden across the street, and the men rushed ahead of them. Behind her, voices rang out in the night, but she didn't stop to find out who they belonged to.

At a black Suburban, the man with lighter hair cranked open the back door while the dark-haired man helped Leo drag Aiden inside the vehicle.

Brynn scrambled in after them, and the car door slammed shut at her back.

They'd laid Aiden across the back-row bench, and the dark-haired man snatched a white plastic case from under the seat. He popped it open as he knelt on the floor beside Aiden while Brynn settled in a second-row bucket seat.

She twisted around and fumbled in the dark for Aiden's hand.

With a cell phone pressed to his ear, Leo flipped on the

vehicle's overhead light and joined the light-haired man at the front of the car.

"We got them," Leo said into the phone. "We're getting out of here."

As the sirens drew near, the light-haired man fired up the Suburban's powerful engine.

"No," Aiden croaked. "Rory."

Brynn gasped with the panic that rioted through her.

"Cian has him," Leo said. "Jack and Noah are picking them up now."

The vehicle eased away from the curb and carried them through the pitch-black night.

"How did you find us?" Aiden asked the man bent over him, swiping at his head with gauze.

"We waited outside for Moretti's men to come for you, then we followed you here."

"When we heard the guns, we jumped the fence," Leo said.

The dark-haired man leaned close. "I think the bullet missed, but you're losing blood." He pressed and held the thick wad of gauze against Aiden's head. "Shea, we gotta get him to a hospital."

Leo relayed that information to the person on the other end of his cell. Through the phone's speaker, a male voice replied, but Brynn couldn't make out his words.

Shea slowed for the stop sign at the end of Moretti's street, and then turned. As they moved further from the chaos, Brynn shook with the adrenaline draining from her body.

Leo stretched to flip off the overhead light, and moments later, a police car going in the opposite direction zipped by them with sirens screeching.

She clutched Aiden's icy hand in hers, and he squeezed her fingers.

Her heart kicked, dissolving some of the tightness in her chest.

"I'm Aiden's brother, Luke," said the dark-haired man. "You must be the sister-wife."

A noise leaked from Aiden and, hyperalert to him, Brynn looked down in time to glimpse the faint smile that touched his lips.

Her heart soared.

Luke's bright grin pierced the murky twilight inside the car. He nudged Aiden. "Welcome to the family, ya kinky bastard."

EPILOGUE

"No, like this—" Aiden puckered his lips to form a small opening, then forced air through to make a soft, melodic whistle.

Pursing her lips, Brynn attempted the tune once more.

A soft breeze kicked off the lake to tease the ends of her hair and warm the soft chuckle that rumbled in his chest.

When she mimicked the melody, a bright smile lit up her pretty face. "Is that it?"

He reclined, stretching out his legs and digging his elbows into the sun-warmed sand. "I think you got it."

Her husky laugh grabbed his insides as she stretched out beside him on her beach towel. "I didn't think you were ever going to teach me the family whistle."

"There's no escaping it now. You're one of us. Have been for a while." He rolled onto his side and smoothed his hand over the still slight but distinct swell of her belly. "Have you thought about names?"

Pink dusted her cheeks. "A little. Have you?"

"Of course. We have a legacy to live up to."

She groaned. "After a saint, a warrior, a king, and a poet,

what else is there? A god?" But she was already shaking her head. "We cannot name our kid after a god. He'll get a complex."

With his fingers, he toyed with a silky strand of her hair. "What about a hill?"

Her eyes narrowed. "Very funny."

"You have something against hills?"

She shot him a telling look. "I know Brynn means hill. Next to a saint, a hill is completely unremarkable."

"Unremarkable? Ever hear of the Hill of Tara? It was the seat of the High Kings and is one of Ireland's most ancient sites. It's a sacred hill, and the heart of Ireland." His tone gentled. "Her history, her courage and her sorrows, her very spirit, were all formed by that hill."

On her face, annoyance had melted into a soft, slippery smile.

Wanting to taste it, he dipped his head. "I love hills," he murmured, right before his mouth brushed over hers.

In the distance, a faint cry carried on the wind.

Aiden lifted his head to see Brie running along the shoreline, her dark hair flying as she skipped through the waves. His mom trailed farther behind, one hand on top of the oversized straw hat she wore as she dawdled in the surf.

Brie waved her arms wildly, and Aiden and Brynn waved back.

"They seem to like it here." Brynn turned her face back to his. "What about you? Do you like it here?"

The upheaval of the past year seemed to press down on him all at once, and his chest heaved with his heavy sigh.

In the aftermath of that fateful night, Aiden and Brynn had stolen away to the island in Lake Michigan where his half brothers lived, and rented a small beachside cottage to hide out while Aiden healed from his wound.

The bullet had grazed his temple, tearing skin and hair

but missing the bones around his eye and his skull. Though his recovery had not been without challenges, he'd escaped with his life and suffered little lasting damage beyond the scar that nicked the side of his forehead before disappearing into his hairline.

Moretti's men had nabbed Rory when he'd gone in search of Brynn, and he'd emerged from his ordeal with a mangled hand and ghosts in his eyes. A year later, he'd never told Aiden about all that had happened to him.

After learning of Alan's duplicity, Siobhan had followed them into hiding with Brie, hoping to shield the youngest sibling from the worst of what was to come.

"I like it," he said. "Though I wish we were here under different circumstances. I wish the last year had never happened."

The tips of Brynn's fingers grazed his temple. "It wasn't all bad."

From their island refuge, they'd worked closely with Agent Kendrick and the FBI, providing enough evidence for the feds to raid Moretti's multiple homes and businesses. Those efforts had led to Manny's indictment a few months later on an array of felony financial charges.

While Moretti continued to fight the charges against him, Brynn's dad had pleaded guilty, cooperated with authorities, and earlier that month had begun his three-year sentence in federal prison.

"No, it wasn't all bad." He caught her hand and touched his lips to the heart of her palm. "But I'm sorry we can't go home yet."

With Moretti's trial ongoing, they'd stayed away, and would not risk returning until it was certain he'd be spending time behind bars. Then, they'd make some decisions about the future of Hathaway Group.

For now, Cian kept watch over things back home, but he

visited the island often to give Aiden updates and hang out with their half brothers. In remission almost six months now, each time Aiden saw him, he appeared stronger and healthier than the last.

Brynn closed her eyes and tilted her chin to the sun. "As long as we're together, we're in the right place."

"You don't want to go back to Chicago?"

"I love Chicago." Her voice softened with her affection. "It's my home. But…."

"But what?"

"There's this house for sale on the east side of the island."

Laughter erupted from him.

"And I was talking to Mina," she rushed to add. "And she says it's not impossible to find a contractor out here."

He cut her off by claiming her lips in a kiss.

When he broke the kiss, he pressed his forehead against hers and lingered over her sweet mouth.

"We're going to be okay," she said. "No matter what happens next."

"I love you." The words rasped in his chest.

"That's how I know we're going to be okay." Her green eyes glinted in the sunlight, and with a glorious pang in his chest, he realized he could see her whole heart reflected in them. "If I can make you fall in love with me after hating me for so long, is there anything I can't do?"

He traced the curve of her cheek with the tip of his finger. "I never hated you. I've loved you from the first moment I saw you."

A disbelieving frown touched her features. "You did a good job of hiding it."

"You're impossible not to love. Believe me, I tried." He stroked a flyaway strand of her hair away from her forehead. "I once thought it'd take a bullet to the head to make me stop loving you, but turns out, even that didn't work."

The light, tinkling sound of her laughter sang in his soul.

～

Thank you so much for reading SAINT.

Next up in the Nolan Bastards series is Cian's story, WARRIOR.

Grab your copy of WARRIOR now.

ABOUT THE AUTHOR

Amy Olle is a USA Today bestselling author of contemporary and new adult romance novels. She enjoys putting her psychology degrees to good use writing emotional, redemptive love stories filled with beautifully flawed characters, cozy settings, and deliciously erotic sexiness.

Amy is living happily ever after in Michigan with her college sweetheart, their brilliant son, and a turtle named George.

When she's not busy burning up the pages in her next novel, she loves to hear from her readers. You can email her at amy@amyolle.com or contact her on social media.